Ghosts of Valhalla

Haunting the Route: A Prequel Novella
Choosing the Slain
Calling the Blood
Waking the Fire*
Raising the Dead*
Seeking the Frost*
Breaking the World*
Drawing the Blade*
Burning the Gods*
Riding the Storm*

*forthcoming

CALLING THE BLOOD

GHOSTS OF VALHALLA
BOOK TWO

AMY CISSELL

BROKEN WORLD PUBLISHING

CALLING THE BLOOD
Amy Cissell

A Broken World Publication
13820 NE Airport Way, Suite K395495
Portland, OR 97251-1158
Calling the Blood

ISBN 978-1-960766-10-6 (ebook)
ISBN 978-1-960766-11-3 (paperback)

Cover Design: Damonza
Edited by Two Birds Author Service
Proofread by Christopher Barnes, Cissell Ink

for liana
love you to the edge of a circle

ONE

Sweat dripped down my face, and my stomach churned as I collapsed to the floor, my pulse pounding in my throat. My vision blurred and wavered.

I swallowed hard, trying to stay conscious and keep the contents of my stomach where they belonged. I'd felt awful more times than I could count in the six weeks since I'd returned to my parents' home in Estacada, Oregon, but never this bad. I took a deep, shuddering breath, then froze in shame and terror. Through the dripping strands of hair that had escaped my ponytail and stuck to my face, I saw my mother.

I hadn't known she was here. I squinted, bringing her into focus. Her expression was completely shuttered.

Fuck. I'd disappointed her. Again.

I pushed myself into a seated position and wiped the tears from my sweaty face, wincing at the sting in my eyes.

"Sorry!" I gasped.

Mom sighed. "You don't have to be sorry."

"Yes, she does," Kara retorted. "That was pathetic."

My chin dipped to my chest, and a flush of shame burned my cheeks.

"Get up." Kara stalked away from where she'd been standing in front of me and paced across the room, never taking her eyes off me. I watched Kara, a Black woman who looked like the grumpiest and most elderly resident of an old folks' home, complete with deep, severe lines in her face and tight, curly white hair.

I used the wall to push myself to my feet, then bent down to pick up my sword. My hand cramped, and I almost dropped my blade. Only fear of Kara kept it in my grip.

"What are you waiting for?" Kara tapped her foot in exaggerated impatience.

My mother offered me a half-smile. I would've preferred an intervention, but I'd take what I could get.

I straightened my spine, shifted my grip to ease the cramps, and shook the tension from my shoulders. I raised my sword and bounced on my toes. Kara would definitely disarm me in less than a minute, but I was not a quitter.

Kara attacked without warning. I'd taken sword-fighting classes on and off since I was thirteen, and the one thing I'd learned about all my opponents is that watching the eyes was more important than watching their body if you wanted to know what was coming next. But it didn't work with Kara. She telegraphed nothing.

One second, she stood unmoving. The next, she rushed inside my guard, and my sword clattered to the ground. Again. At least this time, it was only my sword that fell and not my body. I was covered in bruises from the six weeks of training, and no closer to proficiency than I had been before.

Kara strode to the far wall of my mother's basement training room and picked up the sword oil and a soft cloth. She whipped a towel at me. "Dry yourself, clean your sword, and hit the shower. Be back at seven tomorrow morning, and we'll go again." She finished cleaning her sword without another word, racked it, and left, her steps light and almost silent on the creaky wooden stairs that led to the main floor of my parents' house.

I took the towel and mopped at my face, then walked over to the bench, gulped some water, and started cleaning my sword.

My mother sat next to me. She was fair-skinned and flaxen-haired, or at least that's how she was described in the sagas. In reality, her white skin was tanned from hours outside, and her hair was a dark blonde, rather than the golden color attributed to the Valkyries by the old stories. She was also powerfully built. She would never be described as slim—nor would I—but she had a muscular solidity about her that was inspiring and intimidating.

"You're doing great," she said.

"Yeah, real great," I replied. "My body is more black and blue than white, I spend more time on my ass than on my feet, and I have never gotten a strike on Kara, a woman who is a million years older than me."

Mom laughed. "Not quite a million. And she's your teacher because she's the best swordswoman we have."

"She's also the biggest bitch you have," I muttered under my breath.

My mom gently smacked the back of my head. "She's not a bitch. She's a hard-ass. And no one likes her when she's training them. She'd probably be offended if you did. Her goal is not to be your friend, but to train you to stay alive."

I sighed. Everything she said was true, but it still sucked. "I hurt all over and may never walk again."

"So dramatic," my mother said mockingly. "With those skills, you could skip saving the world from Ragnarök and become a Broadway star. I smell a Tony!"

Teenage Frankie wanted to roll her eyes, but adult(ish) Frankie leaned into her mom and rested her head on her shoulder. "You're ridiculous, Mom."

She slipped her arm around me and pulled me close. "That's my job." After one more squeeze, she let go and stood up. "Take your time, but don't sit too long or you'll stiffen up. I'm going to help your dad finish getting lunch set up. Once you're showered and clean, come eat. You need the calories." She ran her gaze up and down my body and frowned. "And not just because of the amount of energy you're expending with Kara. You are running on empty, Frankie."

I brushed off her concern with the same light tone I'd perfected over years of ups and downs with bipolar, substance abuse, and the resulting health and body changes that went with them. "I'm fine." I met her gaze and pushed sincerity into my eyes. "Seriously. I feel better than I have in ages. I'm just crap at sword fighting at the moment." I set down my sword, stretched, and took another drink of water. "Go help dad. I'll finish cleaning up in here, then take a shower and meet you in the kitchen."

The narrow-eyed look she shot me indicated she wasn't convinced, but she let it go. At least for now.

When she'd left the room, I slumped onto the bench. She was right. I was running on empty. I might have been clean and sober for almost two months, but things were not getting easier.

"You okay?"

A smile crept across my face. I turned around to face Dusana and tried to keep my jaw from dropping. She always looked good—she was a tall, dark-haired white woman whose lush curves needed a warning sign and whose blue eyes were deep enough to capture my soul—but in her tight blue jeans, scarlet corset, and knee-high leather boots, she was stunning.

No! I chastised myself. *Reapers are friends, not fuck buddies.*

"Hey, Dusana," I said, going for casual and not quite hitting the mark. Fortunately, my new friend and secret crush was not the greatest at reading body language, since it took more than a decade as a human to pick up all the skills, and my awkwardness went by without comment. After a moment, I remembered that she'd asked me a question. "Um. Fine. Everything's perfectly alright now. I'm fine. Thank you. How are you?"

A smile flitted across her face. "Love a *Star Wars* nerd almost as much as I love the planning and preparation that goes into the Great Potato Showdown Redux, as your mother calls it. Once you're showered, can we go for a walk?"

My head spun with the pinball effect of her subject changes, but I caught up quickly. "Of course! Showering is good. Food, better. Potatoes best. I'm gonna grab some lunch once I'm clean, and then we can head out. Anywhere in particular you want to go?"

She looked past me, and I knew Archibald had appeared somewhere behind me. "Why don't we figure it out as we go." She reached out and lightly ran a thumb down my jawline.

Friends, I told myself, clamping down on my libido. I was too fucked up now for anything else.

She grinned at me, then walked out of the room. I turned around to face the large, fluffy orange cat in the corner. "How long have you been here?"

He delicately licked his front right paw. "Not long. I missed seeing Kara knock you around. Any better today?"

I finished cleaning my sword, then hung it on the wall-mounted display rack and leaned the scabbard against the wall under it. "No. I'm never going to get it. I'm useless as a fighter. There must be a better role for me."

Archibald walked over to me and head-butted my ankle, then twined around my feet. "You're not just a fighter, Frankie. There is so much more waiting for you. But fighting is going to be a part of it all, and if you can't keep yourself safe, you can't keep anyone else safe. Don't look at this as PE class punishment. You're not running laps. You're learning how to channel the most elemental, powerful parts of your soul and become a weapon."

"I don't wanna be a weapon," I sulked.

Archibald snorted. "You are a Valkyrie. Not only can you escort souls to the afterlife, you can pull them from a person before they're ready to leave. You're already a weapon. The least you owe the world is self-control."

He wasn't wrong. But still...

"I'm not learning how to stop inadvertently stealing souls. I'm learning how to kill people with a pointy stick."

Archibald strode toward the door, tail straight in the air, giving me a view I could've done without. "Tell me later how what you're learning isn't teaching you control." He disappeared before he reached the stairs, and I glared at the point in space where he'd vanished. Why couldn't I learn how to teleport instead of stab people?

With a final huff of disgust and self-pity, I walked up the stairs, skirted the kitchen and living room, and ducked into my room. I shed my clothes on the way to the shower, stuck my tongue out at my reflection in the bathroom mirror, then turned the taps on to just below boiling, letting the scalding water beat out the tension from the fight, my nerves, my crush, and my crazy.

Dusana was waiting for me on the deck after I finished the most amazing grilled cheese sandwich and homemade tomato soup my dad had ever made for me. Hunger added just enough seasoning to enhance his usually amazing food to sublime.

She'd changed out of the corset and sexy boots and now wore sneakers, leggings that clung to her thighs and hips, and a loose, burgundy tunic that did not cover her delectable ass.

Friends. I took a deep breath. "Where to?" I asked. I sat on one of the Adirondack chairs Dad had made during his short-lived but productive carpentry phase to put on my hiking boots. I debated whether the flannel shirt I'd grabbed on my way out would be warm enough, but the September air only hinted at the coming autumn chill, and I'd warm up quickly once we got going.

She gnawed at her lip for a second. "Can you take me to your place?"

I cocked my head. "We're at my place. Well, in as much as I have a place. I can't take you here." *Oh, but you could,* my traitorous brain suggested.

Dusana's brain must've suggested the same thing because she laughed for a second, then covered her mouth with her hand. "I meant your *special* place. The tree. In the woods."

I only hesitated for a second. "Of course. I'd love to share it with you." Funny thing was it was true. I'd been hiding out in that tree since I was seven years old, and in the almost thirty years since, I'd never taken anyone there. But Dusana was safe. I finished tying my boots, then led her down the stairs and into the trees that abutted my parents' yard.

It was impossible to walk side by side in the woods that formed a barrier between my parents' home and the Clackamas River, so we walked single file through the dark green conifers and the shades of brown that made up the late-summer undergrowth. The sweet smell of dying grass baking in the sun rose up to meet my nose with every step, and I smiled. I was sore, frustrated—mentally and sexually—and exhausted, but these woods were home in a way no other place had ever been.

The path was overgrown in places, and the creeping ivy hid obstacles whose locations I knew by heart, but Dusana didn't, so I slowed my pace. "Watch your step up here," I warned, shooting a glance over my shoulder. "There are a few big roots hidden under the vines. I haven't cleared the path since I've been home."

She smiled at me, and I nearly tripped over my own feet when it went straight to my heart. "Thanks for the heads up. I have very little experience in being outdoorsy. It was hard to do much of anything when I was stuck on the road."

I stepped over the largest of the obstacles—the roots of a giant fir tree wrapped around a jagged rock—and paused, holding my hand out to her.

She accepted it. Heat traveled up my arm, spread over my chest, and settled low in my abdomen. As soon as she was on the other side, I dropped her hand and put a few feet of space between us. "What was it like? Haunting Route 66, I mean."

Dusana laughed. "I wasn't really haunting it, Percy was. Although I guess in a way, that distinction doesn't really matter."

She paused long enough that I thought she wasn't going to continue, but just before I threw out another more innocuous but less interesting conversation starter, she spoke.

"It was fun sometimes, especially in the later years. We traveled back and forth between Chicago and Oatman, I don't even know how many times. But there was always something new to see, someone new to meet." She sounded wistful and a little sad.

"You don't have to talk about it if you don't want to. We're almost to the clearing where my tree lives."

"I don't mind. It's nice, actually. The only other person I've ever told is Adele, and who knows where she is anymore. I barely got to say three words to her before she took off, mumbling something about a mission." Dusana took a deep breath, and even though it was mean and a little petty, part of me was pleased she sounded a little winded.

"This is where Percy would make a joke about my job. 'Someone new to talk to, and someone new to escort to the afterlife.' He was so annoying, at least at first. But after a while, when we got used to each other, we were friends. I miss him."

The ache in her voice transferred to my chest. I had a ton of follow-up questions, but none seemed important enough to interrupt her grief.

A couple minutes of silent walking, and the path widened into a small clearing. It wasn't a fairytale glade. It wasn't a circle of soft grass with a bubbling spring, out-of-season wildflowers, and cheerful butterflies. It was bare dirt, pine needles, and dandelions. But the view of the ground wasn't the attraction.

I tipped my head back and looked up. My shoulders unknotted, and the tightness in my chest I hadn't clocked dissipated.

"Whoa," Dusana whispered behind me. "That is a *tree*."

"I know, right? C'mon. You haven't even seen the best part yet." I reached for her hand to pull her forward, then thought better of it and dropped my arm back to my side. I led her through the center of the smallish clearing until we were at the base of the tree. "Look."

She lifted her head and stared at the tree, then turned back to me with a quizzical expression. "What am I looking for?"

I grinned and moved out of her way.

Her mouth dropped open. "No fucking way. What kind of magic-tree shit is this?"

My tree, the one I'd secretly called the World Tree since I was a kid and enamored of the Norse myths my mother told us every night, had huge roots that spiraled out of the ground, serving as a ramp to help me reach the huge low limbs and haul myself up into her branches. Yggdrasil, the real World Tree, was an ash and not a red cedar like this one, but it hadn't mattered to me then, and it didn't now. She might not be Yggdrasil, but she'd been my world tree when I'd needed something magical to hold on to. I snorted. My whole life now was made of magic, and I'd do anything to escape it.

"It's like a ladder," she marveled.

"Exactly like," I agreed. "Follow me." I half-climbed, half-crawled up the initial spiral until I reached the first branch, hopped up onto it, and climbed through the branches until I was about ten feet off the ground.

"This is kind of scary," Dusana said from behind me.

"Oh no! Are you afraid of heights?" I asked. "I didn't think about that."

She laughed, but the sound was strained. "I never thought I was before now, but yeah. Maybe a little."

I grimaced in disappointment, careful to keep my expression to myself. "Let's head back down, then. I can tell you all about the wonder that keeps me coming back to this beauty from the ground."

"Nope," she said. "I've made it this far, and I am not turning around now."

"If you're sure..."

She huffed out a breath. "I'm sure. Let's do this."

I continued climbing, spiraling around the trunk as I hopped from branch to branch. We were over two stories off the ground when I stopped. "We're here. Only a couple more branches, and then you can chill for a while."

"Not sure I'll be able to chill, but I wouldn't mind sitting down against the trunk for a bit before we have to make the hellish climb back down."

"We can do better than that." I took the last couple steps and shifted my weight to turn and watch Dusana. She came into view, and her tight jaw and white knuckles indicated her nerves were even more at the surface than she'd let on. "Look," I said softly.

She turned her head, and for the second time today, gasped. "Wow. This tree is definitely the greatest of all tree-kind."

Several branches grew out from the same place, creating a platform of sorts. They curved a bit as they left the trunk, creating a large, shallow dip big enough for me to stretch out—perfect for sitting.

"When I was younger, I hauled cushions up here in the summer and spent the night in the woods under the stars. I don't have anything out here now though." I paused, then barreled on before I could overthink it. "Being a teenager is hard sometimes. I don't want to downplay anyone else's experiences, but being a closeted lesbian and mentally ill made it worse. If I'd been good at sports, my shortcomings might've been forgiven, but the only sport I liked was cross-country, and I was never fast enough to win."

Dusana stepped into the hollow and effortlessly sank into a cross-legged position.

I continued without looking at her. "Being here"—I waved my hand to encompass the tree and the surrounding forest—"made all my problems smaller, at least for a little while."

"Does it still?" Dusana asked.

"Yes. I can forget the last ten years. Everything I did wrong, everyone I hurt." I smiled wryly and glanced at her. "I can even almost forget how often and thoroughly Kara kicks my ass."

"I am honored you shared this with me."

I sat beside her, much less gracefully and with a pained moan as the muscles I'd been using and abusing for the last few weeks protested. Once I'd arranged myself into the least painful position I could manage, I looked at her. "Why honored?"

"I bet you don't bring a lot of people up here. It's beautiful, and it's obviously a part of you. Thank you for sharing these pieces of yourself with me." She leaned back against the trunk and closed her eyes. "I'm going to lie here for a while and for a moment, I won't imagine how we're going to get down. You should try to relax a bit, too."

She'd barely finished speaking before her breath softened and evened out. I watched her sleep for a few minutes and lay back. I wouldn't mind a nap either, and it'd been a long time since I'd slept in my tree's embrace. The autumn rains would start soon, and it might be a long time before I had another chance.

I closed my eyes and did a progressive relaxation exercise to release every muscle in my body. It didn't work. I was wide awake. For once, the tree wasn't easing my worries. My mind jumped from possible bad weather in the ten-day forecast, to my training failures, to the sudden, powerful craving for a drink. My brain didn't stop there. It dredged up every embarrassing moment from middle school, a falling out with a friend I'd had in vet school that was totally my fault, all the ways I'd screwed up with Gwen. Then it settled on a more recent event.

I relived the accident that had thrown Dusana and me together. I'd watched a little girl die and prevented her twin from following, dooming her to a slow decline into the madness befalling all wraiths —those who didn't die when their time came. Instead, I'd chosen the drunk driver who'd plowed into the family car for death when I shouldn't have.

Tears streamed down my face for the second time today. I curled up into the fetal position and rocked gently. Things were not right, and it might be time to talk to someone about it.

A cold, wet nose bumped against my arm, and I startled.

"What the hell, Archibald?" I whispered. I didn't want to wake Dusana. "Why are you here?"

"Keeping an eye on you, of course," he replied. He collapsed heavily against me and started purring. The vibrations of his body soothed me, and the mad spiraling of my thought pattern slowed and drifted away. "You are not okay."

"Of course I am," I protested automatically.

He didn't reply, just pushed harder into my body and redoubled his purring.

My eyes drifted closed.

THREE

I jogged lightly in place, trying to warm up my stiff muscles before Kara showed up to destroy me again. I rolled my neck. It was achy and stiff, a side effect of sleeping in a tree that neither my father's arthritis cream nor a hot shower had been able to alleviate.

At exactly seven o'clock, the door to the basement swung open and three sets of feet descended. My mother, my honorary aunt and fellow Valkyrie Lena, and Kara. I barely had a chance to nod at the two women I was fairly certain loved me before Kara strode into my field of vision.

"Ready?" she asked. She shed the silky pink dressing gown she'd been wearing to reveal tight black leggings and a bright-pink tank top. She picked up her sword from where she'd racked it the day before, removed the scabbard, and swung the blade around a few times, warming up her wrist.

I mustered a grin, trying for confident, and picked up my sword. "Bring it, bitch."

Kara laughed. "I like the spirit, Frankie. Too bad your skills don't match your mouth."

I didn't wait for her to set herself or prepare in any other way. I attacked, and for a moment, I thought I might be successful. Catching her by surprise gave me an advantage, and I forced her to defend herself against several blows rather than take me out immediately. It wasn't long, however, before she gained her equilibrium. A few seconds later, she blocked my sword, sending a jolt of pain reverberating up my arm. Moving inside my guard, she swept my feet out from under me. I hit the ground hard but didn't drop my sword. A definite improvement over yesterday.

"Get up," Kara said. "Let's go again. You almost had the beginnings of something there for a moment. A spark. Now you have to nurture it."

I scrambled to my feet, pleased to be less sore than I'd been yesterday morning, and readied myself.

Ten minutes and almost half again that many defeats, I was no longer pleased about my mildly sore muscles.

"Get up!" Kara barked for the umpteenth time.

Resilience and persistence had never been my primary personality traits, according to more than one therapist. That'd hurt my feelings in the past, but now I was not only willing to admit they'd been right, but to lean into it as well.

"I am not cut out for this," I gasped. I slid back across the floor and out of her reach. I'd read enough fantasy novels to believe she might whack me with the flat of her sword to get me moving.

"If not you, then who?" Kara asked. She didn't sound nice, but she had softened a bit from her world's-worst-drill-sergeant act.

"I know there are others. Go find one and beat the shit out of them instead." I winced at the whine in my voice. I sounded like a petulant child, a trait that was part of my personality, per my last therapist. The one who had never called me back after I left a message telling her I was maybe having a psychotic break when my Valkyrie powers woke.

Kara's face appeared in my field of vision. "Stop whining. Stop slacking. There are other Valkyries, and if they need it, they'll be trained too. But there is no one else like you. And *you* are here *now*."

"Kara, maybe go a little easier." Lena's soft voice drew my attention. She was a tiny white woman, no more than five feet tall, with short-cropped red hair and piercing blue eyes. She sat next to my mother in one of the three chairs shoved into the back corner of the expansive training room. "She's doing her best and yelling at her won't make her work harder."

Kara snorted. "She is not doing her best. She's hiding behind fear and insecurity. There is more in her. She is a Valkyrie, and fighting is in her blood."

Lena clasped her hands in her lap and leaned forward. "You've had her in here every day for six weeks. Give her a day off."

Kara's voice was harsh. "You of all people know what's at stake here."

"You won't have your warrior if you break her now," Lena said softly.

"I will not lose one!" Kara glared at Lena, then transferred her stare to me. "Get up. Go again."

Archibald walked up and sat between Kara and me, curling his long, fluffy, orange tail around himself.

"Out of my way, Guide," Kara barked.

He didn't move. "Enough, Valkyrie. She will be here and alive to train tomorrow."

Kara spun around and stomped out of the basement, pausing only long enough to grab her scabbard and robe.

Aunt Lena smiled at me. "You're doing a great job, and I am so, so proud of you." She blew me a kiss and followed Kara out of the basement.

I set my sword on the floor and pulled my legs close to my chest, lowering my head to my knees. Archibald brushed against my legs and flopped to the ground.

After a few minutes of silence, he spoke again. "Kara's right, you know. You are not trying as hard as you could."

I shot to my feet so fast that Archibald nearly tipped over. "Seriously? I am down here every day doing my best. How the fuck am I supposed to beat a five-million-year-old Valkyrie? I'm a fucked up, crazy-ass addict who ran home to my mommy and daddy when I screwed up my job and my relationship in the same week. I am useless, and the sooner everyone realizes that, the sooner I can be left alone to whatever fate someone like me deserves."

Archibald got to his feet and walked halfway across the floor. "I'll keep Kara off your back for a couple days while you figure out what you need to do to stop feeling sorry for yourself. If, after that, you want to go back to the kind of life you lived with Ash, walk away. But if you find you want something more and feel a little responsibility to yourself, your family, and this world, then come back here and learn."

He walked toward the stairs but disappeared before he got there.

I exhaled, then bent to pick up my sword.

Maybe I was exhausted. Perseverance and resilience might not be my strong suits, but the nauseating resentment churning in my gut originated from more than my fear of failing. I was not okay. I'd hoped that taking my meds religiously, avoiding drugs and alcohol, exercising, and having a secure place to stay would be enough to fix my fucked-up brain, but apparently not.

My waning mental energy had to be enough though. I couldn't disappoint my family by failing again, and if working with Kara to become a world-class swordswoman was what my mother wanted from me, I would do my best to give it to her.

I brought my blade up and moved through the exercises I'd learned as a child when my mother had first handed me the sword. Once muscle memory took over, I pulled the creepy-ass mannequin out of the corner and tugged off the sheet that covered it. Over and over, I stabbed and slashed until my arms trembled.

The practice dummy blurred, and I swiped at the sweat and tears obscuring my view. My next slash glanced off the dummy's side, knocking the sword out of my hand. It clattered to the floor, the echo reverberating through the room.

"Hey," Dusana said softly.

My pulse jumped even higher than mere exercise had raised it, and I spun around to face her.

Dusana was sprawled in a chair. She wore black leggings and an Indigo Girls T-shirt which fell mid-way down her thighs. I stared. I don't think I'd ever seen her dressed so casually.

"I didn't know you owned T-shirts," I said. I rolled my eyes. What a stupid thing to say. "What are you doing here?" Great. Better for sure. Nothing like a dumb statement followed by a rude question to strengthen a friendship.

"I don't. This is your mom's. It's comfortable. I might invest in a few."

"If you want to try out one that wasn't lent to you by a giant, I have a couple you could borrow."

A smile crinkled the corners of her eyes. "Thank you. I'll definitely take you up on that. As for why I'm here, I heard from a certain furry friend that you had the rest of today and tomorrow off. Do you want to take a field trip with me?"

"Field trip?"

"I don't know about you, but I'm getting a little stir craz— I mean, I haven't spent this long in one place ever, and I need a break. Sorry about the c-word."

Laughter bubbled up before I could stop it. "It's no big deal. I don't like the word crazy to describe a person who is decidedly sane. Calling a fucked-up situation crazy has never bothered me. The other c-word, though? Big fan. It's a very useful word."

A flush stained Dusana's cheeks. "Now I feel really stupid."

"Don't. Tell me about your proposed field trip instead." I dropped into the seat beside her and grabbed a nearby cloth to wipe down my sword.

"Portland."

I cocked my head. "You want to go to Portland?"

"The only place I've been in Portland is that weird not-island where you had your fight with Ash."

At the mention of Ash's name and the reminder of our battle, my stomach tightened. Ash had been my best friend for three years. He hadn't been a good friend, or even a good person, but he'd been with me through a lot of shit. Finding out he was Loki and had been messing with my head fucked me up, and our fight to the near-death still gave me nightmares of fire, pain, and fear.

Dusana continued, unaware of the wave of conflicting feelings threatening to drown me. "I certainly didn't do any sight-seeing. I haven't been many places that aren't along Route 66, to be honest. When I left Oatman, I drove to Vegas, then followed you up here. Let's go to Portland, hit up the huge bookstore, have some coffee, and visit the Japanese gardens or a museum." She clasped her hands under her chin, widened her eyes, and fluttered her eyelashes. "Please say yes."

FOUR

I squeezed my eyes shut and held onto the "oh shit" handle. When I'd agreed to let Dusana drive us to Portland, I had no idea what I was in for.

She laughed, more a squeal of delight, actually. "This is amazing. Percy was always such a stick in the mud about the way I drove, even though he was already dead and I was a reaper of souls."

"He may have had a point," I said through clenched teeth as the centrifugal force of tearing around a hairpin curve pulled my stomach from my body, shook it up, and put it back upside down and in the wrong place.

Dusana snorted. "We're both immortal—or near enough. And I'm a fantastic driver."

"I'm not immortal, and we're not the only ones on the road. There are plenty of innocent drivers out there who could be victims of"—I waved my free hand in the air—"whatever this is."

Dusana huffed out a sigh. "You're almost as bad as Percy." The car decelerated, and my equilibrium slowly returned. "But fine. I don't want my passengers to be terrified. And of course you're immortal. You're a Valkyrie, right?"

"So I've been told."

"How old is your mom? Or your Aunt Lena? Or Kara the battle-ax?"

I cracked my eyes open, ready to retreat into the imagined safety of darkness again if I saw trees whizzing at me like we were jumping into hyperspace, but our speed on the straight, level highway was downright sedate compared to how fast we'd been traveling on the winding road between Estacada and Portland. "That's different. They're actually Valkyries. I'm just a Valkyrie spawn."

"Not how it works. I'm not an expert, of course, but I'd be willing to bet you inherited more than your ability to escort souls to the afterlife. You're not truly immortal; none of us are. But you won't age and die, and you're a lot harder to kill than an ordinary person." Dusana rolled to a halt at a stop sign, then turned left onto a wider and mercifully much straighter road.

She drove into traffic as we approached the freeway into Portland and was forced to slow even more. Her muttered curses, recriminations, and pointed jabs at her fellow drivers were enough to cover my sudden angst at the idea of immortality. Sure, perhaps I should've figured it out on my own—my mother *was* over a thousand years old —but there'd been a lot of other things going on, and my desire to not die in battle had completely overshadowed the possibility that I might not be able to die at all.

"Guess this makes suicide pointless," I said. I'd intended it to be a joke, but my tone was too flat for it to sound amusing.

Dusana stared at the road in front of her, and only the whitening of her knuckles betrayed any emotion.

"I didn't mean..." But that was a lie. I absolutely did mean it. Kind of, anyway. My meds still worked, and my brain chugged on. But the inherent knowledge, present for as long as I could remember, that my destiny was to die by suicide had resurfaced. It wouldn't be soon. I didn't have a method or a plan, the things that were the important distinction between getting therapy or going to a psych ward. But the knowing was always there under the surface.

I looked down at my hands twisting in my lap. I was usually better at keeping this side of me hidden. Talking about depression and suicidal ideation made most people deeply uncomfortable, and the very idea of ending one's own life was considered selfish by a majority of the population.

"Sorry," I muttered. "Bad joke."

Dusana flipped on the blinker, slammed on the brakes, and pulled onto the shoulder in the space of a couple seconds. She jammed her car into park and turned to glare at me. "Don't you ever apologize for saying how you feel. Ever. If you're feeling like ending it all, please tell me. Tell someone. Anyone. But I will never, ever judge you." She grabbed the steering wheel and looked straight ahead. Her chest rose and fell quickly, and her exhalations were loud enough to do any pranayama teacher proud.

"Okay?" I didn't know what else to say. Her reaction was nothing like I'd expected. Most people went along with my "joke" and either laughed awkwardly, ignored it completely, or gave me a lecture on the selfishness of my attitude. And occasionally, they'd end with an exhortation to try meditation.

Her breathing slowed and quieted, and she shifted her body to face me. "I have seen a lot of death. I've been there for more endings than I can count. No matter the cause of death, there is no selfishness in it. Often, there is pain and then the cessation of pain. It doesn't matter why there is suffering, the relief is the same. I would never judge a person for desiring that relief and taking steps to find it. Living can be agony."

"Thank you." I had other words; I was sure of it. Words that could express my shock, my gratitude, and my wonder. But none of them made their way from my subconscious to my tongue.

She shrugged and faced forward again. "You're welcome. And I'm sorry for going off like that. Death is a subject I feel very passionately about—it's a job hazard. There's a lot more judgment about it than I would've guessed. It can be hard, of course. I hate reaping children, especially those who die because of another person's actions, but there is nothing in death that is shameful. However"—she flipped on the blinker and looked behind her—"for all that, I would like you to not feel that way. There may be no shame in death, but there is so much joy in living. I'd like to be there as you rediscover that."

She pulled smoothly into traffic and merged onto I-205 before I spoke again.

"I'm not suicidal right now. I'm just not happy." Ugh. That sounded childish and ungrateful. "I mean, of course I'm happy. My parents welcomed me back with open arms. My sisters are pretty great about me coming back, too. I have a niece named after me, a wonderful new friend, a handsome cat, and a destiny I could've never guessed. And real-live Valkyries to teach me how to save the world. My life is fantastic."

"And yet?"

"I wish I felt more grateful."

"That's bullshit," Dusana said. "You can acknowledge that your life is great without having to be grateful every moment. That whole 'attitude of gratitude' crap is almost as toxic as 'positive vibes only.' All you need to do is acknowledge your feelings as they come and decide what to do with them, but don't try to fake happy 'til you make it. I don't give a flying fuck how uncomfortable some people feel in the face of mental illness. They suck. You do not. End of story."

My shoulder blades melted down my back, and my jaw unclenched for the first time in what felt like forever. "I'm feeling an awful lot of gratitude right now. I don't think anyone has ever yelled at me quite like this before. Usually, I get a lot of admonitions about how I'm doing mental health wrong, but you made me feel a lot better without telling me I should feel a lot better."

Dusana laughed sheepishly. "Eons of experience counseling the newly dead combined with a decade of seeing it from the other side make for some very decided opinions on the subject. Sorry if I came off too strong."

"You came off exactly right," I assured her. "I had no idea how much I needed someone to tell me I wasn't an awful, evil person."

She took the ramp to merge onto I-84 West. "As much as I'd like to promise a repeat performance every time you start to feel shitty, I don't think that's the kind of thing you should count on. Nor is it a role I'd care to play with a friend. I hate to sound like a cliché, but have you thought about getting a therapist?"

And just like that, the tension crept back into my body. "I've had one or two or a hundred, and although some were good, there were a lot who weren't so great. My standards are pretty low, but I would like to believe that I shouldn't leave every therapy session feeling worse about myself than I did when I walked in."

Dusana honked at a red sedan that had sped up to block her merge and flipped them off. "Asshole!" she yelled, even though there was no way they could hear her. "I hope you spend the rest of your life getting paper cuts under your fingernails every damn day."

"Wow. Harsh." I laughed.

"It's up there with cursing someone with constant upper-thigh chaffing, or a persistently itchy spot on their back that they'll never be able to reach," she admitted.

"So in addition to being extremely passionate about death, you're a connoisseur of the best ways to insult a person who triggers your road rage?" I was changing the subject and hoped she'd catch on and not steer us—pun intended—back around to therapists.

"When you spend as much time on the road as I did, originality becomes more and more difficult. Percy and I used to make a contest out of it. He was better at first because he was more familiar with the everyday irritations that would be agonizing if they became everyday occurrences, but after a couple years, I kicked his ass because I'm meaner." She flashed a grin at me that was two parts amusement and one part acknowledgment that she was letting the subject of my mental health go, at least for the time being.

"I wish I could've met him. He sounds like a lot of fun."

"He was, even though the thought of getting excited about visiting the largest ball of twine was completely unfathomable to him." Dusana peered at the map on her phone for a second and changed lanes to merge onto I-5 South. Then she took the next exit for the Morrison Bridge, which crossed the Willamette and would take us into downtown Portland.

"The largest ball of twine is on my bucket list," I confessed.

"I know. You told me that when I gave you a ride ten years ago," Dusana said. "That's one of the reasons I remembered you. That and you could sense Percy, even if you couldn't see him."

"Not because I was wicked hot?" I teased.

"That might be on the list," she said with a grin. "Now, where do we go first?"

CHAPTER

FIVE

I laid back and gazed at the dusky sky, intersected by the soaring green span of the St. Johns Bridge. Dusana was taking pictures of the West Hills across the Willamette River, the bridge framing the variegated greens of the conifers interspersed with the changing leaves of the oaks and maples.

A nearly empty picnic spread lay between us. A couple water crackers, one piece of Beecher's cheddar that was about to meet an untimely end in my stomach, a bit of Brie, and three olives were the only things left.

It'd been an amazing day. I loved books, but I hadn't realized that I was an amateur book lover until watching Dusana in Powell's. It was a fantastic bookstore and the biggest I'd ever seen. Getting lost in there had been one of my favorite pastimes when I was a teenager. But Dusana made noises that weren't for polite company when she got to the middle of the store and did a slow twirl to figure out where to go next. The only thing preventing her from buying more books than the metric fuck-ton she'd ended up purchasing was sheer womanpower.

After books and lunch, we headed to the Japanese Gardens, then

33

hiked up into Forest Park, where we toured the Pittock Mansion and took Wildwood Trail to the Witch's House.

After that, we grabbed food and had a picnic in Cathedral Park. It was one of about a million parks in Portland, and it was definitely in my top five. Lounging under the St. Johns bridge was amazing, and seeing the river made the experience even better.

"We should get up," Dusana groaned. "If I don't move soon, I'm going to become a permanent fixture here. That was a lot of cheese."

I scoffed. "It wasn't that much. I've definitely had more cheese." I spread the Brie on a cracker, popped it into my mouth, and shoved the cheddar in after. Was it sexy and graceful? No. But was it deeply satisfying? One hundred percent yes.

Dusana ate the last cracker, chasing it with the olives. "We will never be able to eat more cheese if we don't get up and move at least a little. You can't possibly expect me to live through a cheeseless future, can you?"

I huffed, rolled onto my side and to my feet, and shoved our detritus into the paper bag it'd come in. "Fine. If you insist. Let's toss the garbage and go for a walk. Killjoy."

Dusana smiled at me and hopped to her feet. It really was unfair that an immortal, ageless being had so much spring in her step. She'd been human for a decade, and she still bopped around like a teenage gymnast. Meanwhile, I was thirty-five and wanted to hobble around, bemoaning my creaky old bones half the time.

I tossed the garbage into one of the many trash bins that dotted the park, then slipped my arm through Dusana's crooked elbow. "Lead on, my lady!"

We strolled arm in arm along the asphalt paths that wound through the park, then walked to the end of a dock and watched the sun set. I stared at the water, watching the ripples break against the dock before finishing their journey to the rocky riverbank.

It was perfect and peaceful. Exactly what I'd needed.

I turned to Dusana, intending to thank her for this gift of a day, when the ripples multiplied and intensified. I stared at the water. Dread raised goosebumps on my arms and prickled my skull.

"We need to go," I said. I grabbed Dusana and pulled her back toward land. It was too late though.

Dozens of slimy eel-like heads broke the surface of the river. They were a silvery purple, and their gaping maws showed off dozens of razor-sharp teeth.

"What the fuck are those?" Dusana whispered.

I reached behind me to draw the sword I'd barely been without for the last couple months, only to have my hand meet empty air. My sword was hanging on the wall in my mother's basement, because there had been no reason to bring it with me. I was on a day trip, I'd be going to all sorts of places that wouldn't let me in with a weapon, and there was nothing dangerous about Portland.

"No idea," I replied. "But we need to get out of here, fast."

"No arguments from me."

I turned around so we could make a run for it. Once we were away from the water, we'd be safe, unless these horrific fishlike creatures could slither on dry land, too.

My heart jolted like I'd been hit with a defibrillator—something that I'd experienced during my post-suicide attempt hospitalization ten years ago. Between us and the end of the dock was what I could only describe as a sea monster. It looked kinda like the creepy eel-things but was as big around as Dusana's car, and its mouth wasn't just a fang-lined tooth factory—it was a horror show. Rows of teeth dripping with what I sincerely hoped was saliva and not venom angled back into a ridged throat that framed a darting, forked tongue.

"That cannot be real," Dusana said. "It's a biological impossibility, and its body doesn't fit together."

"I'll let it know, and then it can peace the fuck out of here," I said. "Once it knows it's imaginary, I'm sure it won't bother us anymore."

"Do you always use inappropriate sarcasm instead of your sword when you're scared?" she asked.

I nodded. My eyes darted around, looking for a way to escape. "Usually. Especially when I've left my sword at home. Can you swim?"

"No. But even if I could, swimming through eel-infested waters isn't a great idea. I know it's only a little ways, but if the girth of that monster is anything to go by, it's going to be more than a minor obstacle. I have a better idea." Dusana glowed a bright blue for a second, and the light scored my vision. A scythe appeared in her hands, and her expression grew fierce. "Kella and I are ready for this."

Dusana pivoted one hundred and eighty degrees and leaped forward, swiping at the small eels writhing in the water. Her scythe cut through them like a hot knife through butter. Their headless bodies sank beneath the waves, and a dozen more replaced them. Dusana beheaded the lot, and two dozen more appeared.

I looked behind us. The behemoth monster had wrapped itself around the pier, and the planks that linked us to land were disintegrating in its coils. Fear, hot and ugly, welled in my chest, and my heart beat a triple-time rhythm. In seconds, there'd be no route back to land, and nothing under our feet but monsters. "Dusana. We have to go."

She swiped at the eels, but this time they dodged, and she only got a half dozen of them.

Twelve snakes appeared as the beheaded ones sank. "What the fuck is going on? This is some kind of hydra bullshit." She swung again.

I grabbed her arm and tugged. "We can take it up with someone later. Now, we have to get out of here before the big snake monster destroys the dock, and we get killed by the little snake monsters. Run!"

Dusana swung her scythe through the water one more time, then pushed by me and ran toward land. She ripped through the monster's neck with her scythe, then was on the other side before I could blink.

The monster roared; my bladder spasmed. I finally understood why people peed their pants out of fear.

"Don't think about it," she cautioned. "Just run and jump. Use its back like a springboard."

I didn't even bother choking back a laugh. "Lady, I am the least springy and most feet-on-the-ground person you'll ever meet."

"And if you don't take a flying leap over whatever this is, you'll be the deadest feet-on-the-ground person. Run and jump. Don't look, and don't let it win."

I squeezed my eyes shut and took a deep breath. I obviously couldn't run down a wooden dock and jump over a sea monster that was not only gushing blood from its nearly severed head but also rapidly healing said gash. But I could at least use some of the training I'd undergone in the last few weeks to evade the teeth and hit the ground running. Probably.

I opened my eyes and scanned my surroundings. The dock behind me was a writhing mass of eels slithering onto the wooden planks in an obscene tangle of slimy bodies. Ahead of me, the dock groaned and splintered under the weight of the sea monster trying to trap me.

Dusana stood on the bank behind it, scythe in hand, and a fierce expression on her face.

I couldn't hear what she said, but I knew, nonetheless.

She wanted me to quit stalling and start doing.

It wasn't a huge leap. The only thing that would make it difficult was an attack mid-flight. The thing was bleeding so much after Dusana's strike that I figured I could handle it.

I spared another glance behind me, did a quick scan of the snaki-ness surrounding me, and ran.

SIX

I opened my eyes. The sky above me was purple with dusk, and the ground under my head was hard and uncomfortable.

A tall, trim, Black EMT pressed an icepack against my cheek. "You're going to be fine, but I suggest not picking fights with invisible eels for the foreseeable future."

"What the hell happened?" It was a question I'd once been afraid to ask. But I'd learned it got me more information than not asking.

"I don't know, ma'am. Your partner said a storm surge took out the dock and a bunch of enormous eels attacked you, but that makes zero sense." He moved me into a seated position. "There are lampreys in the water, but a sighting is pretty rare."

I was missing so much context I didn't know how to respond. Fortunately, his questioning took on an entirely new track.

"Do you have family you want me to call? Or should I leave you with the scary lady?"

I cracked a smile. "I'll be fine with the scary lady."

The EMT grimaced. "Well, if you know her..." His voice trailed off, but the fierce expression on his face didn't disappear.

I waved him away. "She's not scary; she's my driver."

"She hurt you," he said flatly. "It's my job to make sure people aren't in real trouble."

I looked between the EMT and Dusana, who was a few yards away, talking to a couple cops and not taking her eyes off me. "What do you mean, she hurt me? She wouldn't do that."

"How do you explain the bruised cheekbone? I've seen the aftermath of more than enough punches to recognize it immediately." He pulled the ice pack away and prodded my face with gentle fingers.

I winced at the sudden spike in pain, and he dropped his hand.

"Sorry. Just making sure nothing's broken. Wanna tell me what happened?" He handed me the ice pack and rocked back on his heels.

I pressed the ice pack to my aching face and wracked my brains. I needed to come up with something that would remove his suspicion from Dusana and get him and the cops to take off. The last thing I needed was police involvement. The problem was, I didn't remember anything after starting my terrifying leap over the sea monster. I glanced toward the river and saw the wreckage of the dock. Telling the truth—or at least a monster-free version of it—was probably my best bet.

"I don't remember. We had a picnic in the park, then walked onto the dock. Something happened to it, and it started collapsing. Dusana hopped from the dock to the shore easily, but I hesitated too long. I remember jumping, but I don't remember landing. Maybe I hit my head on one of the rocks?" Since I knew Dusana wouldn't have punched me as I hit the ground, and a sea monster attack would've left a much bigger injury, face planting into a bunch of rocks was the most logical, not to mention least graceful, answer I could think of.

The EMT pursed his lips, then rose to his feet. "That's the story she told, although hers had eels in it."

"There were eels. A whole bunch of them on the end of the dock." I shuddered at the memory. "I've never seen anything quite like it, and I hope I never do again."

He offered me his hand, and I let him haul me to my feet. I paused, braced for dizziness that didn't come.

"Let me have one last look at your face, then I'll go away and leave you alone if you want me to."

I dropped the ice pack from my cheek.

"Huh," he said. "It doesn't look like it's going to bruise anywhere near as much as I thought it would. Keep the ice on it, and it'll probably be nearly unnoticeable in a couple days."

He glanced back at Dusana, then at me. "She is fierce. If she's on your side, you are lucky to have a partner like that."

"We're just friends," I said.

A speculative light shone in his eyes for a second, then he shook his head. "She is totally out of my league, isn't she?"

"She's out of everyone's league," I confirmed. I smiled at him and held out my hand. "Thank you. I really appreciate your help and your concern for my safety."

"You're welcome." He shook my hand, then headed back toward the ambulance and his waiting partner.

I walked over to Dusana, who had a polite smile pasted on her face and a look in her eyes that spoke of barely restrained impatience and frustration.

"Hey, officers." It paid to be polite to the men with guns. "Can we leave now? I'm tired and sore, and it's a long drive back."

The taller of the two cops glared at me. "Yes. I have your phone numbers, and as soon as we have enough evidence that you destroyed public property, we will let you know."

Dusana didn't say anything until we were back on the freeway. Night had fallen, and the highway lights highlighted her profile as they blinked by.

"What really happened?" I asked when it was evident that she wasn't going to volunteer any information. Fuck. Was she mad at me for whatever I'd done between jumping and waking up? "Did I hurt you? Is everything okay?"

"Of course you didn't hurt me. You're the one who got hurt. But you are an idiot."

I was taken aback. I'd suspected I'd upset her in some way, but even with that surety, this was not the response I'd expected. "I'm sorry."

She huffed out a sigh. "No, I'm sorry. You're not an idiot. I was scared for you, then the cops showed up. I'm too tense. But you are crap at jumping."

I laughed and was pleased that there wasn't a single note of hysteria in it. "I told you I was no good. I remember running toward the monster, but I don't remember even starting to jump."

"It's probably for the best. It would be one of those images that'd come back to haunt you years later when you're trying to sleep, and your brain insists on playing its 'Most Embarrassing Memories' reel."

I wrinkled my nose and grimaced. "It was that bad?"

"It was that bad," Dusana confirmed, shooting me a sideways glance. "Want me to tell you more?"

"Not really, but also yes. Go ahead."

She signaled, then took I-5 South to the I-84 East interchange. Once she'd merged with traffic, she said, "You jumped, and I knew right away you didn't go high enough to make it over the monster. So I helped. Kinda."

A flush halfway between embarrassment and fear suffused my body. "When you say 'kinda'…"

"I jumped on the back of that slippery asshole, grabbed your arm, and hurled you to shore like a ball in one of those dog toys, then leaped after you. Unfortunately, between my poor person-tossing skills and the momentum of the throw knocking me off balance, you landed on a bunch of rocks, and I landed on top of you. Sorry." Her hands tightened on the steering wheel.

"The EMT was right, then. You did hurt me. Guess it's good our stories matched. He was convinced you'd punched me." I turned Dusana's words over in my mind. "How the hell did you manage to hurl me at all?"

"I'm almost half a foot taller than you, and I am much stronger than I look," Dusana said, grinning at me. "I didn't mean to hurt you."

"Of course you didn't, and I really appreciate you saving me. Again."

She took her eyes off the road long enough to wink at me. "That's what friends are for."

My phone rang, and I let it go to voicemail. Maybe my day off hadn't gone perfectly, but I wasn't going to ruin the end of it by answering the phone just to learn about my nonexistent car's expired warranty.

The ring broke off, then started again.

"You should at least see who it is," Dusana said. "Maybe it is actually something important."

I rummaged through my bag until I found the phone. I had fifteen missed calls and three times that many text messages.

"Shit," I whispered. "Something is seriously wrong."

I checked my messages first. I had texts from just about everyone in my contact list, but the most were from my sister Jackie. I scrolled through the eight from her. They'd all come in the last hour and grew increasingly frantic.

The messages from my other sister were along the same line, but with fewer bodily threats or dire warnings about sea monsters.

Before I could read any from my parents or Aunt Lena, the phone rang again. It was my mother.

"Mom? What's going on? Is something wrong?"

The silence after my questions was so long, I had to glance at the phone to make sure we were still connected.

"Mom?"

"You're okay?" Her voice broke, and I heard fear in her tone.

"Mostly," I said. "I have a bit of a bruise, but nothing worse, which is pretty good, all things considered. Did you know there were sea monsters in the Willamette?"

"What are you talking about?" she asked. "Sea monsters?"

I wrinkled my nose. "I thought that's why you were calling. One of Jackie's messages mentioned them, so I figured everyone was worried about that. If that's not why you're calling, then what's up?"

"You disappeared without a word to anyone," my mom said. The fear was no longer evident. In its place was a tight annoyance. "I thought, after earlier..."

My breath left me in a *whoosh*. "You thought I'd taken off. That I'd run away." My voice was flat and expressionless. Of course they had. Why wouldn't they? "I didn't leave without a word. I told Archibald where I was going, and he was supposed to pass the message on."

"You gave a message to a cat to pass on?" my mother asked in the too-calm voice that meant she'd gone from worried to furious without making more than a pit stop at relieved.

"He's not just a cat," I protested.

"He might be your Guide and a magical creature, but he is still a cat." Her displeasure was so palpable that it poured out of the phone, and my shoulders hunched around it.

"I'm sorry," I said, feeling about twelve years old. "I won't do it again."

Mom sighed. I couldn't see her, but I knew the expression that went with that noise. Her eyes were closed, and she was rubbing her temples with the thumb and middle finger of her right hand. She wasn't angry anymore. She was sad.

"I promise," I said.

"You don't have to apologize. You're an adult, and you have the right to take a day to yourself. I'd love it if you'd let someone know you're leaving in the future, but I'd expect that of anyone who was living with me. I overreacted. We all overreacted. It's me who should be sorry." She sounded exhausted, and guilt knotted my guts. "We can talk about the sea monsters when you get home."

"I love you, Mom."

"I love you, too, Frances Lenore Ström. I'm glad you're safe."

She ended the call before I could say anything else. I slipped my phone back into my purse without answering any of the messages.

"You didn't leave a note?" Dusana asked.

"I told the cat," I replied a little defensively. The meaning of my words struck me, and I started to giggle.

"You left a message with your cat." Dusana snorted; she was giggling a bit now, too.

"He's in big trouble when I find him." I tried to sound serious but couldn't quite manage it. "If he'd done his job, we could've avoided this *cata*strophe."

Dusana's gales of laughter filled the car. She turned toward me and smiled just as we passed under a freeway light, and the glow made her look ethereal. She was so fucking beautiful, and my heart skipped a metaphorical beat.

Forget the monsters and the wrath of my mother. This woman was going to be my downfall.

I was in so much trouble.

SEVEN

There was no one on the back deck when I finally made my way there just before midnight. I'd gotten through the gauntlet of reactions about my "disappearance" and made my escape, promising to update everyone on the sea serpent situation the next morning.

But now the house was quiet, and I could finally be alone with my thoughts.

I was missing something about the confrontation on the dock, and it niggled at me.

I shook my head. If it was really important, it'd probably come to me sometime. Likely in the middle of the night when I was staring at the ceiling, wishing I'd stuck glow-in-the-dark stars to it like I had every ceiling I'd slept under until I'd moved in with Gwen. I'd thought about asking her if it was okay, telling her that they comforted me and I counted them to help me fall asleep, but didn't. I wanted her to respect me as well as love me, to think of me as an adult, and needing glow-in-the-dark stars to sleep was akin to requiring a teddy bear.

But since I didn't have ceiling stars, the real things would have to do. I lowered myself to the floor of the deck and sprawled out on my back, looking for the familiar constellations and trying to identify the brightest lights in the sky. I evened out my breathing and let my shoulder blades slide down my back. It wasn't hard to put myself into savasana, my favorite yoga asana. I preferred meditative pranayama to the more vigorous Vinyasa classes, and no longer needed coaching from a teacher to find my breath and my connection to the earth.

The door slid open, pulling me away from the stars and back into my body.

"What are you doing?" Jackie asked. She sounded more curious than accusatory, which spoke volumes to how much our relationship had mended in the six weeks since I'd reappeared in her life after a ten-year absence.

"Meditating and counting the stars," I said. "Why are you still here?"

"I don't like driving in the dark." My youngest sister was as tall as my mother—easily six feet—but had dark skin and black, tightly curled hair like my father. She was not only gorgeous, she was brilliant, athletically gifted, fierce, and aggressively kind. The polar opposite of me. She dropped beside me and crisscross-applesauced her legs. "Couldn't sleep?"

I pushed myself into a seated position next to her and leaned back against the railings. "Couldn't sleep,"

"You always needed the stars to sleep. You should get some of those stick-on ones for your room."

"How do you even remember that?" Sure, Jackie hadn't been a child when I'd left the state after vet school, but she had been when I'd moved out to go to college.

She tilted her head to look at me, and when she spoke, confusion rode her voice. "When I was little and had bad dreams, I always came to your room. You'd let me snuggle with you, and we'd count the stars until I wasn't scared anymore and could go back to bed. And you had them in your dorm room, then your apartment when you were in vet school."

I shook my head slowly, and a lump formed in my throat. How could I not remember comforting her? Something so significant, so much a part of her childhood, and I had no recollection. "I don't remember. I'm sorry, I wish I did."

"It's no big deal. It was a long time ago." Jackie's eyelids sank to half-mast, and she tipped her head back to look at the stars.

I wasn't always great at reading expressions or tones, but this one was obvious. It was, in fact, a big fucking deal.

"I'm really sorry. There's so much I don't remember. It's not because I want to forget. I don't know what's wrong with me." The helpless feeling that'd been riding me off and on for the last few days returned. Finding a therapist who wouldn't think I was crazier than my diagnosis indicated had to be top of my to-do list. "Do you still have bad dreams?"

"All the time, although now I know them for what they are. Visions of the future. Most of the time. I really hope the one where my teeth fall out while I'm giving a naked presentation on dental hygiene to a middle-school health class is just a run-of-the-mill nightmare."

"Best to refuse all requests to speak to middle schoolers, just to be on the safe side." I grinned at her, hoping I could recapture the rapport we'd been building.

"I intend on avoiding everything to do with teenagers for the rest of my life." She shuddered dramatically and smiled back.

"And when the best baby in the world turns thirteen?" I teased. "What then?"

Jackie wrinkled her nose. "Don't think I haven't thought of that. When Lenore turns thirteen, it's straight off to military school with her. She can come back when she's twenty-five."

I slid my arm around my baby sister's shoulders, and she leaned her head on mine. "Where is my favorite niece tonight?"

"Home with her daddy, probably staying up all night to play violent video games and smoke cigars."

"Important parts of every baby's upbringing." I nodded solemnly. "I'll never forget my first cigar. I think it was right before I started on solid foods."

Jackie dissolved into giggles, and it didn't take long before I laughed, too.

This was perfect. It's what I'd wanted when I came home but hadn't quite dared to hope for.

Peace. Laughter. Family.

The slider opened with so much violence that it bounced off the doorstop.

Kara glared at us from the doorway. "Downstairs. Now."

We scrambled to our feet and followed her inside without hesitation. It was only when I got to the living room that I remembered I was thirty-five years old and didn't have to leap to my feet when someone said jump. Based on the way Jackie stopped short, I suspected the same realization had just come to her.

"Why?" I asked.

Kara whirled around. "Your presence is required." She looked at Jackie. "Yours is not. You may leave now."

I crossed my arms. "You are my trainer, and I will accept your direction while you're teaching me. But you aren't in a position to issue commands anywhere else. We are adults, and unless we're on the battlefield, we deserve explanations before rushing off to follow your directives."

Jackie folded her arms, too. "I'm not a Valkyrie, so you can't tell me where I can and cannot go. Spill, or we're not moving."

Kara took a deep breath, held it, then exhaled with a *whoosh* of breath. Her long-suffering expression was the one my mother always sported when any of us girls got in trouble as children. But we were not children, and it did not work on me. I could wait her out.

"Freyja is in the basement and needs to talk to the Valkyries," Kara said finally.

"That wasn't so hard, was it?" Jackie said in a voice that preschool teachers everywhere used when a toddler finally agreed to share a toy.

Kara didn't reply, just turned around and marched to the basement door.

Jackie and I looked at each other and shrugged.

"Wanna come?" I asked.

"And break up the Valkyrie-only party?" she replied dryly.

"You can be my sidekick. Sidekicks are always welcome." I stuck out my tongue. I knew what she'd say next.

She blew a raspberry at me. "Pffffffft! If anything, you're my sidekick, which means I'm automatically invited. C'mon."

CHAPTER

EIGHT

Jackie and I took our seats and ignored Kara. No one else said anything else about Jackie being there, and Lena smiled broadly at us both.

Freyja stood in the middle of the floor, looking like she had the first time I'd met her. She was taller than any of the other women in the room, which was saying something, since my mom was over six feet tall, and Kara could double as a small giant. Freyja's long, honey-blonde braids brushed her waist, and summer sky blue eyes completed her look as a stereotypical Norse goddess. But that's where the stereotype ended. She wore khaki shorts, a rose-colored, silky tank top that matched the pink in her cheeks, and an unadorned gold circlet perched on her head.

"Ah, finally," she said.

"What's going on?" my mother asked briskly. "You wouldn't show up if there wasn't a problem."

Freyja looked affronted. "That's not the only time I visit."

Lena and Kara exchanged an amused glance but didn't say anything.

Freyja huffed. "Fine. I'll try to come hang out sometime. I under-

53

stand you have potato tournaments. I will attend the next one of those. I love lefse."

"Now that we've established you're here with bad news, how about you get down to it?" Mom suggested. She smiled at the goddess, but a muscle in her jaw pulsed with tension.

The goddess clasped her hands in front of her. "A Valkyrie needs your aid!" she announced with an ominous tone that would've been better suited for "FEAR NOT, FOR I AM AN ANGEL OF THE LORD!"

Kara wrinkled her nose. "Yes. We know. That's where the rest of our sisters are. Rounding up the others who, like Frankie, don't know what's happening to them, and ushering them here."

"I don't mean there are other nascent Valkyries in need of help. I mean, there is one who is alone, confused, and in danger."

"Who is her mother? Where is she?" Kara asked.

Freyja shrugged, a casual motion that belied the strain on her face. "I believe she is Serena's, but I cannot sense Serena anywhere. It has always been easier for me to sense the First and her family." The goddess nodded at me. "The blood of the First, the chosen, runs as true in Frankie as it did in her grandmother, and it calls to me as it calls both the Guide and the other Valkyries."

This was the first I'd heard about my blood being truer than other Valkyries', and I wasn't sure how I felt about it. It sounded too close to something white supremacists who incorporated the symbols of my heritage as emblems of their beliefs and espoused purity would say. Between the trappings of hate and the responsibility inherent in such a statement, there was a lot to take in and none of it good.

I raised my hand, knowing I was being insensitive, and asked, "Can we talk about being the chosen one?"

"Later," Kara snapped. "Where is Serena's daughter?"

Freyja shook her head. "I don't know. She's on the move, but I think she's close. The pull of your Aerie will lead her. She won't find her way here, of course, but the safety it represents is a beacon to my

Valkyries." Her gaze turned distant for a moment. "She has her sword. That should be enough to allow you to find her."

Kara nodded as if that made sense, which of course it didn't.

I gritted my teeth. I'd already interrupted a goddess once, and no matter how many questions I had about swords and chosen ones, I'd table every single one of them until later.

Freyja turned to me, her expression softening. "You have many questions, First. Ask now, and I will do my best to answer them."

"What is so special about me? And how do I stop it?"

Freyja reared back, almost as if I'd slapped her. "Why would you want to? You are a Valkyrie, and you are born to lead your sisters into battle. It is an honor almost beyond comprehension."

"But is there someone else who could take my place?" I pressed. I figured this line of questioning would get me further than telling a bunch of battle-hardened Valkyries that I was in no way interested in glory. "Someone else who could lead an army?"

"No. There are others whose powers are awakening and who have no idea what's going on. But you're the daughter and grand-daughter of the First, and that means you are the one who will lead." She turned back to Kara. "My Valkyries, those who have passed on their power, are disappearing. You must have felt this."

Kara shook her head. "It is more difficult to sense those whose powers have passed on to their daughters."

Freyja took a deep breath. "Six. Six are all that are left of my orig-inal children. The rest of the Valkyries are children and grandchil-dren, most of whom have even less training than Frankie." She turned and snagged my gaze. "The power is waking in them as it woke in you. The potentials will find their way here, and you will lead them in our battle to stop Ragnarök."

Her volume increased as she rolled to the end of her sentence, and her voice reverberated through the room, rattling the weapons on the walls and vibrating my chest like when the bass in a funky song was turned up too high.

"Buffy season seven," I said to Jackie.

Freyja rolled her eyes, and the tension in the room dissipated. "I am trying to give you something to relate to. Pop culture is a common modern language, whereas ancient consequences told only in what you deem myths and legends are not." Freyja sobered, and all traces of amusement disappeared. She pointed at me. "You must find the other Valkyrie and bring her here."

I had a hundred more questions, namely why me, and why couldn't Kara or one of the other "originals," as Freyja called them, lead us into battle? I opened my mouth to ask, but before I could, Freyja disappeared. It wasn't a flashy vanishing. One minute she was there, and the next—gone. Not even a *poof* for verisimilitude.

"You heard the goddess," Kara barked. "We need to get to Portland and find the missing Valkyrie."

My mother stood. "In the morning."

"Katrin—" Kara started.

"No. Frankie is tired, and sending in someone this exhausted would be disastrous. If you want to go yourself, please do so, but Freyja gave this task to Frankie."

Kara sighed and said two words I'd never expected to hear from her. "You're right. Tomorrow is better." Then she looked at me and pointed. "We will leave at dawn. Be ready, and don't forget your sword this time."

It was only then that I realized we hadn't told Freyja about the sea monsters. I glanced at my mother, and she nodded her understanding. "I will let her know," she said, thus confirming my suspicion that she could talk to Freyja at will. "You sleep."

Jackie stood. "I'm going, too."

"No," my mother said.

"I can help," Jackie said stubbornly. "I know what is happening before it happens. I can guide them."

Kara regarded Jackie. "That is a useful skill."

"No," my mother said again, this time more forcefully. "She is untrained and cannot defend herself."

Jackie grabbed my sword and tossed it to me, then pulled another off the wall. "Fight me," she said to me.

"Um, no?" Nevertheless, I unsheathed my sword and stood. I knew Jackie well enough to predict she would absolutely push it.

Jackie pulled her sword from its scabbard and attacked before I set my guard.

I barely blocked her first two strikes, and she took a step back to re-evaluate before rushing forward again.

For a couple minutes, it was all I could do to keep her from breaching my defenses. Every strike I made, she countered instantly, and I lost ground a step at a time.

Finally, I saw an opening and knew exactly how to end this. The movement Kara had been drilling into my brain for the last six weeks surfaced. I took two steps forward and disarmed my sister.

Her sword clattered to the ground, and she shook out her hand.

"Not bad," Kara said, eyeing my sister speculatively. "How much of that was skill and how much was knowing what Frankie would do next?"

Jackie shrugged off Kara's "Not bad," like it wasn't higher praise than I'd ever gotten. "It's about fifty-fifty." She wasn't even breathing heavily, which was supremely unfair. "I've been taking classes for years. I watched Frankie train when I was a kid, then joined an SCA group in college. I drive into Portland three times a week to take classes and spar with others at the Academy. Once I accepted I knew what was going to happen before it did, I discovered my psychic power, or whatever it is, worked best in situations like this. Spur-of-the-moment, high-stress decisions when I don't have time to think or get in my own way are easiest."

Kara eyed her speculatively. I would've flinched under her gaze, tried to make myself smaller somehow, but Jackie met her eyes and didn't back down.

"You will come tomorrow. You are not a Valkyrie, but I will never turn down a battle seer on the eve of a fight. After, we will talk about training." Kara didn't wait around for agreement or negation, just turned and walked out.

Mom didn't follow Kara and Lena out the door. Instead, she marched over to Jackie and drew herself to her full height. Jackie was a good three inches taller than my five-seven, but Mom was over six feet tall. She towered over Jackie but didn't say anything.

They stared at each other for at least a minute before Jackie broke the silence. "You can't stop me, Mom. And if you weren't my mother, you'd know that taking me along is a great idea. Hell, you're willing to throw Frankie to the sea monsters, or whatever else might be waiting, and she isn't nearly as well trained on the sword as I am."

"You have a child," my mom said.

"And you have three," Jackie countered. "I am skilled, I am valuable, and I am going." She handed me her sword and left the basement, leaving me and my mom alone.

"I'm sorry," Mom said.

"For what?" I yawned. The sleeplessness I'd experienced earlier was finally catching up with me, and ceiling stars or no, I'd be asleep ten minutes after crawling into bed.

"Not arguing more against sending you into battle."

I shrugged. I hated it—hated that it hadn't seemed to occur to her there should be an argument, but I couldn't be angry. Not now, anyway. "Sounds like it's my destiny, so what's there to argue about?"

Mom sighed. "I don't know. Maybe nothing. The gods know I never had a choice." She stepped forward and grabbed my shoulders.

The closeness forced me to look up and meet her eyes.

"I love you, and I am so proud of you. Do not ever forget that, no matter what happens." She dropped a kiss onto my forehead and released me.

"No matter what happens?" I repeated. "What is likely to happen?"

She smiled. "You're going to kick some ass, that's what's going to happen. I'll see you in the morning before you leave. Sleep well."

"I love you, too," I said.

She walked away, leaving me alone in the training room. Fear tore through me, but it was no match for exhaustion. I walked out of the basement, turning off the lights behind me as I went, then found my bed and pulled the covers over my face.

I closed my eyes, imagined the night sky, and counted stars in my head until I got too tired to worry about tomorrow. Only then did I fall asleep.

CHAPTER
NINE

Dawn sucks.

I'd seen more sunrises in the last few weeks than I had in the months and years before, and although I liked seeing the sun come up, it still wasn't my preferred time of day.

At least in late September, dawn wasn't at stupid o'clock. I splashed cold water on my face, trying to wake up. Once my vision cleared enough to no longer be considered bleary, I contemplated the clothing available in my dresser. I had the same combos I had when I'd arrived. I owned one pair of blue jeans, two pairs of yoga pants, running tights, two sports bras, two tank tops, three graphic T-shirts, and one hoodie, as well as a small variety of underthings. I might not be in danger of ending up on the streets, but I still didn't have any money to waste on anything but food, and therefore couldn't buy non-essentials like clothes.

If I'd told Mom and Dad that I was down to four pairs of underpants without holes in them, they would've taken me shopping, but there was something especially embarrassing about asking your parents to buy underoos when you were in your thirties.

I put on my black running tights emblazoned with gold skulls, the tighter sports bra, a black tank top, and zipped my soft black hoodie up over it. Black socks and sneakers completed the look. Other than the gold skulls on my tights, I was ready to stalk the shadows. Definite RPG Rogue energy.

I regarded my reflection, spent a moment wondering if I needed more color in my wardrobe, then decided my aesthetic was perfect as it was.

My door rattled with the force of someone knocking, and my heart skipped several beats.

"Are you up? You'd better be up. It's go time."

I pulled open the door, interrupting Jackie in mid-knock. "Dude. Lady-dude. What the actual fuck? There's no need to bring the entire house down."

Her grin resembled a rictus more than happiness. "Just making sure you're awake! Don't want to be late. Kara might skin us and make us into rugs."

"Are you nervous? You don't have to go." I was sure as shit nervous and wanted to stay home.

"Of course not! Why would I be nervous? Everything is super great, and I wanted this, and it's peachy keen and also A-OK." Her voice had crossed the line from anxious to hysterical. She was about thirty seconds away from needing to breathe into a paper bag.

I grabbed her by the hands and led her to my bed. "Sit. Breathe. I'm going to get you a glass of water. It doesn't matter if we're late." She looked like she was going to protest, so I held up my hand to interrupt her. "Fifteen minutes isn't going to make a huge difference in the overall scheme of things, and it'll be easier if no one in the car is hyperventilating."

I darted to the kitchen and filled a local-brewery-logoed pint glass with tap water and took it back to Jackie. "Drink this."

She downed the glass in three long gulps, then pressed it to her forehead. "I'm fine," she said. I had a feeling it was more for her own benefit than to reassure me.

Another couple minutes passed before she opened her eyes and looked at me. "Thank you."

"No problem. Seems like the least I could do. Are you ready? You can stay here if you want, you know."

She shook her head. "No. I'm going with. You're going to need me today. But after this, I'm calling Aunt Sasha. It might be time for me to work on my shit. Can't be a superhero with a Valkyrie sidekick if I don't know how to use my superpowers."

"As a person desperately in need of someone to sidekick for, I support this idea." I wrinkled my nose at her. "And now that it's at least thirty minutes past dawn, should we go see if our lateness has made Kara foam at the mouth?"

"You are a very bad person," Jackie said. "I kinda love it."

CHAPTER
TEN

Kara didn't say a word when Jackie and I walked in, only making two checks on the clipboard she held.

After a few minutes shuffling my feet and waiting for the rest of the crew to show up, I realized this was the rest of the crew. Kara, Jackie, and me.

"Um. Shouldn't there be more people? Are Mom and Aunt Lena joining us?" I asked.

"We are finding one Valkyrie. Three people are enough," Kara said. "In fact, one person would be enough. However, you are a trainee, and your sister is a stowaway. So, we are three."

"I'm not a stowaway since you agreed I could come," Jackie said.

Kara didn't answer my sister. "Get your swords and any armor or other weapons you need, but remember that we need to be discrete."

I didn't bother with anything besides my sword. Nor, I noticed, did Kara. Jackie, however, strapped on a Kevlar vest and pulled her blue hoodie over it.

"Follow me," Kara said.

I did as commanded and trailed after her, Jackie on my heels.

"Are you scared?" Jackie whispered, coming up on my left side as we jogged to keep up with Kara.

"Fucking terrified," I replied. "But what are we going to do? I have to rescue someone if I can. Besides, since she's a Valkyrie too, maybe that means she can take over once she gets here. I need a month off, a therapist, my own place, and *Xena, Warrior Princess.*"

"An old TV show is your comfort place?" Jackie asked.

"Um, yeah. Totally the show and not feelings about any of the characters."

Kara, who I'd assumed, wrongly it seemed, had a car parked in front of my parents' home, headed down the long, conifer-lined driveway away from the house. Fog swirled through the trees, giving the early morning an other-worldly feel.

"I'm human," Jackie reminded me. "And while I might be straighter than the pole Annalisa Johnson dances on, Xena has a special place in my...heart."

"Annalisa Johnson? The band nerd from high school?" I asked, more to distract myself from the fear that I couldn't shake off than any desire to have a conversation about someone I'd barely known fifteen years ago.

"Band nerd was her best quality. She tried to get the school to take away my valedictorian status because she 'had proof' I wasn't a virgin."

"Not sure that's a thing." Something tugged at me before snapping away like a weak rubber band, and I shivered. The driveway felt interminably long, and Kara's car was nowhere to be seen.

"It was enough to get me kicked off the cheerleading squad." She sighed. "I don't think Annalisa is an exotic dancer. And now I feel like shit comparing her to one as an insult. That was uncalled for. Exotic dancers are way cooler than Annalisa."

I nodded. "It was a little rude and out of character but also hilarious."

"You've just described my whole personality."

Kara stepped backward between us and grabbed our arms, jerking us forward. Just as suddenly, she let go.

Jackie stumbled into me.

"What the hell, Jax? I know I just said you were rude, but..." I looked around. We weren't on a gravel driveway. Fog no longer curled from the ground.

Two-story cinderblock buildings drew up on either side of us, and the light from the early morning overcast sky barely touched us in the shadows.

"Where are we?" I whispered.

Kara whipped around. "Portland. Isn't this where the goddess said we'd find the missing Valkyrie?"

I looked around. I'd had a lot of friends from Portland, and even lived here a couple summers, and felt confident I could navigate the city pretty well for someone not actually from there. But I had no idea where we were.

"How'd you do that?" I asked. Finding our missing Valkyrie was obviously top priority, but if I knew how to teleport, it'd be a lot easier to avoid Kara's training.

"Just stepped through," Kara said absently. "You'll learn how as you progress through the training."

I stared at her. Teleportation was kind of a big deal, and a Valkyrie perk I would've mentioned sooner, had I been her.

"Did you know you could do that?" Jackie asked.

"Not a clue," I replied. "It'd be nice to get the whole training manual all at once."

Kara glanced over her shoulder at us. "No one would take the long way around and do the necessary training if they knew the shortcuts. Now shut up."

Jackie and I froze in our tracks. I might not know how to teleport to find a missing person, but I knew enough to stop talking on a mission when someone way more experienced than me told me to.

"Run," Jackie gasped. "We can't stop here. Run!"

"Which way?" Kara asked without hesitation.

"Follow me."

Jackie took off in a straight line, leading us from the narrow alley we'd arrived in and across a small street. She veered to the right, crossed another street with nary a care for the cars coming from both directions, then darted into a sheltered alcove that served as a doorway to a local business—a boxing gym, from the looks of it.

"Are we safe?" Kara asked.

Jackie took a deep breath, then nodded. "For now."

"What happened? Was someone there?" My eyes darted from side to side, like I'd see whatever threat Jackie sensed.

"Not yet," Jackie said, a little absently. "But there would've been soon. And not someone we want to tangle with today."

"You have much talent," Kara said to Jackie, making me feel, once more, like a third wheel. "I look forward to spending time with you once you have been fully trained in your gift. In the meantime, I would be honored if you would consent to training with me as I train your sister."

"That would be so great!" Jackie threw her arms around Kara.

To my shock, Kara hugged her back. "It has been a long time since I've had the pleasure of working with someone skilled in the ways you are."

I sighed. Of course. It wasn't that I wanted to be number one with Kara. That didn't matter, and I really didn't like her that much, anyway, but damn. I was the fucking Valkyrie, whether I wanted to be or not, but Jackie was the one being celebrated.

"Any idea where to start looking?" I asked, envy and impatience making my voice harsher than I intended.

"None," Kara said after gracing me with a long, laser-pointed look that saw right through my jealousy. "But you should. Her blood calls to yours."

I strained my senses but felt nothing.

Jackie did a slow semi-circle, then stopped, face pointed toward a bank of shadowed buildings diagonally across the street. "I'm getting a sense of trouble across the street. Could be your missing Valkyrie, or it could be a drug deal about to go wrong."

"Do you usually sense mundane problems?" Kara stepped out of the doorway and stared in the direction Jackie was looking, as if she could see through the walls into whatever lay beyond. For all I knew, that's exactly what she was doing.

"Sometimes. Enough to avoid traffic accidents, anyway. But usually, it's all about Frankie." *Sorry*, she mouthed at me.

I didn't know why she felt the need to apologize for that, so I smiled but said nothing.

"And if you think about your sister walking into that building?" Kara asked.

Jackie blanched. Her breathing quickened, and she shook her head emphatically. "That is bad. Really bad. Something's in there. Something that wants Frankie more than anything."

"I hope it's not more sea serpents," I muttered.

"We're not too far away from Cathedral Park," Jackie said, a note of hysteria riding the edge of her voice. "Maybe they grew legs."

Kara drew her sword, prompting Jackie and me to do the same. A group of young women walked by, holding paper coffee cups in cardboard sleeves, and talked about the new Indian restaurant down the street. One glanced toward us, and her eyes widened when she caught sight of our swords. She turned back to her friends, but before she could say anything, Kara looped her free arm through mine and pulled Jackie close with her sword arm. She took a step toward the group of women, and for a moment, I thought we were going to confront them.

I stumbled over a jagged break in the sidewalk where tree roots were attempting to escape the concrete confines of the city. When I regained my balance, I realized we were in front of the building Jackie had warned us about. The walls were smooth, uninterrupted by either doors or windows.

"Find a way in," Kara whispered at me harshly.

"Why not just walk through the walls?" I replied snarkily. "Doors are so mundane."

"Your sister sensed danger inside, and whatever it is, you are the target. Stepping into unknown peril would be stupid, and stupid Valkyries are dead Valkyries." The unvoiced censure hunched my shoulders.

I walked down the street toward the end of the building, assuming I'd find a door on the other side. As I walked, I trailed my fingers along the wall. Three quarters of the way to the corner, they hit a seam. I looked at the section of wall. At first, it looked as smooth and featureless as the rest of the building, but gradually a rectangular outline appeared in front of me. It had no visible hinges or a knob, but there was no mistaking what it was. "I found a door," I whispered.

Kara and Jackie abandoned their searches and joined me.

"Of course, it won't do us much good if we can't open it," I said.

"All doors can be opened," Kara said. "Where is it?"

I cocked my head. Maybe Kara's eyesight was failing in her old age. Ha. As if. I put my hand on the wall where I'd first felt the seam. "Right here. You can feel it."

Kara put her hand next to mine and wonder bloomed on her face. She traced the outline and then stood back. "That is amazing. I don't know how this magic works, and I would dearly like to."

I bit my tongue so nothing sarcastic would fall out of my mouth.

"Of course, now that I can see it, I can open it." Kara sheathed her sword, turned sideways, and jabbed her elbow into the side of the building at approximately knob-height. The door opened a crack.

"More Valkyrie magic?" I asked.

"Nope," Kara replied. "That was a good old breaking-and-entering skill I picked up a couple hundred years ago. There's a place on old doors that, with a solid blow, can disengage the lock. Now, silence."

She pushed gently, and the crack widened. The darkness that spilled out made me recoil.

"This is wrong," Jackie said, echoing my thoughts. "But I don't know why."

"The light out here should break through the darkness inside, not the other way around." I shivered with the wrongness of it.

Kara drew her sword again. "We go in slowly. Do not get separated. If it is as dark inside as this would indicate, we cannot trust our sight. Stay aware, listen, and follow your instincts. No stabbing anything unless you're positive it's an enemy."

There were so many things wrong with this scenario, and I opened my mouth to voice them.

Jackie reached out and squeezed my hand. "It will be okay as long as you're not in there alone. Stay close."

I squeezed back, then dropped her hand and nodded. "Okay. Let's do this thing."

ELEVEN

The darkness swallowed Kara. She didn't gradually fade into shadows. One moment she was there, then she wasn't. Her footsteps were the only indication she hadn't disappeared. I took a deep breath and followed her in.

I'd expected total blackness. Instead, light blazed, blinding me.

Red spots danced in my vision, and I blinked, trying to dispel them.

I only had time for a quick look around, long enough to notice the enormous wood-paneled room boasted no windows, no other doors, and no furniture of any kind. In fact, except for the large column in the center of the room to which a person was tied, it was completely empty.

The door slammed shut, and the lights went off again, blanketing us in unnatural inky darkness.

"Can you get us out of here?" Jackie asked Kara.

"Probably," was her totally not reassuring answer. "Let's go grab our Valkyrie and give it a shot."

I held my left hand out and brushed against Kara. "Wait. Do we know that's a Valkyrie? Could it be a trap?"

"The goddess said there was a missing Valkyrie in Portland, my *steps* led us here, and your sister identified this building as our likely target. One of the things you'll learn is to trust your instincts and those of your sisters."

I opened my mouth to tell her that my every instinct screamed something was wrong, but she didn't give me a chance. Kara hoisted her sword, and a faint blue light emanated from it. She strode across the floor with a confidence I couldn't imitate, and Jackie and I had no choice but to follow her or get separated—and possibly left behind.

"What is your name?" Kara demanded loudly before she'd even stopped walking.

"Hope," the person whispered. "Please, help me before they come back."

"Who's your mother? Why should I cut you loose?" Kara asked.

The prisoner drew in a quick breath. "My mom's name is Serena. Aren't you here to rescue me?" Her voice was louder now, matching Kara's in volume.

"Depends on who you are. I am here for someone specific and have no time to waste rescuing the wrong person."

"I don't know," she wailed. "All sorts of weird things have been happening to me lately. Then some lady showed up—and I mean showed up out of thin air—and told me that if I went to Portland, someone could help me. I don't know why I listened to her. It was obviously a setup to kidnap me. But here I am, and I really, really want you to cut me down now, please."

"What kind of weird stuff?" I asked, even though I was pretty sure I already knew.

She barked out a short, nearly hysterical laugh. "'I see dead people' is so cliché, but that's what's happening. And they talk to me. Need my help. And you know what? I *can* help them. I don't know what I'm doing or why, but I'm sending them somewhere." Her near-hysterical tone crossed the line into full panic. "I'm probably going crazy, right? I don't know what crazy feels like. I have more willpower than that, but this has got to be it, right?"

"You're not going crazy," Kara soothed. "I'm going to cut you down now. Then I can take you somewhere safe where you can rest and find out what's been going on."

"There's nothing wrong with crazy," Jackie said. "Some of the best people have a mental illness."

I shot my sister a grateful look I knew she couldn't see.

"Sure," Hope scoffed. "But I'll take sanity any day of the week. At least I hope I still will. I don't want to end up in a straitjacket in a padded room eating crayons."

The rough sound of a knife sawing through rope thankfully shut the potential Valkyrie up before I could decide whether I was pissed off or depressed by her characterization of mental illness.

A thud followed by a clumsy stumble announced that Kara had succeeded in freeing Hope.

"Thank you," Hope said. "Now what?"

The lights flared to life again. We were no longer alone.

Several horrifically tall figures ringed the room. The skin of the lanky, gaunt figures glowed an ashy blue.

"What are those?" Hope gasped.

"Draugr," Kara barked.

Draugr, soldiers not chosen for Valhalla or Fólkvangr but instead taken by Hel, were not quite zombies, but they were closer than anything I've ever wanted to come across.

"They reek," Jackie said, gagging.

"It's the grave stink," Kara said. "These are recently risen, or they'd smell worse. The rot hasn't set in yet."

I swallowed, trying to force down the nausea.

"What do we do?" the possible Valkyrie asked in a tiny, girlish voice that irritated me for no good reason.

"Everyone, hold on," Kara commanded. She grasped the newcomer's arm, and Jackie and I circled Kara's wrists with our hands.

This time, a sensation of falling and the resulting stomach drop accompanied Kara's step forward. When my feet hit solid ground again, I fell to my knees and retched.

I didn't vomit, but the sour taste of bile in my saliva brought back memories of too many nights of drinking. I spat, trying to erase the taste from my mouth and my mind.

"Holy shit," Jackie gasped. "That was so much worse than before. What the hell just happened?"

I looked up from my position on the ground. Kara had her hands on her knees and was sucking air. "No idea," she gasped. "Dark magic interfered. Need a chair and a shot of whiskey. Maybe several shots."

I climbed to my feet with the help of a nearby tree. We'd been deposited in my parents' driveway in view of the house.

The new recruit hadn't said a word, but she looked around with wide-eyed wonder. Now that we weren't in imminent danger, I got a good look at her.

In the light, her feminine features were immediately evident. She was a white woman, a couple inches shorter than me, and her delicate facial features were enhanced by large, blue eyes and honey-brown hair that framed her face. She wore faded denim jeans, a black tank top, and a black leather jacket too big for her slight frame.

In other words, her look was almost an exact duplicate of my aesthetic. In fact, she was a more delicate version of me. Instead of that making me warm to her, though, I glared. It was rude, but I couldn't help it. She rubbed me the wrong way.

"Thank you," she said and held out a hand. "I don't know what's happening to me, but I'd love a shower, a comfy place to sit, and that whiskey you mentioned."

Kara shook Hope's hand. "I am Kara, the tall Black woman in front of you is Jackie, and the shorter blonde next to you is Frankie. Before we get into explanations, we need to get to the house. No sense in standing out here on a gravel road in the middle of nowhere."

Hope did a slow circle, her face scrunched up and eyes wide in confusion. "What house? I don't see anything."

I exchanged a glance with Jackie. Sure, the house was at the end of a long driveway, but it was clearly visible.

"*Magic!*" Jackie mouthed, wiggling her fingers in what she must have thought was a mystical manner.

I rolled my eyes and grinned.

Kara laughed and held out her arm. "You will in a minute. Come with me." Kara led the way up the driveway. Hope followed, and Jackie and I trailed behind. I lagged, hoping Jackie would take the hint and fall back with me.

"What's up?" she asked once Hope and Kara were far enough in front of us that they couldn't hear us. Probably.

"Does any of this feel wrong to you?" I asked.

Jackie stopped and put her hands on her hips, knocking back the handle of her sword as she did so. "A better question is, what doesn't feel wrong?"

"It was too easy. We showed up at the exact right place, found a hidden door, and rescued a special Valkyrie who'd been kidnapped for nefarious purposes and left unguarded in the middle of a room. We didn't even see the draugr until she was free, which gave us plenty of time to escape. The bad guys are never that incompetent outside of the movies. It's not right."

I expected her to dismiss my admittedly specious fears, but instead, she pursed her lips and nodded. "I'm not saying you're right, but this morning didn't go the way I expected, and that almost never happens. I can be surprised, but you're right—it should've been harder to rescue our wayward Valkyrie."

"I don't want to look a gift horse in the mouth or anything…"

"Why would you? Horses' mouths are—" Jackie shuddered, then winked. "There's something not quite right about all of this, but until we have more to go on, let's just ride this wave and pretend everything's cool. If Hope isn't on the up-and-up, we don't want her to know we're onto her, right?"

My sister's logic was spot-on. "Hey, thank you." I started walking again.

She matched my pace. "For what?"

"Listening to me. Not dismissing me or calling me crazy."

Jackie snorted. "You're not crazy. Well, at least not the way common vernacular would have us believe. And you are smart, intuitive, and connected to all this. If you say something's not right, it's worth investigating. Besides, no reason not to be cautious. Things are fraught AF, so let's not fuck around."

I winced, and my chest tightened at her words. It was dumb. I was dumb. But I couldn't stop myself.

"What's wrong? What'd I say? I'm so sorry!" Jackie grabbed my arm.

I thought about prevaricating, about laughing it off. But too many misunderstandings had damaged our relationship, and I wasn't about to do anything to continue down that path. "It's dumb..."

"It's not. I can already tell," Jackie said. "Spit it out."

I sighed. "Ash used to say things were 'crazy AF,' which, in his world, was defined as, 'crazy as Frankie.' It shouldn't bother me, and I know you didn't mean it that way, but I can't hear 'AF' without hearing him. I'm not asking you not to say it, of course."

"Dude! Look at me!" She grabbed my arm and wrenched me around. "All you have to do is say you hate it, and I will stop. I might fuck up at some point, but always call me on it. It might be a common expression, but if it hurts you—and I hope your so-called friend Ash spends eternity sliding naked down a rusty razor banister —then I don't want to say it. So, consider it erased from my vocab. Now let's get back to the house, see if there are breakfast potatoes, and watch Mom interrogate the newbie."

CHAPTER

TWELVE

L ena, Dusana, Mom, and Dad were all in the kitchen, breakfast preparation in full swing.

Mom raked her eyes over Jackie and me. Once satisfied that we'd returned unharmed, she smiled warmly at Hope. "Hi, welcome to the Aerie. For as long as you need, it will be your home as well as mine. Kara will show you to your room. Once you're settled, please join us for breakfast. After that, we will talk."

I snagged a sausage from the table and eyed the spread. To my disappointment and shock, no potatoes of any kind graced the table.

Mom correctly interpreted my wide-eyed dismay. "I know it's unusual, but we are skipping potatoes for this one meal."

I squinted at her. "Are you okay? Is something wrong? Are you my real mother?"

Mom laughed. "I promise everything is fine. No need to worry about anything at all."

"She lost the potatoes," Dad said, flipping a half-dozen pancakes one at a time on the large griddle.

"How does one lose potatoes?" Jackie asked. She poured a large

79

glass of fresh-squeezed orange juice and drained it in several long gulps.

Lena rolled her eyes and placed a platter of breakfast sausage on the table next to a stack of plates. "They've been like this for an hour. I'm doing my best to ignore them."

"Someone is in trouble, as soon as I figure out who the culprit is," Mom declared. "I shredded potatoes for hash browns, walked out of the room to grab my phone in case any of you needed me, and when I came back, they were gone." She looked at Dusana with narrowed eyes.

Dusana held up her hands. "I swear on my life I would never take your potatoes. Not only have I come to realize how much they mean to you, to this entire family, but I also love hash browns and wouldn't jeopardize my breakfast for anything."

Hope and Kara walked back into the room. Hope stared at the group in the kitchen, jaw slightly open. "Are you arguing about potatoes?"

Mom dried her hands on her apron and held one out toward Hope. "Not seriously. I'm Katrin. You must be our missing Valkyrie."

"Am I?" Hope whispered. She didn't take my mom's hand, instead tucking hers behind her back. "What's a Valkyrie?"

For the first time, I felt sorry for Hope. She knew as little as I had a few weeks ago.

"She's Serena's daughter," Kara said. She pushed into the kitchen and took the coffee Lena held out to her.

Lena walked forward and pulled out a chair. "Why don't you sit. We'll make you a plate, and we can help you figure out what's going on."

I picked up a plate, took a couple pancakes from the pile next to dad, added a few chicken apple sausage links, and filled a small bowl with some of the mixed-fruit salad. I set it all in front of Hope, shoved the butter and syrup over to her, and poured her a glass of OJ.

Hope wrinkled her nose at the plate and looked at me. "You expect me to eat all that? So much fat and empty calories." She shuddered and pulled the bowl of fruit closer. "I'd rather do a few lines of cocaine than fill myself up with that poison."

Okay then. It was going to be like that, was it?

I pasted a smile on my face, picked up the rejected food, and headed to the other side of the table. I slathered butter on my pancakes, doused them in syrup, and took a huge bite. Once I'd chewed and swallowed, I speared a sausage with my fork, dragged it across my plate, and shoved half of it into my mouth, catching the sticky drops with my finger before they could drip onto my shirt.

Hope watched my performance with what could only be described as horror.

"Have as much fruit as you want," Lenore said.

Jackie put her hands on her hips and glared at Hope. "Pancakes are nothing like drugs, you know. You're a guest here, so don't yuck our yum."

Hope's expression became downcast. "I am so sorry. I wasn't trying to imply that your breakfast wasn't good. I'm just"—she gestured at her slim, muscular body—"really into keeping in shape. That's not everyone's focus, and that's okay. We all have different relationships with food, and all bodies are perfect just as they are."

I shoved another bite of pancakes into my mouth before I said something regrettable. I hadn't been my best self after my Valkyrie powers had woken either, and I hadn't even been kidnapped. I caught Jackie's eye and shook my head.

My mother's smile looked as forced as mine felt, but there was nothing but warmth and kindness in her tone. "You'll need something besides fruit. What else would you like for breakfast? If we don't have it here, Marty can run into town."

"I usually eat a poached egg, one-quarter cup of fat-free plain yogurt, and one slice of gluten-free bread." She looked down at the fruit. "This fruit is fine, though. Don't go to any trouble on my account."

"I can poach you an egg, and we have plain Greek yogurt, if that would suffice," Dad said with zero inflection.

Ha. Hope was not winning friends and influencing family.

She fluttered her eyelashes at my dad, and his expression shifted from one of careful neutrality to amusement.

"I'm really hungry. If you could please go get me something I could eat, I'd appreciate it so, so much." She tore her gaze from my dad's face. He lost control and let a wide grin split his face. "Or… maybe Frankie can go fetch me some food since she's done eating—at least I hope she's done. That was a *lot* of food."

I finished my pancakes in three large bites, ate my last sausage, and slurped my orange juice as loudly as possible. It was only after my obnoxious display that I remembered Dusana was in the room. Dusana, the woman I was definitely not trying to impress. Shit. Nothing like making a good impression. I stood and nodded at Hope. "I would love nothing more than making sure you're well taken care of. If you give me a list and some cash, I'd be happy to get you whatever you need for the next couple days."

"You want money?" she asked in her little girl voice.

I shrugged. "You want food. It's not free."

"We'll cover it," Mom said smoothly. "Frankie, the car keys and my wallet are on the table by the front door. Hope, if you want anything besides gluten-free bread and nonfat yogurt, let Frankie know."

"I'm sure there's no skim milk or low-fat cheese here, so some of that would be great too. And a bottle of Champagne if they have anything like that in your town." She simpered at me. "Thank you, Frankie. You're simply the best."

I exited the room without another word, picked up Mom's keys and wallet on my way out the front door, and didn't let my tight grin fall until I unlocked the car and got in.

I hadn't even started the car yet when Jackie and Dusana climbed in, Dusana in the front seat and Jackie behind her.

"I am going to murder her," Jackie said.

Her fierceness was such a contrast to her attitude six weeks ago, and it was almost enough to make up for Hope's absolute cuntiness.

"I'm a reaper, so I can send her on," Dusana said. "Strictly speaking, it's not allowed. I'm supposed to wait for people to be dead before I reap them, but I might make an exception in her case. Although you might have to do it, Frankie, since she probably believes in your gods."

"We are not murdering anyone," I said as I started the car. I seldom had the opportunity to be the voice of reason. "She had Valkyrie powers thrust upon her with as little warning or foreknowledge as I did, then was sent to Portland by a mysterious woman—probably Freyja—without an explanation. She ended up kidnapped, rescued by us, and confronted with blue zombies. Anyone would be stressed and wanting comfort food." I headed down the driveway toward the highway that led into town.

"Sure thing, Sis," Jackie said. "I bet she's usually the kindest, nicest soul in the world."

"I don't want to be judgy. Actually, that might not be true, but low-fat cheese, fat-free yogurt, and gluten-free bread are not comfort food," Dusana added.

"I'm reserving judgment on the gluten," Jackie said. "I dated a guy with celiac once, and it was not good if he got glutened up."

"Fair," Dusana said. "Guess my judgment-free zone had some judging going on. Can I still make fun of the idea of low-fat cheese and fat-free yogurt being comforting?"

"One hundred percent," Jackie said.

"Stop it, both of you." I tried to sound stern but ruined it by laughing. "I want to give her the grace in this that I didn't get from Ash." I hadn't said his name once in the six weeks since he'd tried to kill me and I'd done, well, whatever I'd done. I hadn't killed him, but I definitely stabbed him pretty good. And now he'd come up twice in twenty-four hours.

"A wooden bridge made with rotten planks would be more supportive than Ash," Jackie said. "You don't have to make a special effort to be better than that."

"I met the bastard," Dusana said. "He's cruel and conniving, but at least he smells better than his daughter."

Jackie undid her seat belt and scooted far enough forward to look directly at Dusana. "Wait. His daughter? What the actual fuck? Frankie, did you know about this?"

"No clue what you're talking about. But you need to buckle up." I flipped on the left blinker as I approached the stop sign but made no move to turn.

"Fine, but we're not going to get in an accident or anything," Jackie muttered. She slid back and rebuckled. "So did he, Frankie? Have a kid, I mean?"

I took a left onto the highway toward Estacada. "Ash didn't have a kid, at least as far as I knew."

"He's Loki, right?" Dusana asked patiently.

"I guess…" Adele and Kara had been certain about that, but it was hard to believe. Ash was androgynously beautiful, but he was no Tom Hiddleston. "And if he's Loki, he has kids. Weird-ass kids."

"Hel is the most humanesque one, isn't she?" Jackie asked.

Dusana shuddered. "Humanesque kinda sounds like grotesque. Good description though. She was so beautiful when I met her, but then she let her mask slip and turned into a horror-show right in front of me."

"What was it like?" Jackie asked. "Was she Cate Blanchett hot?"

"We need to get our heads out of the MCU," I said. "I love the Thor movies, but knowing we might run into the thunder god puts a damper on my movie enjoyment. There's no way he's gonna be a lovable himbo."

Jackie sighed. "You're right. I'll let it go. Dusana, please tell me about Hel."

"When she dropped her mask, I almost vomited on her," Dusana admitted. "There were maggots in her eye sockets, and the stench…" She gagged. "It was awful, and that was even before the vague threats."

This was unfamiliar territory. "Threats? You never mentioned them before," I said. Sure, there were a lot of things about Dusana I didn't know, but meeting Ash and being threatened by Hel seemed like big ones to skip.

Dusana flushed and shrugged. "Adele knows, and so does your mom. Probably Lena and Kara, too. I'm sure they discussed it. It's not that it slipped my mind. It's more that you had a lot going on, and I didn't want to get in the way of all that. Anyway, Hel showed up in a bar in Oatman when I'd been on this plane for only about a year, told me not to help a mysterious woman, 'or else.' She came back right before the events in August, said pretty much the same thing, and took off. I haven't seen her again."

"But you met Ash?" I prodded. The light in front of us turned red, and I pulled to a stop behind a pickup with a gun rack in the back window and a large Confederate flag bumper sticker.

"Yeah, about three days before you passed through town. He was posing as a creepy motel clerk and almost ensnared me. He wanted to know how to kill a reaper. I was mortal then, but he didn't seem to know that. It was like he hypnotized me. I told him things I hadn't meant to but got away from him before he could kill me. A couple days after that—the day we met again, actually—Hel showed up in Oatman. She basically said the same thing Ash had. 'Don't help the pretty girl, blah, blah, blah.'"

The words "pretty girl" derailed my thoughts, and I almost missed what Dusana said next.

"It was weird, though. I don't think they shared information, just a common goal—ensuring I didn't help you. They're obviously both bad guys, but each playing their own game, if that makes sense?"

"It surprises me not at all," I said. The parking lot at the Thriftway was crowded, and I shut up long enough to concentrate on finding an empty spot.

"That is a cool mural," Dusana said, taking in the colorful painting on the outside of the grocery store.

"There are murals on buildings all over town," Jackie said. "We'll have to walk around and check them out."

"Not now though. I don't want Hope to wait any longer than necessary for her low-fat cheese." I walked forward, pulling Jackie and Dusana in my wake.

"Gods forbid," Jackie muttered. "Pretty princess might expire."

Dusana took the lead and grabbed a shopping basket. "She's not right. I can't put a finger on it, but there's something off about her. Something more than her shitty attitude."

Jackie nodded. "Kara doesn't seem to have any doubts. Hope knew Serena's name, and we walked right to her, but I don't like it, and not just because I don't like her."

While I thought, trying to push out all my personal bias, I perused the yogurts and selected the cheapest one. "I don't like her either, obviously. But I was being serious before when I said that everything she's gone through might make her awful. I did not have the best reaction when I saw my first dead person. In fact, I screamed and ran away without helping him. So, her attitude is perfectly understandable."

"But..." Jackie prodded.

I sighed. "But...there's something off, and every instinct I have is screaming at me that she isn't quite right."

"Kara said to listen to your instincts," Jackie said. "And for once, I agree with her. Hope cannot be trusted."

THIRTEEN

It didn't take long to get back to my parents' after we'd picked up the bread, yogurt, and cheese. I didn't even bother looking for Champagne. I wasn't interested in walking down that aisle. I'd been sober for almost two months, and no matter how aggravating Hope was, I felt a little sorry for her. But I would not jeopardize my sobriety to make her happy.

When we got back, the stack of pancakes on the long kitchen table was taller than when I'd left. Nothing else looked like it had been touched at all.

Hope clapped her hands. "Oh, thank you, Frankie! Now, we can all finally brunch." Her tinkling laugh filled the room. "Well, most of us. I guess you had a head start on that, didn't you?" The smile she pointed at me looked kind and humorous but raised my hackles, nonetheless.

Mom and Lena exchanged a look, but instead of the suspicion I harbored, they seemed amused. Lena's right eyebrow quirked upward, and my mom's lips twitched.

While Hope dug into her nonfat yogurt, I scanned the others around the table to gauge everyone's reactions.

Jackie and Dusana sat next to each other at the opposite end of the table from Hope. After Dad loaded his plate with pancakes and doused them with more syrup than should be legal, he joined them.

Kara put two pancakes and two sausages on her plate, added only enough syrup to moisten them, and filled the rest of her plate with fruit. She set her plate down and poured herself another enormous cup of black coffee before sitting next to Hope.

Mom and Lena hit that space between Dad and Kara, both in pancake treatment—moderate amounts of butter and syrup—and spacing. They sat in the middle of the table, which was big enough to seat twenty, closer to Hope than Jackie.

I filled my favorite mug with coffee, added a liberal glug of half-and-half, and plopped down next to Jackie. My stomach growled. I wrapped my arms around my midsection and tried to suppress the flush of embarrassment trying to rise.

"If you're hungry, get some more food," Dad said.

"I'm fine," I said, accompanied by an even louder rumble.

Jackie huffed, got up, and picked up a plate. A couple moments later, she set two pancakes and four sausages in front of me, sliding the syrup jug over as she sat down. "Eat," she commanded. "One of the nice things about being in tune with your body is listening to it rather than someone else. You're a calorie-burning machine right now. You need fuel."

She sat next to me, tore a large piece of pancake from her stack, and bit down savagely.

I took a much daintier bite than hers—I'd done my dramatic eating earlier—and chased it with my coffee.

Jackie swallowed. "Besides, food is delicious, and eating is pleasurable."

Dusana wiped the last vestiges of syrup from her plate with a final bite. She picked up her coffee mug and wrapped her hands around it, then leaned back in her chair. "That was magnificent. I love breakfast more than almost anything. My first meal was pancakes, and I've had a soft spot for them ever since."

"You're kidding," Jackie said. "You don't talk about yourself nearly enough. I want to know everything about you immediately."

Dusana's eyes widened, and she glanced at me.

"She's kidding," I said. When Jackie made a noise of protest, I amended my statement. "She's mostly kidding. She definitely wants to know everything about you, but she can be a little patient, especially if you dole out bits and pieces of your personal history and keep her hanging on Scheherazade style."

Dusana didn't look convinced exactly, but her shoulders relaxed down away from her ears.

Dad spoke up for the first time since he'd sat. "Jackie, you're going to scare Dusana away, and then you won't get any stories."

Jackie and Dad bickered about the best way to extract information from someone, Dad voting for quiet patience and Jackie for a full-on frontal assault.

Dusana scooted her chair closer to mine. "It's not that I mind sharing stories of my life, it's just that I haven't done that before, and I don't know quite how to do it. The only person who knows anything about me that's more than surface-level is Adele. It's kinda hard to tell acquaintances I'm only ten years old, at least technically in Earth years, and Percy and I never stayed in one place long enough to have anything more than casual."

"It's your story, and you can tell it in your own time. She's not the only one interested though. I'm not as pushy as she is, but I am looking forward to hearing what it's like being a brand-new person after eons of amorphous immortality."

"Breathing was weird. I nearly choked on my first drink of water, and pancakes were a delightful surprise. Bodily functions were, and arguably still are, the worst part of humanity. Being made mortal was a punishment, but giving me an angry, malfunctioning uterus crossed the line into cruel and unusual, if you ask me. How people deal with all the cramps, headaches, bloating, and irritability, much less the mess, is beyond me." She glared at me, like I might have had something to do with her menstrual cycle.

"There are things you can do that help. I mean, you probably already know, but there are a lot of options. Do you have a doctor?" This was not the conversation I'd thought I'd be having over pancakes, but sharing was caring.

"I went to a doctor one time to discuss getting rid of these cursed reproductive organs. However, since I am of 'child-bearing age' and yet unmarried, my request was denied. My assertion that marriage to someone who could impregnate me was highly unlikely fell on deaf ears, and I was advised to come back when I was in my forties." Dusana's anger was palpable; the heat of it pulsed against me.

"That's obviously bullshit." I needed to change the subject almost immediately, but something she'd said caught my attention. "How old are you? I mean, what does your driver's license say?"

"According to my completely fake ID, I'll be forty in two weeks." She sighed. "I hope Adele is back by then. I've never had a birthday without Percy and Adele, and though Percy can't be here right now, it'd be nice to have a familiar face nearby."

This subject change was not producing any more positive results than the last couple. I needed to find something more cheerful up my sleeve.

Jackie broke off her conversation with Dad and spun around to look at Dusana. "There is no way anyone is allowed to get away with not having a birthday party, especially not for such a big milestone. Adele will be here, as will all of us. There will be streamers, cake, probably potatoes if I let Mom have any part of it, and maybe a stripper."

"No strippers," Dusana laughed. "And a party isn't necessary. It's not like I'm actually turning forty. I'm an ageless entity temporarily taking corporeal form. Age is meaningless."

Jackie laughed and clapped her hands. "Too late, reaper. In fewer than five minutes, Becky will know there's a party to plan, and there is no way to stop her when cake is on the line." She pulled out her phone and started texting.

"I've never had a party before." Dusana sounded wistful. "Not sure now is the time for it, though. There's a lot going on."

"Celebrating each other is always important," Dad said. "And there are seldom convenient times to pause in life. Let the girls throw their party."

Jackie put down her phone and pointed a finger at Dusana. "Your party will be the bright spot we all need." Sadness flashed across her face, but she quickly replaced it with a smile. "Especially me."

FOURTEEN

At precisely 7:00 a.m., I walked into the basement, sword in hand, the same as I had every morning bar two for the last six and a half weeks.

After breakfast yesterday, Kara, Aunt Lena, Mom, and Hope had sequestered themselves down here for hours, and I'd gone to bed before they'd emerged. Hopefully today, it'd just be me and Kara. I wanted to ask her impression of Hope to see if it was anywhere near mine and she was being polite the day before, or if she was fully on board with "Hope is the best" the way she'd seemed.

I warmed up my muscles, moving through the exercises Kara made me start every session with. I finished and checked the clock. It was 7:20. Five minutes of pacing later, the door at the top of the stairs creaked open.

I stilled and readied myself. Sometimes Kara attacked without warning, but this time I'd be ready.

Instead of the fierce, old Valkyrie, Jackie made her way down, sword in hand and baby Lenore strapped firmly to her chest.

"Sorry I'm late! I thought John had the day off and could watch Lenore, but he got called in to work, and so here we are." She flopped in a chair, dropped her sword with a clatter that made me wince, and looked around, seeming to realize we were alone. "Where's Kara?"

"No clue." I hung my sword on the rack and sat next to Jackie. I reached toward her, then paused. "May I?"

Jackie lifted Lenore out of the carrier and handed the baby over. She arched her back and groaned. "This kid is getting heavy. I don't know how much longer I'm gonna be able to run around with her strapped to me."

I cradled her in my arms and booped her tiny nose. "Who's the most beautiful baby in the world?" I crooned. "Lenore is. So beautiful and so sweet."

"You wouldn't say that if you'd been up with her all night," Jackie grumbled. "Of course, she's wide awake and happy now, whereas I'm exhausted and grumpy with bags under my eyes that are too big to fit in the overhead compartment."

"I've never been on a plane." I tickled Lenore's tummy. She giggled and reached up to touch my face.

"Seriously?" Jackie asked. "Never ever?"

I thought about it while I bounced Lenore up and down. "Maybe when I was younger, but when we took family vacations, it was almost always a road trip, wasn't it?"

"Ugh, yes. So much camping." She shuddered. "But we went to Hawaii one year and Iceland the year I graduated from…"

"And I was already gone." I didn't take my eyes off Lenore. I didn't want Jackie to see the pain and guilt in my expression.

"But still, never after that? You didn't go to visit Gwen's family or anything?"

"Nope." I leaned down and nuzzled Lenore's nose with my own.

"Are you afraid of flying?"

"Not exactly," I hedged. "The chances of dying in a plane crash are pretty slim. It's a very safe mode of travel and allows a person to visit all sorts of places that they wouldn't get to go otherwise. It's just so…high."

"I love that you have a weakness," Jackie said. "Makes you a little more human."

I stared at her. "I am nothing but weakness. I'm a mentally ill addict who can't keep a job or a girlfriend."

"Don't be ridiculous. You're here and you're sober. If that's not strength, I don't know what is." Jackie retrieved her sword from where she'd dropped it, something that would've been guaranteed to incur Kara's ire had she been present, then began her own series of warmups. She moved slowly at first, then faster and faster until her movements were nearly a blur.

I watched for fifteen minutes, rocking the baby without taking my eyes off my younger sister. "You are really good," I said when she slowed down. "Way better than me. Too bad you're not the chosen one."

"Whatever, Buffy." She grabbed a towel to wipe the sweat off her face. She wasn't even breathing hard, which was supremely unfair. "I'm the brains, and you're the muscle. I can defend myself, but I don't have to lead a bunch of women into battle. The only way that'd be cool is if I got a flying horse."

"If one shows up for me, you can have it. There is no way I'm leaving the ground, much less on an animal that shouldn't even have wings."

Jackie laughed and collapsed in the chair next to me. "Speaking of animals, where's your cat? I haven't seen him in a couple days. I thought he might push his way into our rescue mission yesterday, or at least show up to examine our new recruit."

"No idea. He's been gone since Dusana and I got back after the sea-serpent incident. He said he wanted to investigate the river and needed to do it alone. He'll be back. He's never stayed away for more than two days. And you're right; he's definitely gonna have opinions about Hope."

The door to the basement opened, and I hopped to my feet to stand next to Jackie.

Kara appeared in the doorway. "Jackie, we need to talk to you. Come up to Katrin's office."

Jackie looked between Kara and me. "I'll hand Lenore off to Dad. He always says he doesn't get enough time with her. Then we'll be in."

"Just you," Kara said. "Frankie can watch the baby." She disappeared from view.

Jackie's gaze swung to mine. "I don't understand. Why me and not you?"

I shrugged, hoping the hurt and rejection weren't evident on my face. "No idea, but it's no big deal. Go ahead. I'll hold on to the baby a little while longer, then hand her off to her grandpa."

"I'll tell you everything I hear. Promise." She held out her pinky finger, and I hooked mine around it.

"Thanks. Now go. You don't want to keep Kara waiting."

Jackie brushed a kiss across Lenore's forehead and ran up the stairs. She looked back at me from the top, then walked out the door.

"Guess it's just you and me, kid," I said to the baby. The hurt I'd been holding back broke free. I was supposed to be the fucking chosen one, so why was I excluded from the big discussions? And why did they want Jackie? It wasn't that I begrudged her inclusion. I hadn't been kidding earlier when I'd said she would've been a better Valkyrie than me, but she wasn't one.

I waited for the tears of rejection and disappointment. They didn't come. Maybe I'd cried too much in the last few weeks to have anything left but emptiness.

"I hope you grow up happy," I said to Lenore. "You are too wonderful to deserve the darkness that lurks in every corner of my mind." I snagged her carrier from where Jackie'd left it and walked upstairs. "I will do everything in my power to keep you safe and innocent for as long as I can. Even if I have to do it on my own."

Dad was on the back patio, reading a book on woodworking. He didn't protest even a tiny bit when I handed Lenore over.

"I have to run into town again," I said as casually as I could.

He rolled his eyes. "More yogurt?"

"Not this time. I'm just having a desperate desire for ice cream. Full-fat ice cream."

"It's pretty early, but I won't judge if you promise to bring some back for me." He looked around and narrowed his eyes, then lowered his voice. "And no one else. It'll be our secret."

"You got it, Dad. Chocolate peanut butter?"

"Always. Keys are on the table by the front door. See you later." His attention turned back to Lenore before I'd even walked through the sliding glass door and back into the house.

The door to Mom's home office was closed. I could hear a murmur of voices from within. I paused for a moment on my way through the house, but I couldn't make anything out.

I snagged the keys and headed to the car. I should be used to being excluded. I'd been fooling myself, thinking I was anything more than the muscle, as Jackie named me.

I was nothing more than a weapon, and a faulty one at that.

CHAPTER

FIFTEEN

Of course, nothing had been open at eight-thirty. So, after a heads-up text to my dad, I took a three-hour drive through the Mt. Hood National Forest to Government Camp, over to Hood River, then back down the Columbia River and south back to Estacada.

I pulled into town, parked a few spaces down from the corner ice cream shop, and dropped my head onto the steering wheel. I needed direction—something more than training to occupy my time and my brain. And probably a therapist who wouldn't recommend me for in-patient care when I told her I was a Valkyrie with a talking cat.

Actually, the prospect of a psych ward might be optimistic. It was more likely I'd end up in police custody.

I sighed. Ice cream might not fix everything, but it would help for a while.

I got out of the car and stared at the front door of Time Travelers Brewing. They were open and served food. I hadn't had breakfast, and I was hungry. Ice cream would be great for dessert, but maybe I should get a sandwich first.

I walked into the brewpub and took a seat at the bar. A server pushed a menu over. I perused the food selections, but it was the beer menu my gaze stuck on.

My mouth watered at the thought of a real West Coast IPA or a hard cider made with local apples.

A familiar voice pulled me away from the menu, and I glanced up. John, Jackie's partner who was supposed to be at work, was sitting in a booth in the back corner of the bar, and it sounded like he was arguing with someone.

"Can I get you something to drink?" the server asked.

I looked down at the options again. "Do you make the root beer?"

"Sure do, and it's pretty good," she replied.

"I'll have a root beer and the sliders, please." I pushed the menu back to her with a shaky hand. I should probably send Sketchy John an edible arrangement as a thank you for distracting me.

I narrowed my eyes at him and stared. Eventually, he looked up and saw me. He smiled and waved, then went back to his conversation. Maybe he wasn't so shady after all if he was waving instead of skulking.

I was halfway through my meal when John approached. "Hi Frankie! I would've thought you'd be training with Jackie and the scary lady."

I pasted a smile on my face before I answered. "I'm just taking a break while Jax and Kara work together for a bit. I thought you were at work today and couldn't watch Lenore."

John waved his hand toward his flannel-clad dining companion. The lumberjack of a white man sported a blond man-bun and looked perfectly at home in the Pacific Northwest. "Business lunch."

The man waved his fingers at me, a gesture almost too twee for such a mountain of a human. It might have been my imagination, since it was dim in the back corner of the bar, but it looked as if he'd smirked at me.

I glanced back at John. "Business lunch? At a pub? I thought you worked in finance."

He shrugged, a small smile playing around his lips. "A brewpub is as good a place as any, and they have non-alcoholic options. And even finance managers have business, you know."

Heat rose and threatened to flush my skin. I straightened my shoulders. "The root beer is delicious."

"I must get back to my meeting. It was nice to see you. Give my love to your parents, and let Jackie know I'll be home by dinnertime." He walked back to his table, bent and whispered something to the other man, and dropped what looked like a wad of cash on the table.

The men exited. I didn't take my eyes off them, making no effort to hide my scrutiny, until they were out of sight.

"Do you know them?" the bartender asked.

"The one in the suit is my sister's sketchy partner, John. Never seen the other one before." I pushed my plate away from me. I had one slider left, but I'd lost my appetite. John had done nothing suspicious, but this interaction rubbed me the wrong way, regardless.

"Your sister's boyfriend is a good guy and a great tipper. He brings a lot of people to lunch here." The censure in her voice was slight but undeniable. I was being a jerk about a perfectly nice man.

"He must be decent if my sister loves him," I said. "Thanks for the reminder that not all men are crap."

She laughed. "There are a few good ones left, and John is one of them. Don't give him too hard of a time."

I handed over a couple twenties my dad had passed me before I'd left the house. Living with my parents was helping me stretch out the money I'd found in Ash's car, but if I didn't want to ask for an allowance, I'd need to find a job, and soon.

I walked back into the bright autumn sunshine and squinted against the glare. There was a help-wanted sign in the brewpub window, and for a brief, ill-advised moment, I considered applying.

Nope. That would be a terrible idea. I might be almost two months sober, but today proved I wasn't doing as well as I'd thought.

I walked around town, taking in all the magnificent murals on the sides of buildings, and doing an inventory of what had changed since I'd left. Answer? A ton. There were a couple new-age crystal shops, and an upscale jewelry store with gorgeous pieces I could never afford. One building housed a used bookstore that sold paperbacks for a dollar, but I couldn't afford that store either, because there was no way I'd walk out of there with just one.

One business snagged my attention. A tattoo shop advertising as "therapeutic." I'd always found the process of getting inked almost meditative, but therapy? I pulled up the website on my phone. In addition to regular tattoos, they did a lot of cover-ups and post-mastectomy ink. The part that really lured me in was the scar hiding and beautification.

I looked down at my left forearm and the lines of scars parallel to my wrist. I had a semi-colon tattoo on my arm, but the idea that something could hide the shame of being easily identified as a cutter or make it somehow attractive, or at least acceptable, intrigued me. I didn't know what scar beautification entailed, but I needed to find out.

I took a picture of the door and saved it to my "favorites" album. Before I walked away, the door opened and a gorgeous Asian woman walked out.

"Can I help you?" she asked. She had short, spiky black hair with bright-pink and blue streaks in it. Her frame was lush and curvy, and she wore denim shorts that stopped at the top of her thighs. Her tight, pink V-neck T-shirt was emblazoned with a sequined dragon.

"Um," I said, once again displaying my renowned conversational skills.

"I'm Grace Kim." She held out her hand. "Are you considering a tattoo?"

I shook the hand of the gorgeous person speaking to me, then gathered my courage to reply. "What's scar beautification?"

She smiled and swept her arm back toward the door. "Would you like to come in? I can tell you what I do and show you some examples of my work."

I walked into the shop and looked around. There were animal heads all over the walls, which made me cringe. Wait a minute... I walked up to one and looked more closely. It was a jackalope. I did a slow circle. None of the skulls were what I'd come to expect when looking at trophies. A unicorn and a dragon faced off on opposite sides of the room, and the others looked equally fantastic.

Grace smiled at me. "I usually judge a person by how they react to my decor," she confessed. "It might be unfair, but the slide from a little horrified to intrigued delights me. Now, why don't you take a seat on the couch, and we can talk."

I settled onto the red couch and tucked my right ankle under my left thigh. "I have scars on my arm," I said with no preamble. "I know they can't be covered up—they're not flat enough—but I want to know what can be done to hide them. Make them less noticeable."

Grace took a seat opposite me and grabbed a photo album from the low table between us. "First off, creating art that will detract from your scars is something we can absolutely do. But that's not what scar beautification is." She flipped the album open. A forearm tattoo sleeve of a ship at sea took up the entire first page. Waves tossed the wooden ship, and its sails were tattered. When I looked closer, I realized the weather-wearing on the ship, the cuts in the sails, and the whitecaps were all scars.

"If your scars are raised, we'll have to take a different tack." She flipped the page. A greyscale skull with a river pouring out its mouth greeted me. This time, I didn't have to look hard for the scars. The vertical lines of the waterfall were raised scars, each with a large boulder tattooed at the top of them to create the illusion of the water separating and flowing back around them. Fainter scars were visible in the skull itself. "This is beautification."

I held out my arm. "Can you do anything with this?"

Grace grasped my arm and turned it back and forth to catch the light. I had thirteen raised scars, each about an inch-and-a-half long, running in parallel tracks up my forearm, and several smaller, fainter ones between them. Bisecting the shorter ones was a single scar from the inside of my elbow to my wrist.

"There are possibilities," she said finally. "Tell me what you'd like to see there. What are you interested in? What would be meaningful?"

I mulled it over for a minute, but only one answer came to me. "A Valkyrie symbol. The runic wings would be great if possible. But I'd like to keep the semi-colon as part of it."

Grace pursed her lips, then pulled up her phone and scrolled through. She turned it around and showed me a picture. "Is this what you had in mind?"

I nodded. "That's perfect."

Grace put her phone away. "Something like that will only be a couple sessions and run between two and three hundred dollars."

That was so much money, and most of what I had left. It was a really stupid decision, but... I looked at the skull and waterfall and something lit in my chest. I wanted this. I wanted to look at my arm and see who I was now, not who I'd been in the past. "Okay. That sounds reasonable."

"Let me take a picture of your arm and get your contact deets. I'll sketch out a couple ideas and send them to you in two or three weeks, then we can book a date to get started. Do you live around here?"

"I'm staying with my parents just outside of town, although I'm looking for a job and a place to live in Portland." I tilted my head. I hadn't intended to say that last bit. Hadn't really thought about it before.

Grace took several pictures of my arm. "Ugh. Job-hunting is the worst. So glad I get to do this instead of making coffee or serving drinks."

After handing over a fifty-dollar down payment and giving her my phone number and email address, I stood. "Thank you. I look forward to hearing from you."

Grace surprised me by hugging me before I walked out the door.

"Everything is going to be okay," she said. "Go get some ice cream and forgive yourself. You deserve all the good things." She closed the door behind me without waiting for a response.

I stared at the storefront for a few seconds, then walked across the street and got two milkshakes and went home.

SIXTEEN

Dusana and my dad were in the kitchen when I returned. Sunlight streamed through the window over the sink, brightening the already cheery walls. I handed Dad's chocolate peanut butter shake over and smiled guiltily at Dusana. "Sorry."

She waved my apology away. "No worries. I'll just make you treat me some other time."

"Deal." I glanced toward Mom's office. "Are they still in there?"

"They are, but they should be wrapping up now," Dad said.

"Where's the baby? Did she get called into the meeting too?" I'd meant it as a joke, but a little of my bitterness seeped through.

Dad gave me a knowing look, but answered in the spirit in which I'd meant it. "She is in there, but in hungry mode, not acting in an advisory capacity."

Before I could ask more questions, the door opened. Jackie and Lenore were the first ones out, and based on her thundercloud expression, Jackie was not pleased. Lena and Adele, whom I hadn't seen in a few weeks, were the next to exit.

Dusana stood up, a broad smile on her face. "Adele! I didn't know you were back!"

Adele, a tall, angular white woman with deep lines on her face and long, grey hair streaming around her shoulders, glanced at Dusana. "We'll catch up in a bit." She and Lena left the house without a second look at anyone. A few moments later, an engine started in the driveway.

Okay. This was getting weird.

Kara preceded my mother out of the room and stalked to the basement door. "Frankie, downstairs, now. We have to make up for the training you missed this morning."

I opened my mouth to protest. Not only had missing training that morning not been my fault by any stretch of the imagination, I was really, really full of ice cream.

Kara paused and held my gaze.

My return stare was blocked by Hope and Archibald walking out of my mom's office in what looked like serious, quiet conversation. I nodded at Kara. "Be down in a couple minutes. Just need to change."

Jackie followed me to my room and dropped onto my bed, cradling Lenore in her arms. "I have to leave for a few days."

"Where are you going?" I shucked my jeans and put on leggings, then traded out my T-shirt for a tight tank top.

Jackie smiled so tightly I worried her jaw muscles would cramp. "To visit Aunt Sasha."

Sasha was our dad's formidable older sister. She'd always intimidated me a little with the way she seemed to see right through me. Which, according to my secret-keeping family, it turns out she probably could. She had the same gift of seeing as Jackie, but with significantly more years of experience and training to back it up.

"Gonna get a few lessons on how to hone your gift? Are you leaving Lenore with John?"

"Nope. I'm supposed to bring the baby, to see if she has the sight, too." The tension in Jackie's voice echoed her expression.

I opened my mouth to tell her I'd seen John in town, but her explosion stopped me.

"I cannot believe they're sending me away!"

Lenore squawked and waved her arms at her mother.

"Sorry, baby girl," Jackie crooned to her daughter. "At least I don't have to leave you behind, even if I am abandoning my sister and my training for this stupid trip."

"Why can't she come here?" I asked. "Everyone else has already shown up. She'd fit right in."

"An excellent question, and no one had a good answer for it," Jackie said. "They wouldn't tell me why I needed to go or why it had to be right now. Just that I needed to 'trust them' and 'not tell Frankie too much.'" Jackie clapped her hand over her mouth. Her eyes widened. "Shit," she mumbled from behind her hand.

I squelched the hurt. "Seriously? They told you not to tell me too much? What kind of chosen one am I if I don't get to know what's going on?"

Jackie dropped her hand and grinned at me. There wasn't a trace of guilt on her face. "I can't believe I let it slip that they're being a bunch of douches. For the record, Mom is not in favor of keeping you in the dark, and I think you'll probably get more information from her tonight."

"So, what is going on that I'm not supposed to know about?" I asked, petulance staining my voice.

"I honestly don't know a lot. I think they talked through the really big stuff before I got invited in, but from what I could gather, something's gone wrong with gathering the other Valkyries. Sounds like Aunt Sasha has flat-out refused to help Kara—I got the impression they have a long and antagonistic history. But she volunteered to train me at least, so I could be 'of some use,' as Kara put it." Jackie put Lenore on the bed, then stood and paced. "I don't know enough to put it all together. Most of what I have is nothing more than guesses and conjecture. Other than the fact they need a seer on their side, and my skills are not nearly honed enough to be of use in battle."

"Battle?" The cookies and cream shake I'd eaten earlier solidified into a rock in the pit of my stomach. "Is there going to be a battle?"

Jackie stared at me, head tilted to one side. "What do you think we're doing all this for? You're in weapons training, you're supposed to be leading an army of Valkyries to find the gods and lock them up before they can start Ragnarök. Were you planning on waving your sword around threateningly and scaring the enemy away?"

Since that was exactly what had been in my head when I dared think about it at all, which wasn't often, I changed the subject. "When do you leave?"

"ASAP. I'm going home right now to pack and tell John he's on his own for a couple days. I cannot get a hold of him, and he's not replying to my texts." She regarded her phone as if it was to blame.

"I saw him today," I blurted. "In the Time Traveler."

Jackie narrowed her eyes. "You were in a bar?"

Defensiveness threatened to overtake me, but since I'd very nearly done what she wasn't quite accusing me of, I squashed it down. "I had the sliders and a couple glasses of root beer."

"That's okay then."

Honesty compelled me to keep going. "I almost ordered a beer though. Seeing John was the only thing that stopped me. I didn't change my mind because it was the right thing to do." I hung my head, shame suffusing me as I admitted to Jackie what I hadn't yet admitted to myself. "I ordered the root beer because I was afraid of getting caught."

Jackie reached out and took my hand. "Hey, that's okay. You've chosen to stay sober for yourself, but if you don't always do it for that reason, that's okay, too. There's no shame in doing the right thing for a not-quite-right reason. If it helps in the future, just know that I can *always* see you, should I choose to. Or at least, I assume that'll be the case once Sasha imparts upon me her great wisdom." Jackie rolled her eyes and dropped my hand. "And speaking of, I'd better get going."

She scooped Lenore up. "Who was John with, by the way? I thought he was at work today."

"He said it was a business lunch. His dining partner was an absolute giant hipster, complete with man bun and flannel."

Jackie relaxed infinitesimally. "If he talked to you and introduced his dining companion, then that's alright."

I opened my mouth to tell her the whole encounter had felt off but swallowed my words. She didn't need my weird feelings to distract her. Instead, I put an arm around her shoulder and side-hugged her. "I'll miss you. Say hi to Aunt Sasha for me and hurry back."

"Take care of yourself, and don't let Kara keep you ignorant. You're part of this, and you deserve to know what they're planning for you." She opened my bedroom door and left, stopping in the living room only long enough to grab Lenore's diaper bag and exchange a few words with our parents.

"Family dinner tonight, Frankie," Mom said. "Just you, me, and Dad. We have a lot to talk about. But now, you'd better get downstairs. You need to be ready, and Kara is the best person to get you there."

Buoyed by the knowledge that my time in the dark was almost over, I went downstairs. I could handle a few hours of Kara. After all, that was what I'd done almost every day for weeks. No big deal.

SEVENTEEN

Wow, was I wrong. It wasn't just Kara waiting for me. Hope was down there, too. She'd changed into workout gear I recognized as Kara's since I'd seen her a half hour ago and was battling full tilt against Kara.

She was good. Like phenomenally good. She got a few hits on Kara, much to my slack-jawed amazement.

"That's enough," Kara said. "You did good. Let's take a break."

Kara was winded, something I hadn't even known was possible.

Hope smiled at Kara. "That was fun! It's been a long time since I felt like I was actually sparring. Most of the time, I hold back long enough to make my opponent feel good about themselves before I destroy them."

Kara laughed and picked up her water bottle. "Frankie, warm up. You and Hope are next. Pay close attention to Hope's technique. She's nearly perfected what I want you to practice." She looked at Hope. "Hold back as much as you can while keeping Frankie working. She hasn't had the advantage of twenty years of daily practice the way you have. She's coming into this late and has a lot of catching up to do before she's ready."

Hope dabbed at her brow with a pastel-pink towel. "Of course. Don't worry, Frankie. I'll go easy on you."

I suppressed my instinctual retort that she could go as hard as she wanted, because I'd just seen her fight. If she came at me as hard as she could, I'd be on the ground crying for mercy inside of thirty seconds. Instead, I pushed as much warmness into my expression and voice as I could. "I appreciate it. I didn't see much, but from what I observed, you are fantastic. Much better than I could even dream of being."

To my surprise, Kara interrupted me. "Don't be ridiculous, Frankie. Once you get out of your own way and surrender to your instincts, you'll be as good as Hope, maybe even better. The only one stopping you is you."

My mouth dropped open. That was the nicest thing Kara had ever said to me. It might be the only nice thing she'd said to me since the night I'd met her. I was suddenly infused with the desire to prove her right and make her proud. My glance swung back to Hope just in time to see cold anger directed at me. She masked it quickly, but I would never forget the sheer animosity with which she'd regarded me.

"Are you ready?" she asked in a clipped tone.

I brought my sword up. "Whenever you are."

Her promise to hold back notwithstanding, she attacked me with so much speed and force it was all I could do to defend myself. I couldn't hold my position or get a single blow in. I might have had the potential to be better than her someday, but it was clear that someday was a long time off.

Sweat dripped, stinging my eyes, and fell onto the mat. I dashed my free arm across my face, trying to clear my vision. Hope took that opportunity to redouble her attack.

I parried her blows, and she didn't land a strike. After a couple minutes, my arms shook, and I could barely hold my sword.

"Enough," Kara said.

I dropped my arm to my side and stepped back. Hope didn't

respond to the command as quickly as I did, and a resounding *whack* hit the right side of my ribcage.

I hadn't seen it coming and hadn't had a chance to move out of the way.

My knees buckled, and I hit the ground.

"Oh no!" Hope said. "I am so sorry." She held out a hand to me. I regarded it with suspicion. The blow had felt purposeful, but I was also certain that she wouldn't do anything further, at least not under the watchful eyes of Kara.

Still, though... Hesitation never hurt anyone.

"Go," Kara said to Hope. "You could have pulled that blow, and you did not. Find a shower. Change your clothes, and I will speak to you later."

Hope's mouth quirked downward, and she met my gaze. "I am so sorry," she said, insincerity riding her tone. "I didn't realize we'd stopped."

I continued to ignore her hand. She dropped it and left the basement.

"She did that on purpose," I told Kara. I pushed myself to my feet and glared at my trainer.

Kara nodded once. "She did. There is no denying it. She dislikes you, and I do not know why."

"Ha!"

Kara cocked her head to one side. "You know why she doesn't like you? Please explain."

"You call me the *chosen one but* exclude me from your planning meetings. You include her, then tell her I will probably be better than her. You are fucking with everyone all the time. No one trusts you, and no one particularly likes you. I am never going to start a Hope fan club, but I get why she's pissed off."

"It is because of me?" Kara looked dumbfounded.

"Probably not entirely," I conceded. "But you're not helping things. Either you trust me or you don't, but leaving me out of things doesn't make me trust you. And you can tell her she's the best thing since sliced bread, but if you tell her I'm the bee's knees and that I outrank her, she's gonna do her best to eliminate the competition."

Kara took a deep breath, stared at me for long enough to make me feel uncomfortable, and nodded briskly. "I have misjudged the situation. You are doing well, if not excelling in the same way Hope is. I will speak to her, then you, again. We will find a way for the two of you to find balance."

I wanted to protest that it was the worst idea I'd heard in a very long time, but she was gone before I could give voice to my fear.

I cleaned my blade and hung my sword on the wall, then headed upstairs to face the family.

CHAPTER

EIGHTEEN

By the time I made it upstairs, the house was empty except for me, Mom, and Dad. They sat drinking tea at the small kitchen table—the one we'd seldom used growing up because our house had always been full, and we usually ate in the dining room. Even though we were pretty far out of town, we'd played host to all my friends when I was growing up, and Becky's and Jackie's, too—when they got a little older.

I never could quite figure out what made my place the destination for the few friends I'd spent time with, but looking around now, I finally got it. My parents might not have been the cool ones who bought their kids booze and looked the other way during parties, but this home emanated comfort, caring, and love. And my folks were always there with rides, advice, and hot meals.

Now that I was back, I felt the warmth this house exuded.

"Thank you." I sat across from them and smiled, fighting back the rising emotion. No one needed to see me tear up.

"For what?" Dad asked.

"For this." I gestured around the cheerful yellow of the kitchen, to the warm wood floors with the grain nearly worn out in the high-

117

traffic areas, the antique table with the white linen tablecloth embroidered with violets around the edge, and finally encompassing them. "I wish I'd realized this when I was younger, but this wasn't just our house. This was home. For me, for my friends, for everyone who needed it. I am so, so lucky."

Mom smiled and reached for my hand. "You're welcome. Everyone deserves a place to belong. We worried for so long that you didn't feel like you fit in here, but I'm glad you did then, and that you do now."

Dad took my other hand. "We love you so much, and we are so glad you're home. But maybe save the thank yous until you hear what your mother has to say."

Mom glared. "Marty, that is not how we broach a difficult subject."

"It's not how you do it. Your method is to beat around the bush until the main point is lost, drop it in with no warning and the least amount of finesse possible, then serve ice cream." Dad shrugged unrepentantly. "My way is better."

Mom huffed but didn't argue. "We owe you an explanation," she said to me.

Dad elbowed her, and she rolled her eyes.

"Fine. *I* owe you an explanation. Things are happening much faster than we thought they might, and there is a lot of information swirling around right now."

My smile tightened. "Is there? I'm not aware of any."

"And that's the problem," Mom said. "You are the first Valkyrie to wake in over a thousand years. Those of us who bore daughters to take our places are weakened. Each of us had the same experience. The gods and the sword claimed our daughters, beginning the process of channeling our Valkyrie powers into you all and weakening us. In a Valkyrie's twentieth year, she should come of age, and the full measure of power should finish its transfer from mother to daughter." She folded her hands, bit her lip, and looked up at the ceiling.

I recognized that look. She didn't want to say what was next, and I sure as shit didn't want to hear it.

"Just spit it out, Mom. I can take it."

"The twenty years between bearing a daughter and having her take her place as a full Valkyrie are difficult. I cannot retire and leave my sisters at reduced strength, even though my strength is waning. In addition to ushering the chosen to their appropriate afterlife, we are still responsible for keeping our gods in check, and that is difficult when one is lacking the full measure of power they wielded for centuries."

"What do you mean, 'keeping the gods in check'?" I asked. "I don't remember any of that from the old stories. Valkyries were created to serve the gods, not to watch over them."

"Managing up is a business buzzword for a reason," Dad said. "Have you ever noticed how many middle-aged white men are in positions of power, even though they are not particularly good at what they do? It's easier to leave an incompetent god in place and mitigate the damage as much as possible while working around him than to try to oust him. A petty god with too much power can make life very difficult for a lot of people."

"Not to mention, firing an immortal being is almost impossible," Mom said. "Odin may claim credit for our creation, but the Valkyries have always worked most closely with Freyja. Part of what we do is ensure the gods don't get bored and start a war to liven things up."

"Okay, they may be part of the 'boys will be boys' club, but that doesn't mean they'd start Ragnarök because it was a slow news year," I protested.

Mom held my gaze for long enough to make me squirm. "Do you really believe that? Or have you not clocked who is responsible for most of the acts of violence, both small and large, in the human world? Take that aggression and lack of impulse control and add immortality and a sense of impunity. That is a recipe for the apocalypse."

She had a point. "Okay, fine. The gods are a bunch of douche-bros. What does this have to do with me?"

"The Valkyries have not been at full strength for about thirty-five years. I was the first of my generation to have a baby, and when everything seemed as it should at your birth, others followed suit. There are twenty-four Valkyrie at all times. Five are originals, including Kara and Lena. In the second generation, there are nineteen. Ten of those chose not to give birth and the other nine are like me—the mothers of potential Valkyries whose powers didn't wake when they turned twenty. For the last thirty years, our power has diminished even though yours never reached full potential."

A knock on the door interrupted her story.

"I'll get it," Dad said. "Keep talking, Katrin. If you lose steam now, you'll never finish."

"Right. Drink?" She stood, grabbed a pitcher of iced tea from the fridge, and poured three glasses. After sitting again, she continued. "When your power awoke in that fire where you parted the veil, I felt it, but I didn't know what was happening. I called my mother, then Lena, to see if they could help."

"Your mother? I thought she was dead." My voice sounded flat rather than accusatory, which was what I'd been going for, but Mom got the picture anyway.

"Oh, she is," she hastened to reassure me. "Once a Valkyrie passes on her powers, she lives a normal lifespan. But dead doesn't always mean gone, at least not for those of us who can part the veil between the living and the dead. Anyway, once I described what I'd felt, Mom said it sounded like the power transfer had completed, which enabled you to hold on to Gwen's spirit and keep her from death, and my gifts were gone. Or mostly, anyway. I can still see things no one else can see, and obviously talk to my dead mother. But I can no longer travel the Bifrost and leave Midgard, and I can't choose the slain, nor fulfill my oath to keep the gods under control."

Dad walked into the kitchen bearing two enormous pizza boxes.

"You're doing exactly what I said you would. You're telling her important stuff, but not the hard part."

"You're the First. It's an inherited position, rather than one based on longevity. The power is strongest in the First, and your connection to the goddesses is deeper. Not only are you the oldest of the third generation of new Valkyries, you are the daughter of the oldest in the second generation—that's me—and you are the granddaughter of the first Valkyrie," Mom said. "That is why you are the one who will lead the armies into Ásgarðr to stop the gods from starting Ragnarök. All Valkyries are powerful, but our family has the added burden of leadership. That's why Kara is riding you so hard."

"And that's why you're keeping me in the dark? Like one does to their leaders?" I asked, not bothering to disguise the snark.

"In part. The rest of the Valkyries know that the third generation is finally waking, but no one yet knows you're among the woken. They assumed because I had three daughters, none of you got the full measure of my power. Therefore, no one's wondered about you.

"Kara and Lena are spreading the news that we will take in all the new ones for training since my home is the most secure on this plane —the Aerie for our sisters. Only humans without a single drop of supernatural blood can find this place without an escort."

Dad grabbed three plates from the cupboard and stacked them next to the steaming pizza boxes.

"We don't want people to know about you until you're strong enough to defend yourself. Although I've never been able to prove it, I believe there is a traitor in our ranks. Someone is feeding information to the gods. If I'm right, they know you're a threat to their plan to start Ragnarök, because you can unite the Valkyries to ride against them. The longer we can keep you under wraps, the better."

"And you couldn't just tell me this from the beginning?" I asked. "How does keeping me ignorant hide me any better?"

"That is an excellent question," Dad said. He set a large plate in front of me with two slices of Canadian bacon, black olive, and pineapple pizza.

"What you don't know, you can't accidentally betray," Mom said. "For the record, I disagree with this stance, which is why I'm telling you now. Kara and Lena outvoted me earlier—they're the only ones who know how much power you have—and since I'm no longer the leader of the Valkyries, I couldn't overrule them. And once the majority of Valkyries present have voted, the rest cannot do anything else."

"So, I can overrule them, but only if I know who I am." I took a bite of pizza and chewed. "Did they forbid you to tell me the significance of being your daughter?"

"Obviously not," Mother said. "They only told me that I could not tell you the news we've received and the plans we're making. They did forbid me to tell Jackie, Becky, Dusana, or anyone else whose word they couldn't compel."

I thought about what to do next. I had so little information and no knowledge of how the Valkyrie sisterhood worked. "Why didn't they forbid you to tell me why I'm being left out?"

Mom smiled. "I might not have the power to lead anymore, but I have not lost my ability to direct conversations and influence decisions. I was willing to go along with them as long as it didn't harm you. And now they are. I can't tell you what they're hiding from you, but *you* can compel them to." Her grin turned positively evil. "And I can tell you all sorts of other things about them to use as blackmail if they choose to be difficult about it."

I thought back to my final conversation with Kara. "I don't know about Aunt Lena, but I don't think Kara will fight me. Not now."

"Finally," Dad said. "I hate secrets, no matter how well intentioned they are. If no one ever asks me to keep another secret again, it'll be too soon."

"Does Hope know who I am?" I asked. "She must. She's heard me referred to as the chosen one, and while she was pissed off, she didn't seem surprised."

Mom nodded, and her mouth flattened into a thin, disapproving line. "She's the daughter of Serena, whom Kara knows well and trusts implicitly. Kara saw no reason not to tell her."

"You disagree?"

"I have been unable to contact Serena to confirm Hope is her daughter. It's possible she's exhausted and weakened from the power drain that occurred when Hope's powers awoke, but I'd like more confirmation than a name. Hope claims to have no idea what's happening to her but is better trained than anyone I've met in ages. Something about her doesn't add up. Watch your back around her, Frankie."

I shivered and goosebumps raised on my arms as a wave of nausea rolled over me. "Goose walked over my grave," I said when Dad eyed me curiously.

"What did you say?" Mom asked with an intensity I'd seldom heard from her.

"Nothing. I shivered and felt a little sick, so I said the bit about the goose and the grave. Nothing weird."

Mom was on her feet and out of the room in seconds. "Frankie, call Becky and Jackie and get them here immediately. Martin, I'm going to need your help to get in touch with everyone else. One of my sisters is dead."

NINETEEN

It took a couple hours for everyone to arrive after we called them in. Becky and Devin showed up first, followed by Dusana, Archibald, and Lena. Kara and Hope rolled in about an hour after we'd called everyone. Jackie and Lenore were the last to arrive, and Aunt Sasha came with them. Neither Sasha nor Jackie looked thrilled by the turn of events.

"Go away, Jackie. Stay with your aunt for a few days," Jackie muttered. She poured herself a cup of coffee after handing Lenore over to Becky. "Oh, ha ha ha! Just kidding. Instead, drive two and a half hours, then turn around and come right back." She glared at no one in particular. "Nothing I love more than spending five hours on the road with an angry baby. John's not coming, by the way. Since I was going out of town, he headed to Seattle to visit his sister."

She poured a generous glug of cream into her coffee, added a teaspoon of sugar, and stomped over to the largest recliner—the one Mom usually claimed—to curl up with her bucket of coffee cradled in her hands.

The rest of our assembly found places to settle in our expansive family room. Lena and Kara looked as shaken and pale as Mom but hadn't said anything.

"What's going on?" Becky asked. She had baby Lenore cradled in her arms and was tucked under the protective arm of Devin. "Not everyone here is a magical prodigy and knows what's happening."

I don't know if anyone else heard the bitterness in my sister's voice, but I did. She was not happy about being the ordinary one.

"One of our sisters died," Mom said. "But I'm not connected the way I was before, and I don't know who."

Kara leaned forward. The exhaustion and grief in her eyes made her millennia of years weigh heavily on her face. "It was Göndul. One of the originals—one of the only five of us remaining. I've known her for thousands of years, and I felt her death. It was brutal." A sob choked her. Lena slid over and wrapped her arms around Kara. The old Black woman took a deep breath and continued. "It was brutal, but I didn't see who did it."

Kara looked around the room, and I wasn't sure if she was assessing our guilt or hoping someone knew more than she did.

"I felt it, but only a little," I said. "Just a wave of nausea and goosebumps."

Lena shifted in her seat, drawing attention to herself but didn't remove her arm from Kara. "You'll feel more in time as your connection to us grows. And Göndul was part of us since the beginning. She was the second created after your grandmother Hilda, and all of us have known her since we came into being. She was formidable, almost as much as Hilda. It would not be easy to take her out."

"But surely she was old," Hope said. "How hard can it be to kill an elderly woman? For that matter, she may have died of natural causes."

The look Kara shot Hope nearly pierced my soul, and I was barely in her line of sight. "She was a Valkyrie. We do not age, we do not become feeble, and we do *not* become easy targets. From the time of our creation until we pass our powers to the next generation, should we so choose, we are Valkyries. We are strong. Göndul was no more an easy target than you are."

Hope looked like she wanted to argue the point but wisely chose a different path.

"This is unprecedented," Lena said quietly. "We are immortal, and our number has always been twenty-four. Without a successor for Göndul, we are lessened."

"How, though?" I asked. "If we are immortal, and Göndul has survived for thousands of years, how did this happen?"

Lena shook her head. "It's impossible. Katrin's home, our Aerie, is singular in that the shielding is all-encompassing to keep out anyone supernatural who hasn't been shown the way. Just like this house, Valkyries each have their own sort of shield. Our power, and thus our existence, is invisible to other supernaturals who don't know who we are."

"I don't understand," Hope said. I felt a surge of warmth and gratitude toward her for saying first what I would've had to.

"This house"—Mom waved her hands around—"is invisible. You probably couldn't see it until you were invited over the threshold of my property. Odin himself couldn't set foot in this house. But each Valkyrie has the same mental shields. Odin could show up in my funeral parlor, but he wouldn't know what I was unless either I or another Valkyrie told him."

Hope scrunched up her nose. "So, if someone told Odin a Valkyrie lived in Estacada and worked at the funeral parlor, could he see you if he showed up there? Or would they have to show him a picture or something?"

The look my mom shot Hope showed she was even more suspicious than she'd let on. "He'd have to be introduced to me as a Valkyrie, much the same way the introduction to this house would need to be deliberate. A supernatural pizza delivery person wouldn't see the place for what it was—they'd just not find it."

"None of this matters," Kara barked. "Our sister was murdered. We must find her body, celebrate her, and avenge her."

It sounded like the correct order of operations, but the twisted grin on Kara's face was still unsettling.

"When was the last time anyone talked to her?" Aunt Lena asked. "I haven't spoken to her for more than six months. She loved the sea, though. We should look to the shores for signs of her. Were any of the others close to her?"

Mom shook her head before Lena even finished the question. "No. She was always a loner, but in the past few decades, she drifted further and further away from everyone. I reached out a few times, and our exchanges were always polite, but she never initiated contact."

"That was my experience as well," Kara agreed.

"Is there any chance at all that she had a kid?" Hope asked. "And maybe that made her less powerful?"

"No," Kara said. "If she'd passed on her power to another, we wouldn't have felt her death as profoundly."

"I have an idea where to look," Mom said. "The last time we spoke, she agreed to meet for drinks in Portland. I think she lived on the Oregon coast."

"It's too dangerous for you to go," Dad said. "What if the murderer is still there? You aren't at full power anymore."

The look my mother leveled at my father was enough to take down buildings. He didn't back down though. Finally, she sighed. "Lena, would you like to go for a drive? It's smarter to have two people, anyway, especially if we're dealing with someone who can kill a Valkyrie."

Lena nodded. "We will find her, and we will bring her back. We will also find an appropriate location to celebrate her life and mourn her passing."

"I will also come," Archibald said, earning a surprised look from Sasha and a startled jump from almost everyone else. He hadn't spoken since he'd walked into the room and curled up under the end table. Almost everyone, including me, had forgotten he was there. "I won't be much assistance against a murderer, but I will be able to sense Göndul when we're near."

"As should I," Lena added. "It is what we do, after all. Escort the souls of the dead to the afterlife."

"Wouldn't someone already have done that?" Hope asked. I was definitely warming toward her now that she was asking all my questions. "I mean, I haven't run across any dying people, but from what I've heard, you show up before they die so you're on hand to help out with the transition. So, someone should've been there when she died. Another Valkyrie, right?"

"Not necessarily," Mom said. "It's true that the Valkyries who died after surrendering their powers to the next generation have been escorted by one of their sisters, but Göndul was immortal. Her death was impossible, so a guide to the afterlife wouldn't have been called."

"Regardless of whether her soul remains or not, I will be able to find her," Archibald said. "Besides, it is not as if you can keep me from accompanying you. It's easier to agree."

"Fine," Mom said rather begrudgingly. "We'll leave in the morning."

THE GATHERING BROKE up almost immediately, although since most people were staying at my parents' place, it wasn't a scattering so much as a wandering off. My mother, Kara, Lena, and Sasha—who'd known Göndul—disappeared with a bottle of vodka to mourn. Hope headed to her room to do whatever it was she did when she was alone. After tucking the sleeping Lenore into the playpen in Mom's office, Becky, Devin, Jackie, and Dad sat around the kitchen table playing a boisterous game of Pinochle.

"Want some hot tea and a beautiful sky?" I asked Dusana, the only one besides Archibald and me still in the family room.

"That sounds divine. I'll meet you out back in five minutes."

I made two cups of peppermint tea, snagged a couple blankets, and headed through the family room toward the patio. "Are you coming, Archibald?"

He hadn't moved from his spot under the end table yet, and although he looked supremely comfortable, he was wide-eyed and too alert.

"Yes, but only if I can have a blanket as well. It's cold, and my fur can only do so much to keep me warm."

"Of course, your majesty. I will find the thickest and softest blanket I can."

Archibald nodded solemnly. "As is my due, peasant."

I barked out a short laugh, grabbed a third fleece blanket, and went outside.

Dusana was curled up in one of the Adirondack chairs, feet tucked beneath herself. She'd added a sweater, a hoodie, and a thick jacket over her T-shirt. A wool beanie peeked out from beneath the hood, and gloves lay on the table next to her.

"Cold?" I asked with a grin, handing over her cup of tea and settling the blanket on her lap.

"I spent most of my life so far in the desert southwest," she said. "Percy and I took Route 66 all the way to Chicago once a year or so, but I always timed it for spring or autumn. Most of the year, we were warm. Or I was, anyway. As a ghost, he didn't feel temperature anymore. I don't know if I've ever sat outside for any length of time when it was a million degrees below zero."

I laughed and took a sip of my tea. "It's forty-five. That's barely cold enough for blankets."

"Don't mock my temperature tolerance," she chided. "I'm actually surprised you're not feeling the cold the way I am. You were in New Mexico for the last decade."

I pulled the blanket around me and curled up in my chair. "I am a little," I confessed. "But something about this place is so familiar that it's not bothering me."

Archibald was buried so deeply in his blanket that all I could see were the tips of his ears and his whiskers. "Valkyries don't feel the cold much. You shouldn't either, reaper. Now that you're not quite mortal anymore."

"Well, I do," she retorted. She set her tea down long enough to pull on her gloves. "Are you okay? Do you know what's going on yet?"

"Not really. I know how to find out now, but Göndul's death kinda disrupted all that. I'll tell you what I know, though."

"Not now," Archibald interrupted. "Your mother's house is protected from outside ears, but there are plenty of people here who don't need to know. At least not yet."

"That's probably a good idea," Dusana said. "And I can wait until we're truly alone to discover more about you."

My body temperature rose enough that I almost didn't need the blanket anymore. Her discovering more about me sounded like a fabulous idea. I licked my lips and let my thoughts take a few tentative steps down that path.

Dusana continued, hopefully oblivious to the fantasy taking shape in my mind. "I'm exhausted. I thought I had enough energy left to watch the autumn stars come out in this arctic wasteland that is Oregon, but I need sleep. There are things I want to tell you, too, but like Archibald said, now is not the time." She stood, shed her blanket, and picked up her tea. "Goodnight, Frankie." She squeezed my shoulder when she walked by, then disappeared into the house.

"Just you and me now, Archibald," I said to the fleecy mound next to me.

There was no response. Cats could sleep anywhere.

I slid my chair over and put my hand on the fuzzy pile of cat and blanket next to me. My hand sank down until it hit the chair. Archibald had disappeared.

I sighed, took a long drink of my tea, piled the two abandoned blankets on top of me, and leaned back to watch the stars.

It was just me.

CHAPTER
TWENTY

The sun crept toward the horizon as we completed the penultimate leg of the journey to say goodbye to Göndul. The drive to the Indian Beach trailhead had been pretty. The hike to the Tillamook Rock Lighthouse Viewpoint had been gorgeous and creepy. The trees were lush, even this late into the year, but the forest had a feeling of watching and waiting, although what for, I couldn't tell.

After half sliding/half walking down the sketchy path from the top of the bluff to the beach, we met Lena at the water's edge and looked out over the Pacific Ocean at the Tillamook Rock Lighthouse. The squat, white lighthouse was on a tiny, rocky island about a mile offshore. From here, the decommissioned lighthouse appeared tiny against the expanse of dark blue waves and the grey and blue sky. A wave broke over the rocks, momentarily erasing the island from view.

"How the hell are we supposed to get out there?" John groused. Jackie's partner had made it back from Seattle just in time to accompany her and Lenore to the funeral, and apparently, he was not happy about it.

"Patience," Kara said. "Not everyone is here yet."

I looked around and counted. The only person I didn't see was Adele, but I hadn't expected her anyway.

An eerie descant flowed in the breeze and surrounded us. Kara turned around and held out her arms. "Sisters."

I followed her gaze. A dozen or more women in shining helmets, white tunics, breastplates, and greaves streamed toward us. Kara and Lena stepped forward and, as they did so, their casual clothing turned into the same kind of armor worn by the others.

I looked closer. A few women carried helmets but weren't wearing the rest of the costume.

I wasn't sure of the difference, and now didn't seem the time to ask.

Kara turned and met my eyes, then Hope's. "Frankie, Hope. Come forward and meet your sisters."

When I hesitated, Jackie shoved me gently.

I walked toward Kara, and the jeans and T-shirt I'd donned before Jackie and I had driven to the coast flowed away from me. I looked down. I was garbed similarly to the others but didn't have a helmet. I stole a glance at Hope. She had the whole kit and caboodle. I didn't know why my helmet hadn't shown up, but if it made people underestimate me, that could only be a good thing, right?

Once Hope and I drew abreast of Kara and Lena, they took our hands and led us to the others. Those in the full Valkyrie regalia strode forward and joined hands, including Kara, Lena, Hope, and me in the circle.

Power, grief, and love with an undercurrent of anger pulsed through the link. The others were here to mourn their dead sister, but they wanted vengeance, too, and they would only wait so long before they took it. Before *we* took it. The longer I stood here, the more I felt the call of the Valkyries in my blood. They were my sisters, just as much as Becky and Jackie.

I was a part of something much bigger than I'd known about,

bigger than I could've ever believed. I would fight and die for these women, and they would do the same for me.

We stood until the sun dipped its fiery toes in the water, and the music faded away.

The buzz of a helicopter drowned out the crashing waves, and a few moments after that, it landed a few hundred yards away.

I looked at Lena, who smiled. "Frankie, Marty, Becky, Devin, Jackie, John, Baby Lenore, Dusana, Hope, and Zofia. You're first."

The named group surged forward, but my feet refused to move. There was no fucking way, not in a million years, that I was getting into that contraption.

"Frankie?" Dusana asked. She held out a hand toward me, but I shook my head adamantly.

"Isn't there a boat or something?" I asked.

"No," Kara said. "It's a helicopter or you come with me."

Relief at not having to fly took hold. Stepping with her hadn't been great, but it was much better than being in a giant metal death trap. "Great. I'll come with you instead."

"See you there, then." Dusana caught up with the group and climbed into the helicopter.

Twenty minutes later, the helicopter returned. This time, there were fewer people to make the trip. Once it took off, I looked at the women who were left. There were twenty-one, and all of them in full Valkyrie regalia, complete with helmet.

"I guess we're all 'stepping' then?" I grinned. I didn't know why we'd had to do helicopters when the Valkyries could've served as teleportation assistants, but maybe it was some kind of taboo thing. I'd ask later.

"Oh, we're not stepping," Lena said. "We are going to fly." She put two fingers between her lips and whistled shrilly.

A cloud appeared on the western horizon and sped toward us with alarming speed. It quickly morphed into a herd of horses. Horses with wings. Winged horses.

"Pegasi," I whispered. "We're flying on horseback. That is so much worse."

"There is nothing better in the world," said one of the Valkyries I didn't know. "Once yours chooses you, you'll understand."

The herd landed, and all but one of the pegasi—pegasuses?—trotted over to a Valkyrie and nuzzled her. In unison, the Valkyries mounted. Kara reached down and offered me her arm. I wanted to refuse. This was worse than a helicopter, but I'd already been kinda difficult about the whole thing and didn't want to be the weird scaredy-cat at the Valkyrie funeral.

I sucked in a breath and let Kara haul me up behind her.

"Hold on!" she said.

I wrapped my arms around her waist and closed my eyes as tightly as I could.

"Watch," Kara commanded in a voice that brooked no argument.

I opened my eyes. The pegasus without a rider ran toward the water. With a tilt of its wings and a thrust with its back legs, it launched into the sky, circled twice, and headed to the island.

I hadn't known it was possible to grip Kara harder, but I found the strength to do so. When it was our turn, the launch left my stomach behind on the beach, and my head swam. I kept my eyes resolutely on the horizon and off the crashing waves below. Logically, I knew that pegasus crashes must be even rarer than helicopter crashes, but that didn't mean passengers didn't routinely fall to their deaths.

It wasn't long before the herd began spiraling downward. I clenched my jaw to keep from screaming. This was worse than the worst roller coaster I'd ever been on. I sincerely hoped that I'd never have to experience that again. Maybe instead of a pegasus, I could have a regular horse. Or, better yet, a rocking chair. That was more my speed.

The pegasus's hoofs touched down with a clatter, and the air whooshed out of my lungs in relief.

I slid off the back of the animal and stood on my own two feet. I had an urge to melodramatically kneel and kiss the ground, but a quick glance around at the bird shit and the sea lion population lounging on some rocks not too far away cured me.

I turned around in time to see Kara press a soft kiss to her pegasus's head, right above his nose, and stroke his jaw lightly. She whispered something into his ear and stepped back. He launched himself into the air, and once the rest were airborne, they wheeled off and flew back to the mainland.

"They're not staying?" It surprised me, although not as much as the fact that I had actual opinions about what was proper funeral behavior for flying horses.

"They wait for Göndul's mount, then they will conduct their own memorial," Kara said. "Come with me. We do not want to keep the others waiting. The sun is setting, and it is time to say goodbye."

CHAPTER

TWENTY-ONE

A wooden canoe drifted out to sea. Flames licked at the sides, rendering the boat nearly invisible.

I sat and watched with the others. We were lined up along the western edge of the island, sitting on the cold, hard, damp ground. No one spoke.

The service had been less than I'd expected. Göndul's body had been examined by each of the Valkyries, excluding me and Hope, before Kara and Lena wrapped her in a funeral shroud and placed the body in the boat. Lena held aloft a torch, and Kara and two others walked forward, lighting their torches from hers.

The four of them held their torches to the kindling in the canoe until it caught fire, then pushed it away from the shore. They doused their flames in the water and joined hands.

When the fiery boat disappeared from view, the four Valkyries returned to the group. Grief creased their faces.

"We are diminished," Kara said, her voice harsher than usual. "There should be four and twenty gathered here in celebration. Instead, we are fourteen strong and two novices. Where are the

139

others? Anja, where is your daughter? Has she not yet come into her power?"

A short, white woman with dirty blonde hair, slight frame that was almost frail, and wearing jeans and a denim shirt walked forward, nodding deeply. It wasn't quite a bow, but it spoke of obeisance and demonstrated how much everyone respected Kara.

"I don't know," Anja said, clasping her hands in front of her. "When Katrin informed me the next generation was finally waking, I called Riley and asked her to come home. I haven't heard from her since." Her voice wavered for a second, but she gained control before she spoke again. "That was three days ago. It is not unusual for us to go a few days, even a week or two, without speaking, but she will always text me back within a few hours. Since she's supposed to be on her way home, it is worrisome."

Kara reached out and placed a hand on Anja's shoulder. "You don't have to hide your worry and fear. We are not men who deem any emotion but anger to be weakness. We are your sisters."

Anja's shoulders shook. Mom walked forward and slung an arm around Anja, leaning in to whisper something to her. I didn't know what it was, but in my imagination, she was reassuring the other woman that her kid was unlikely to disappear for a full ten years like I had.

Pressure against my lower shin drew my attention. Archibald head-butted me in the manner of cats everywhere when they were both showing affection and demanding attention. I kept my eyes on the women in front of me but squatted to scratch behind Archibald's ears.

"She's not talking about you," Archibald said softly. "She wouldn't. She shared her pain at your absence with her sisters, but she never spoke negatively about you."

"And how do you know that, cat?" I whispered. "It's not like you were here, right?"

He looked at me, forcing my hand off his head, then slowly and deliberately winked.

I rolled my eyes at him and stood in time to see Anja step out of the circle of my mother's arms.

Kara reached out and took Anja's hands in hers. "Did you feel the power leave you? Are you sure her powers have woken? I know there was some uncertainty, given the, um..." Kara hesitated and bit her lip. "...unusual circumstances of her birth."

I took a step forward. An uncertain Kara was not something I'd expected to see tonight.

"It left the day after I spoke to Riley," Anja confirmed. "I nearly collapsed when the weight of it left me. It was freeing and yet devastating to lose the connection to the goddess I'd known for a thousand years. I remember when it awoke in me, and how overwhelming it was. If it hadn't been for the support of my mother and sisters, I might have gone mad, and I knew what was happening and what to expect. I called Riley immediately but received no response."

"We found Hope, daughter of Serena, bound in a room full of draugr," Kara said.

A collective intake of breath startled me. "They did nothing but guard, and even when we took her, their response was understated. We need a list of the missing and their last known locations. I haven't felt any other deaths." She paused and looked around. When no one offered any statements to the contrary, she continued, "Nor can I feel anyone who isn't here. Either their deaths are being kept from us, which seems unlikely, or they are alive but imprisoned, in which case we need to find them and rescue them before our numbers dwindle even further. Göndul did not have an heir to take her power. We cannot let that happen to anyone else. There are too many missing to hope we can find them all, so we must first concentrate on those who have not yet given birth."

The minute she stopped speaking, an electric shock tore through my body. My spine bowed, and a scream tore from my throat.

I don't know how long I was lost in the pain of having my guts ripped from my living body, but it was way, way too long. Once the screams died in my throat, leaving me raw and drained, I looked around, expecting to see everyone's eyes on me.

Instead, I saw fourteen women on the ground in a similar state.

"What the fuck?" Hope asked, looking around. "Are you guys okay?"

She'd recovered a lot more quickly than me, and from the looks of it, the others were in even worse straits. Whatever happened seemed to take out the oldest harder.

"Regan is dead," Kara croaked. "And it was not a peaceful death."

TWENTY-TWO

Three hours later, the group, less Dusana and my bio sisters and their families, were sitting in a rough circle around a long table that'd been set up in the basement training room of my mother's house. Kara passed around a bottle of whiskey, something that had me salivating and stepping back simultaneously.

"We have no time to lose," Kara said. "We have six missing Valkyries and another of our sisters is dead. We have to find everyone and bring them to the Aerie."

"Why here?" a tall Asian woman with long, silky brown hair and light-brown eyes asked with a thick Scandinavian accent. "Katrin is no longer one of us, and she holds no power. Her child is untested, untrained, and unlikely to wield the authority and power present in her mother and grandmother. It would be better to meet in the Heart."

"The Heart?" I asked. My excitement at learning new things had waned significantly in the last few weeks when everything was learning, and nothing was just fucking telling me what I needed to know.

No one answered, but Mom looked at me and mouthed, "Later."

Kara took a deep breath, and the look of pained patience I'd become so familiar with shuttered her face. "The Heart is a wonderful meeting place. However, most of us live in the United States now, and every single one of the missing are from the Western US. The Aerie is the closest safe house, Mari."

Mari crossed her arms. "It's not as safe as the Heart. It will never be as safe as the Heart. Frigg herself has blessed our ancestral home and promised her protection. It is sacred to Freyja and has served as our haven for millennia."

"None of that is in debate," Kara said evenly. "However, for our sisters who are missing, it will be easier for them to get here than Tromsø."

My mother rose from her seat halfway down the table. From the set of her shoulders and the tight smile on her face, I could tell she'd barely been holding herself together. Her voice was just as steady as Kara's, though, when she spoke. "My home is not the Heart, but it is the Valkyrie Aerie in North America. It has not been claimed by Frigg, but Freyja has honored me with her presence more than once."

Mari sneered. "Easy words for someone who is grasping at the power she lost through promiscuity and carelessness. Saying you have Freyja's blessing is nothing more than an empty claim. Produce the goddess, if you're so confident she would back your pathetic grabs for power you no longer have a right to."

My jaw dropped. Not in a million years would I have expected this kind of infighting in a group so close knit they felt each other's deaths.

"Mari, what is wrong with you?" Kara asked, apparently almost as surprised as me. "No one would ever accuse you of being easy-going, but this is beyond the pale."

Mari looked around, eyes wide, and shook her head. "What...?" She squeezed her eyes shut and rolled her neck. "I don't know. I'm so sorry. Katrin, I am so sorry. I don't know what came over me."

My mother smiled tightly at Mari, clearly not quite ready to forgive and forget. "Your apology is heard. And, as I do not claim to command the comings and goings of the goddess we all worship, I cannot produce her to prove my home has her blessing and protection. But I agree with Kara that my home is the best location to serve as our command center and safe house."

Mari nodded and sat down, a bemused expression still on her face.

"Does anyone else want to voice disagreement or alternate plans?" Kara asked, looking around the table. I followed her gaze. The other Valkyries shook their heads. I was so involved in observing the others that I missed Kara's glance falling on me.

When I looked at Kara, I found her staring at me. "Frankie?" she prompted.

I gaped at her, not sure what she was asking.

"Are you okay with Katrin's home serving as our meeting place, command center, and safe haven for those who need healing and protection?"

I nodded, not trusting my voice.

"Decided," Kara said. "Now, let us discuss next steps."

THREE HOURS LATER, my eyes were heavy, and my mind was exhausted. Other than the early resolution that the Aerie was the safest place on this continent, no other agreements had been forthcoming. Two hours ago, I'd gotten up to use the restroom, then pushed my chair as far away from the table as possible.

Hope dropped into the seat next to me and handed me a bottle. "Do you think it's always like this?"

I eyed the bottle of whiskey but didn't take a drink. "I hope not. It seems petty, right?"

"So petty," Hope agreed. "You'd think after a million years of life, they'd be better at agreeing on stuff. Like, does it matter that much who does what, as long as it all gets done?"

I snorted, then clapped a hand over my mouth. A quick glance at the others told me that my indiscretion had gone unnoticed. "I would've expected a group of immortal Valkyries who've known each other forever to come to an agreement faster than college kids tasked with a team project."

Hope's grin was genuine, and for the first time I felt myself almost warming to her. "Take a drink and pass the bottle back," she said. "I think I'm gonna need a lot more of that."

I tipped the bottle to my lips. The searing smell of good whiskey hit my nose, and I inhaled deeply, letting my eyelids flutter closed. My god, it smelled so good. I could feel the memory of the burn of the liquor as it slid down my throat, and I couldn't remember the last time I'd wanted anything so badly.

I took one more deep breath, inhaling the rich smokiness, then regretfully lowered the bottle. I looked at it, pushing against my desire to tuck it into my jacket and make a run for the nearest dive bar where if anyone knew my name, they certainly wouldn't tell anyone else.

I closed my eyes, forced my hands to unclench, and handed the bottle to Hope. "Be my guest."

Hope took the bottle and took a quick swig. "I forgot you don't drink." She wiped her mouth on the back of her hand before taking another swallow. "What's up with that? Are you some kind of alcoholic?"

The word hit me hard, and even though it was the right one, hearing someone else say it hurt in a way I hadn't expected. I forced a smile. "Some kind."

Hope eyed me like she was waiting for me to elaborate, but instead, I retrieved my bottle of water from the floor next to my feet and took a gulp of that.

"Sorry," Hope said, rolling her eyes. "I guess sharing isn't caring after all." She stood and walked back to the table where the rest of the Valkyries as well as the "retired" ones were still debating their next moves.

My mother caught my eye. She smiled and gave me a thumbs up before jumping back into the fray.

It might have been condescending if it'd been anyone else but having that visible signal of my mom's approval was warm enough to displace the imaginary burn of the whiskey I hadn't drunk.

"Frankie, get back here," Kara commanded.

I sighed, stood, and picked up my chair to sit at the table again.

"We're ready for you to decide," she declared.

I wrinkled my brow and stared at her. "Ready for me to decide what?" I asked.

"What we're going to do, of course. You're First among us now, and the deciding vote will always be yours. So, tell us, Valkyrie Queen. What is your command?"

TWENTY-THREE

I stared, speechless, for much longer than was polite, much less comfortable.

"I'm sorry, what now?" I asked. "I'm no queen, and if I was, I'm sure you would've mentioned it at some point before right now in front of a bunch of strangers."

My mom cleared her throat. "Queen is the wrong word," she said. "Kara is teasing you. But you are the granddaughter of the First, and that means you are now First among us all."

"That sounds like some bullshit," I said.

"Hear, hear," Mari muttered. She might've calmed down after basically calling my mother a slut, but she was clearly not a happy camper.

Her agreeing with me shouldn't have been so upsetting, but somehow, I felt even worse than I had a couple minutes ago. Still, I had to keep trying. "Shouldn't Kara or Lena be First? After all, they're part of the original class, right? That makes a lot more sense than some random crazy lady who's been a Valkyrie for about two months making any decisions."

Kara shrugged. "We didn't make the rules, Frankie. I'll guide you and advise you as you want, as will your mother, who held this position for more than a thousand years. But ultimately, this is who you are, and you cannot shirk your responsibilities."

Zoning out during the discussion had already come back to bite me in the ass. I scrambled to come up with some kind of answer that would be acceptable and prove I'd been listening when I'd been focused on feeling sorry for myself and the bottle of whiskey being passed around instead.

"Um..." I said, dredging up every last ounce of cleverness I'd been storing for just such an occasion.

Mom rolled her eyes, the ghost of a grin floating around her lips. Hope's eye roll echoed Mom's, but her sigh of disapproval was all her own.

Kara pursed her lips. I couldn't read her expression, but disappointment mixed with disgust seemed most likely.

The Valkyries stared at me while I struggled to come up with something to say. The disappointment I imagined on Kara's face was not as carefully hidden on about half of theirs. The rest of them had a variety of expressions, ranging from neutral to mild hope. Only Mom looked cheerfully confident. And I was about to prove her faith was misplaced.

"Maybe you'd like to sleep on it?" Lena suggested.

Gratitude surged through me; I'd never loved my honorary aunt more than at that minute.

I nodded in what I hoped was a regal manner. "That's an excellent suggestion. Since I am so new to being a Valkyrie, I'd like the chance to review the options and seek the advice of those more experienced than me before agreeing on a course of action."

I don't think I fooled anyone, but at least I didn't have to announce I hadn't been paying attention.

"That's that, then," Mom said. "If you want a haven, and I recommend you all take me up on this, you are welcome to stay here."

Mari got to her feet. "If we're dismissed, I have places to be."

The door burst open, slamming against the wall and sending my heartbeat soaring. I coughed and choked as the saliva I'd been in the process of swallowing caught in my throat.

Adele strode into the room. I hadn't seen the tall, grey-haired white woman since she'd disappeared after the conference I hadn't been invited to, and I'd never seen her like this.

She was crackling with energy, and not metaphorically. The surrounding air was charged, and visible shocks of static radiated from her, making her look like she was the center of a controlled, but nonetheless roiling, thunderstorm.

Not for the first time, I wondered who she was. She obviously had power, but she wasn't a Valkyrie.

Mom stood before Adele made it no more than a few steps into the room, and Kara and Lena followed suit.

"What's happened?" Kara demanded.

Adele paused and took a deep breath. The electricity around her quieted a bit. Two more breaths, and it dissipated to barely notice-able levels. She looked more like one of the static balls ubiquitous in Spencer's Gifts than a living storm.

"I found them," she said in a voice made horrible by the quiet, calm delivery.

There was no doubt in my mind the state in which she'd found the six missing Valkyries, but I asked anyway, in a voice so flat I barely recognized it as my own. "Are they dead?"

Adele nodded with a short, sharp jerk of her chin.

Mari fell heavily back into her chair. "Are you sure?" she whispered.

"I'm sure," Adele replied. "I have secured and hidden their bodies so no human will stumble across them. They can be cele-brated and mourned in a place of your choosing after you examine them."

Zofia leaned forward and clasped her hands in front of her on the table. "Bring them to my home. It isn't as secure as Katrin's, but it's on the water, it's remote, and it will be a fitting place to send them off from."

Kara nodded slowly. "That is a generous offer, and one we will take you up on. So many funerals."

"Didn't you feel these deaths? We all felt Regan die—even me, who is the newest. How could five others die, probably by someone else's hand, and none of us notice?" I asked.

Kara smiled, but there was no warmth in it. "That is what we need to determine." She looked around the room at the remaining Valkyries, both past and present. "I don't have the power to insist you stay with Katrin, but I strongly urge you to do so. We are already too few, especially for what's coming. We cannot afford to lose anyone else. Not only for tactical reasons, but emotional ones, too. Each death lessens our numbers and decimates our hearts."

Zofia opened her mouth, but Kara didn't give her a chance to protest. "We will hold the funerals at your home, but you cannot stay there."

"Cannot?" A dangerous edge rode Zofia's voice. "You don't have the power to command me, Kara. My mother outranked you. I am the Fourth."

"And I am Third," Lena said softly. "But I would not command you, nor would I count our place in the ranks like that. You are right that only one person has the power to command you to do something you don't want to"—she shot a quick glance at me—"but I would ask you to consider how many have been lost, and how your death would affect us."

"Fine," Zofia said. She crossed her arms and clamped her mouth shut.

Silence descended on the room. Hope reached forward and grabbed the whiskey bottle off the table. She took a long swig, then passed it to her right. I watched the bottle make its way around the group and breathed a sigh of relief when the Valkyrie on my left passed it to the one on my right behind my chair.

I broke the silence. "Is there anything more that can be done tonight?"

No one answered, so I took that as a no.

"If not, why don't we find space for you all to sleep?" Where, I wasn't sure. The house was filling up rapidly.

The Valkyries streamed upstairs, following my mother, and left me alone in the basement. I took a deep breath, metaphorically girded my loins, and headed upstairs.

TWENTY-FOUR

Morning dawned too early, and Adele's summons to the training room came before I'd finished my rushed breakfast of scrambled eggs, toast, and raspberry jam.

Fortunately, the full contingent of Valkyries wasn't there. In addition to Adele, Kara, and Lena, there were three Valkyries—Zofia, Mari, and another I hadn't officially met.

She held out her hand and introduced herself. "Susanna. Second generation, daughter of Mist."

I took her hand and replied in the same way. "Frankie, third generation, daughter of Katrin."

She laughed. "I know who you are." Susanna was a tall, fat, white woman with short, tousled brown hair, sparkling brown eyes, and an infectious smile. She wore a hot pink tank top that showcased her powerful arms and shoulders, spandex shorts that hit just above her knees, and sneakers the same shade as her shirt.

Mom and Anja, the only former Valkyries in the room, walked down the stairs.

Mari glowered at me. Apparently, her animosity from the night before still lingered. "Well?" she demanded. "Have you had time to decide?"

I swallowed around the lump in my throat. I could do this, right? I took a deep breath and exhaled noisily. I could definitely do this. It'd be like taking charge of a group project in college, but instead of an 'A,' I needed to ensure no one else died. Easy-peasy.

I put as much authority into my voice as I could muster. "Zofia, Kara, and I will go with Adele to find the bodies of our fallen sisters. Once we recover them, we'll take them to the lighthouse on Zofia's property and summon everyone else."

Mom gave me a thumbs up, and a flush of pride and satisfaction suffused me.

Mari pointed at me. "And what about me? Do you expect me to cool my heels here when you're taking the glory that should be mine?"

The crack of skin against skin echoed through the room. Mari's hand flew to her cheek where a white handprint appeared.

Lena stood inches away from Mari, her hand still raised. "You forget yourself. You don't have to agree. You can argue as much as you want. But you do not accuse the First of chasing glory when what she's doing is searching for the bodies of our sisters. That is not glory. That is loss and pain. It is not an honor to seek the dead."

This was not what I'd imagined my first decision would look like. I didn't want to cause more dissension in the ranks, especially not with my first decision. I opened my mouth to ask Mari to come with us, but Kara held up a hand to forestall me. I swallowed my words.

Kara walked forward and stood next to Lena. "The First has spoken, Mari. There are times for debate and times for action. This is the latter. There will be no further arguments."

Mari muttered something too low for me to hear and stalked out of the basement, slamming the door at the top of the stairs with teenage-level dramatics.

"Um." My brain stuttered, and I shut up. There had to be something I could do to mitigate the situation and make Mari like me. "Now what?"

Lena's smile didn't quite erase the sadness in her eyes. "Now you head out with Adele, Zofia, and Kara."

Adele tossed her long, grey braid over her shoulder and tapped her foot. "The longer we delay, the more likely it is someone will stumble across the bodies."

I shrugged on my black hoodie and grabbed my sword. I hoped I wouldn't have to use it, but I did not want to be caught unaware again. "I'm ready. Whose car are we taking?" I crossed my fingers behind my back that our journey wouldn't involve any air travel.

"No cars," Kara said. The hint of humor dancing in her eyes made me believe she knew how much I dreaded flying. After a pause long enough to make the nervous butterflies in my stomach turn into bats and try to escape, she continued. "Since Adele knows where we're going, we'll step there."

Relief washed over me. "Perfect. Great. Definitely the most efficient way." I shut my mouth, clacking my teeth together. Babbling wouldn't up my street cred.

Adele and Kara conferred. Kara sheathed her sword in her back scabbard and reached out her hands. I took one, Adele took the other, and Zofia grasped Adele's free hand.

I took a deep breath and braced myself.

The ground shifted under my feet, and I stumbled a half step, dropping Kara's hand. Cool, damp air surrounded me. Fog sheathed the conifers surrounding me and flowed through the underbrush, creating an otherworldly feeling.

"Where are we?" I asked once I caught my breath.

"The Olympic National Forest," Adele said. "Temperate rain forest. This way." She walked into the fog and disappeared. I hurried after her, desperate to not get lost. Kara and Zofia fell in line behind me. After a couple seconds of walking, the forest opened in front of me and a trail appeared.

Adele waited on the trail. Serenity and joy had replaced the dourness I'd gotten used to seeing on her face.

"I love it here," she whispered. "The trees around the Aerie are wonderful, of course, but something about this place stirs my soul and reminds me of home." Mournfulness shadowed her face, a cloud skimming the sun. "I haven't been home for centuries."

Kara wrapped an arm around Adele's shoulders and squeezed her tightly. "When this is over, when it is safe again, you and I will go back and roam the Northern Wilds. I swear it to you."

Adele stepped out of the circle of Kara's embrace. "I look forward to that day. First, though, we must secure the gods who threaten us and our peace." She sighed, and her shoulders drooped. "Your sisters are close. Follow me."

The melancholy that Adele's joy in her surroundings had briefly lifted shrouded us again. The fog thickened as if it, too, grieved.

Five minutes later, Adele turned off the trail and scrambled over a fallen tree nearly as wide as I was tall. When Zofia, Kara, and I joined her, she placed her index finger over her lips in the universal "shhh" gesture, then beckoned us forward.

We skirted a large, perfectly circular clearing devoid of the otherwise ubiquitous fog. I peered through the branches at a cheerfully bubbling spring framed by bright green grass. Yellow and purple flowers that only bloomed in early summer waved in the gentle, fragrant breeze. Only the knowledge that impossible had the potential to be deadly—and Adele's careful avoidance of the clearing—kept me from giving into my desire to lay in the sunshine and let the sounds of water lull me to sleep.

I started to wonder if Adele was leading us on a wild goose chase when she finally stopped in front of a large hill. She ran her hand slowly over a boulder partially buried in the hill, and it rolled away, revealing an opening.

"Are you a hobbit?" I whispered, awestruck.

Adele chuckled softly. "Not even close. This is not my home, nor would I live in a hole in the ground."

"It is a tomb," Kara said. "Our sisters lay within."

The reminder of why we were there sobered me. "Of course. I didn't know them, and I apologize for my levity."

"It is of no matter," Kara said. "When we stop laughing in the darkness, despair will take us, and we will be lost." She walked into the cave.

CHAPTER

TWENTY-FIVE

Illumination blared to life at the same time the stone rolled back to seal us in.

We stood in a large, domed, oblong cave. The walls, ceiling, and floor were all rough-hewn rock, and industrial-looking fluorescent lights hung down at regular intervals.

"How did you get electricity out here?" I asked.

"I didn't. It's magic, and before you ask, it's not mine and I don't know how it works. It belongs to the caretaker of this place." Adele turned her back on me, forestalling further questions, and walked to one end of the long room and pulled back a grey sheet, revealing six bodies laid neatly side-by-side on the floor.

Kara's hand flew to her mouth as a loud cry was wrenched from her. Her grief echoed off the walls and pulled tears from me.

Zofia knelt at the feet of her fallen sisters and passed a hand over the face of the Valkyrie nearest her. "Not a mark on any of them except Regan. If they were mundane humans, it would be easy to assume they'd died in their sleep of natural causes."

"They are not mundane," Kara said tightly.

"Of course not," Zofia replied absently. She pulled a small,

161

zippered bag from an inside pocket on her black jacket and opened it. Quickly and efficiently, she drew a vial of blood from each of the Valkyries, then stowed it away. "I'll get this to my lab when we leave here and see if I can determine whether they were drugged. In the meantime, there is no clear cause of death."

She pushed to her feet and crouched next to each body in turn. "There are no marks on Prima, Prudence, Arya, Mathilda, or Agnes." She moved to the last body in the line and reached out, took the chin in a gentle grip, and turned the head from side to side. "Regan has significant bruising on her face consistent with a fist fight." Zofia let go of Regna's head and picked up her arms, pushing back the sleeves. "There are defensive bruises on her arms as well. No cuts one would expect from a sword, no bullet wounds, and no evidence of blood loss. From my initial examination, her visible injuries are minor and no cause of death can be determined."

"Now what?" Kara demanded. She knelt on the floor next to Zofia and cradled Regan's head in her lap.

Zofia shrugged helplessly. "I can do autopsies if you wish. We felt Regan die and we know it was painful. I didn't sense the deaths of the others." She paused and looked back and forth between me and Kara.

I shook my head, and a second later, Kara did the same.

"I didn't even know they were dead until Adele brought us the news," Kara admitted.

"This sounds ridiculous, but I believe they died simultaneously. Regan was the most powerful, and she fought back. That could be why it was her death we felt. Her pain and ferocity overwhelmed our senses." Zofia stood and stretched.

"Who could do such a thing?" Kara asked.

"Only a god could kill a Valkyrie," Adele said.

Kara shook her head, negating Adele's words. "Not only a god. There are monsters out there that could do the same. Dragons, the world serpent, Fenrir-wolf, Odin's warriors, and the undead armies of Hel would also be able to slay any of us."

"A human could do it if they had supernatural help and knew what to do. A paralyzing drug of some sort would aid them," Zofia added.

I took a deep breath. "Right now, it does little good to speculate. Let's move our fallen sisters to Zofia's lab. I don't know if this is anathema to the customs of the Valkyries, but I recommend Zofia perform autopsies in addition to running a tox screen."

Kara nodded in brisk agreement. "If it will help us determine how they died, an autopsy is the best course of action."

"I don't need to autopsy all of them," Zofia said. "I think it is safe to assume they all died the same way. I will autopsy Regan—her death was the most violent—and Agnes. If there are more differences between them than I expect, I will move on to the rest."

"That sounds like a plan," I said. "Kara, how shall we move the bodies?"

"I will go first with Zofia to her home to familiarize myself with it, then come back for our sisters."

Adele stepped forward. "That will not work, at least not efficiently. You will be able to step out of here, but when you come back, you'll find yourself in the same place where we arrived earlier today." She shrugged. "It's the magic of this place, and not something I can easily dissipate."

Kara pursed her lips. "It could still work, but you are correct in that it is not ideal."

I grimaced, knowing that what I said next was could make my day even worse. "What about your pegasi? Would they be able to come directly to you, or would the magical barrier keep them out without Adele to lead them as well?"

Kara quirked up an eyebrow and looked at Adele.

"I don't know," Adele admitted. She looked chagrined, clearly unused to saying those three words.

"If they can come to us, how does that eliminate our quandary?" Zofia asked.

"Perhaps we can create some kind of bier that can be suspended between your mounts, if that's possible, and they are amenable, I mean. If we can fly out with everyone on the bier between you two, Adele and I could"—I gritted my teeth—"ride behind you."

Kara and Zofia shared a long glance, almost as if they were communicating telepathically. For all I knew, they were. Teleportation couldn't be the limit of the mysterious Valkyrie powers no one had given me the handbook for.

Finally, Kara broke the silence. "It's worth trying to see if they can come to us and asking if they are willing. Frankie, this is a good plan."

It decidedly was not. No good plans involved me being up in the air where I could easily plunge to my death.

Adele whispered something in a language I didn't understand, and the boulder rolled away from the opening. The lights inside the cave blinked out as the morning sunshine streamed in.

When I climbed through the opening into the forest, Kara and Zofia stood side by side with their eyes closed. Zofia's arms stretched to the sky, and she was moving her lips in a soundless chant. Kara's arms hung by her sides, and the furrows around her mouth that bespoke her great age deepened as a blissful smile spread across her face.

Kara opened her eyes. "They come."

TWENTY-SIX

The four of us settled on the soft, mossy ground to wait.

"They choose us, you know," Kara said after a couple minutes.

"Pardon?" I'd been lost in my own thoughts, and the swirling images of tattoos, Dusana in a red corset top, and my desire for a house and job didn't fit with Kara's statement.

"The pegasi. They choose us. No one knows where they come for, and it's not something they talk about, but when a new Valkyrie finally comes into her power, her sword sings and her blood calls out to her sisters. For those of us who were the original Valkyries created by Frigg and Freyja, we were chosen from our original families as infants, and the power of the goddesses infused us. We are all within a year or two of each other. You know Hilda, your grandmother, was First among us. Göndul was Second, and Lena is Third. The power is strongest in the First families, but it is not insignificant in the Twenty-Fourth."

Zofia interrupted. "There is seldom cause to even discuss rank. Until recently, dissention was rare, and only the First's position mattered."

Kara laughed softly. "Zofia is Fourth, her mother was Geirönul, and I am Fifth. That was her gentle way of telling me she doesn't often remind anyone she outranks me."

"Only when necessary," Zofia teased.

This. *This* is what sisterhood sounded like. I'd missed this with my sisters when we were younger, and we hadn't quite gotten there again, although we were close.

With a faraway look in her eyes, Kara took up her tale again. "When Hilda turned twenty, Frigg and Freya came to the training house where we'd been raised by the greatest warriors of the time. They gave her three swords and told her to choose one and secret away the others until she needed them. She selected one, unsheathed it, and blue light enveloped her, hiding her from view. When the light dissipated, she was clad in shining armor, wearing a blue cape, and crowned with a helmet.

"A herd of winged horses appeared on the horizon and landed in the meadow. One by one, they came forward to regard her. Finally, one stamped her foot and ruffled her wings at the others. She had chosen. The pegasi departed, and from that moment until her death, Hilda and Pellenir were inseparable. It was like that for each of us, although no one but Hilda kept the swords they hadn't chosen to pass on to their daughters and granddaughters."

My jaw dropped. "Are you saying—?"

"She is," Zofia said. "The sword you carry was a gift from Frigg and Freya to your grandmother thousands of years ago."

"It was different for the second generation," Kara said.

Zofia nodded and took up the story. "Our mothers gave us our swords at birth. We didn't choose them; they affirmed us. Because none of us grew up in a warrior woman training camp, the swords kept us safe and alive until such time as we could protect ourselves. And on my twentieth birthday, rather than a ceremony with my peers and a herd of horses showing up, I received a visit from Freyja and Frigg, and I received my armor. Shortly after, a single pegasus showed up to choose me."

"None of that happened for me. No armor. No horse. No visit from Freyja and Frigg." I hesitated. "Actually, Freyja stopped by to talk to me while I was on my way home from Santa Fe."

"We don't know why your generation is different," Kara admitted. "When your twentieth birthday came and went, with no changes, some believed it was the goddesses' way of letting us diminish naturally. The others of your generation are all ten years and more younger than you, and each of their birthdays passes without note. Riley is the youngest—she is twenty-one. By the time she came of age, no one even questioned why her powers didn't emerge."

Something Zofia said finally hit me. "What do you mean, the swords keep us alive and safe?" I demanded. "Is that why..."

Kara nodded. "Yes. Your sword kept you alive when you attempted suicide."

Rage and gratitude swirled through me, each fighting for dominance. "My mother knows," I said flatly. It wasn't a question. "Does Dad?"

"I'm not sure," Kara said. "Katrin shares much with Martin, but he is not privy to all our secrets. You'll have to ask them yourself."

"When this is all over, I will. Whether she told him or not, she must have had her reasons. She'll need to explain them to me, but I'll at least give her the benefit of the doubt."

"There's hope for you yet," Kara said cryptically.

Before I could ask more questions, Zofia and Kara stood, their faces raised toward the sky.

"They're here."

CHAPTER

TWENTY-SEVEN

For the second time in three days, I stood at the edge of the Pacific Ocean, this time in the San Juan Islands in northern Washington, and watched burning boats drift out to sea. The flying horses that had been the Valkyries' companions in life flew after them. I hadn't learned much more from Kara and Zofia after my plan had worked, but Kara told me that no one knew what the pegasi did after their Valkyrie died. They flew away with the others and were never seen again.

"This is worse than I suspected," Kara said to me as the fiery crafts disappeared into the vivid colors of the Pacific sunset. We watched from the shore, standing a few yards away from the rest of the Valkyries. "Seven dead is bad enough, but in such a coordinated manner by someone who knows too much about us is terrifying. We have to find the nascent ones and bring them here, whether they want to come or not."

"How many are there?" I asked, not taking my eyes off the ocean. I could still make out the horses flying behind the boats, and I wanted to watch until they, too, disappeared.

"There are ten in the third generation," Kara replied. "You, Hope,

169

four whose mothers are missing, and the children of Anja, Zara, Mickey, and Astrid."

"You said there was something unusual about the circumstances of Riley's birth. What was it?" It probably didn't matter, but I didn't want to risk missing a clue.

"When she was born, many thought that Anja had been the first Valkyrie to give birth to a son." Kara shrugged. "They were all wrong, but it wasn't until Riley was fifteen that she came out to her mother. When Anja gifted her daughter with a sword, it claimed her in the manner of all new Valkyries."

My thoughts churned, and a theory slowly built. "If it was assumed she wasn't going to be a Valkyrie at her birth, maybe she isn't on the radar of whoever's taking the Valkyries out. How many unrealized Valkyries have died? Would we even know if any of the eight missing potentials are still alive?"

Kara nodded before I finished my question. "The power is waking in everyone, and we would feel it if it was extinguished from this world."

I tore my eyes away from the ocean where the boats and horses had finally disappeared. "How do we find them?"

"We can track their swords if they're carrying them," Mom said, joining our group.

I tilted my head at her. "You can? Then how come you didn't know I was alive before I showed up?"

Mom sighed. "You weren't yet a Valkyrie, and we can only find you when the magic of the Valkyrie mixes with the magic of her sword."

"And when the power hit me and left you?" I prodded.

A look of pained embarrassment marred her expression. "I didn't initially understand what was happening. I'd spent so many years assuming the power hadn't passed to you, resigned to the fact that I would hold this position forever, weakened though I was, that when the power transfer did happen, I convinced myself I was coming down with the flu. It wasn't until I saw you that I understood what had happened."

"But the missing Valkyries' powers have awoken, and their swords will sing to ours," Kara said.

"And that's how we'll find them and call them home," Mom added.

I looked between them. "Why do I get the funny feeling that you're going to put this on me?"

Kara smiled grimly. "It won't just be you. There are too many missing, and you've no experience in searching for a lost sister. But you will have to coordinate our efforts." She held up a hand to forestall the protest she assumed—rightly—I was about to make. "We will advise you, but you are the most powerful among us, or will be once you're fully realized, and you need to get used to leading. If you don't take the reins now, the others won't develop the trust in you that your position warrants. And if they don't trust you implicitly, they may hesitate to follow orders in the heat of battle. That would be disastrous."

I sucked in a breath. What she said made sense if I accepted the premise that I'd be the most powerful. But this was not something I'd ever wanted for myself. "Can I abdicate?"

"No." Kara's harsh tone brooked no arguments. "This is your birthright, whether you want it or not. It is in your blood, and the sooner you come to accept your position, the sooner the Valkyries will be a cohesive unit, even if our numbers are diminished."

"Basically, suck it up, buttercup," Mom said. Then her eyes and voice softened. "It's hard and confusing, but I'll be here for you as long as you need me to be. You're not alone. We might be pushing hard to remind you you're the leader, but you're only first among equals. There will be few occasions outside of battle where you'll be called on to actually give orders rather than suggestions. Generally speaking, we are an egalitarian group who seldom disagree."

"Last night was an exception, I presume," I grumbled.

Kara nodded. "That was atypical. Mari is one of our more prickly members, but she's never crossed the line into personal insults."

I filed that away as a reference. It might mean nothing, but just as Riley's birth had been unusual, and a concerted attack on Valkyries was unprecedented, this might be another piece of the puzzle.

"What now?" I asked.

Kara glared at me. "Has nothing I've told you sunk in?"

It had. I knew what she wanted me to do, but I was afraid. I might never have been a follower, but I wasn't a leader, either. I was a "march to the beat of my own drummer, far, far away from other people" kind of person.

But Kara's and Mom's expressions were uncompromising.

I sighed. "We need to convene back at Mom's house. Invite as many people as we trust to a conference, and brainstorm ideas on how to find your missing Valkyries. Then, we'll divide into teams for safety and go out and save as many as we can."

"*Our* Valkyries," Mom said.

"What?" I cocked my head and looked at her.

"You said, 'Your missing Valkyries.' They are *ours*. You are one of us now, and you'll never have to be alone again."

TWENTY-EIGHT

I sat at the huge table in the training room, propping my forehead in my hands. The stress headache that'd appeared when the Valkyries, Adele, Dusana, Aunt Sasha, Jackie, Dad, and me had convened this morning to talk about our missing grew in intensity.

Everyone agreed that search parties needed to be sent out. No one argued that tracking the missing swords was the best method.

However, when it came time to divide people into groups, I started getting pushback. Carina insisted she was better suited to looking in Seattle because she'd lived there a few decades a hundred years ago, while Zofia said her claim to the city was stronger since she'd lived in the San Juan Islands for the last thirty years and visited Seattle frequently.

In the end, I assigned both of them to Seattle, took all other search area claims into consideration, and drew names to round out the teams when no one volunteered to head to Boise.

I dispatched seven teams of grumbling Valkyries. Sasha, Baby Lenore, and Jackie followed them out the door to head back to Sasha's house in Eugene to get started on Jackie's psychic training that'd been interrupted by Göndul's death and funeral. Adele had disappeared again to do whatever it was she did. I was finally ready to take a deep breath and let go of the tension riding my shoulders, at least as soon as my headache agreed with me.

Dusana sat down next to me and squeezed my right shoulder. "You okay?"

I nodded and lifted my head to look at her. "That was intense. Is it always like that?"

"I have no idea. I've never done a lot of committee work. Reaping is assignment-based, and after I got stuck in this mortal body, I was mostly on my own. The only person I ever argued with was Percy." She smiled sadly when she mentioned the ghostly companion she'd been tied to for a decade after he'd refused to move on in a timely manner.

She obviously missed him even though she'd said his eventual choice to step into the After, as she called whatever lay beyond death, was long past due.

I sighed and stood up. Mom and Lena were waiting for me to lead the eighth and final search party to White Salmon, a small town on the Washington side of the Columbia River. "Do you want to come with?" I asked Dusana, not sure what answer I hoped to hear.

"Nah. I'll hold the fort down here with Becky and your dad. I've got a book to read, and some alone time to savor." She graced me with a smile.

Mom popped her head into the room before I could come up with anything intelligent to say. "Frankie, we need to get on the road."

"On my way," I replied. I bit my lip and looked at Dusana.

She made a shooing motion. "Go. Find your missing Valkyrie. I'll be here when you get back."

IT TOOK JUST over an hour to get to White Salmon. It was a cute town overlooking the Columbia River. Mt. Hood rose to a rounded point above the river, its flanks sporting only a smattering of snow this early in the autumn.

I stood on the main drag and did a slow circle. Nothing sinister stood out. No one called to me, and everything looked too friendly and nice to be hiding a bunch of Valkyrie-kidnapping draugr. Portland wasn't a gritty anarchistic hellhole, but it was a city, and every city has more than one place to stash a zombie army.

"Aunt Lena? Mom? Any ideas?" I turned around again, stretching my senses.

Lena narrowed her eyes and stared up one of the side streets. "I'm getting a strong pull toward Soča."

I followed her gaze. "What's Soča?"

"It's only one of the best wine bars in the Pacific Northwest," Lena said.

"We're not going to find our missing Valkyrie in a wine bar," I said, trying to push the thought of Champagne by the glass from my mind. I rarely drank wine, but there was something about bubbles. Right now, I heard the same call as Lena.

"She's not in the wine bar," Mom said, glaring at Lena. "We are not going into any drinking establishments in White Salmon."

"Young lady, I am three thousand years old, and if I want a glass of grenache, I can damn well get one."

Mom whacked the back of Lena's head. "We are not talking about this in front of Frankie. Now behave."

Lena grimaced. "I am so sorry, Frankie. I didn't mean to…"

I laughed and waved away her apology, trying not to let the embarrassment of having my addiction acknowledged take over my brain. "It's not a big deal. I live in a world where alcohol is everywhere. People drink, and I don't want to make anyone feel weird about it."

"Still, I'm sorry," Lena said.

"Apology accepted. But you know we won't find the Valkyrie in a wine shop, right?" I smiled, hoping my expression looked as unbothered as I wanted it to.

"Did you say you were looking for a Valkyrie?"

I spun around. A short, curvy woman with dusky skin, shiny black hair, and light brown eyes stood behind us.

Mom laughed. "Of course. Who doesn't want a warrior woman?"

To my surprise, the stranger busted out laughing. "Truth. I'd let a Valkyrie tie me up and take me to Valhalla any day of the week. Alas, the only one I've met recently doesn't seem to be into chicks, and trust me, I tried." She thrust out her hand. "I'm Stacy, by the way. I work at Soča." She pointed at the wine shop behind us. "And if the last week is any indication, you'll find your Valkyrie in there, drowning whatever sorrows she has in glass after glass of Champagne."

Lena snickered, and Mom elbowed her in the ribs.

"Thank you," Mom said.

"No problem," Stacy said. "Now, if you'll excuse me, I've got to get to work pouring Champagne for pretty girls." She raked her gaze over me. "First one's on the house. Especially if you tell me you're a Valkyrie, too."

I pushed a smile onto my face and hoped it didn't look as frozen as I felt. "I appreciate the offer, but I don't drink."

Stacy shrugged. "Come in for a phony Negroni instead, tell me your life story, and we can take it from there."

Her carefree flirtation did a lot to lighten my mood. "I'm only in town for another hour or so, but I'd love a phony negroni. No promises on the life story though. Not nearly enough time."

"I seriously have to run. See you in a few!" Stacy dashed the half block uphill and disappeared through the front door.

"Well, guess I'm getting a free drink," I said. "Wanna see if there's a Valkyrie in the wine bar?"

"This is why everyone should always listen to me," Lena said. "My instincts are rarely off, and I'm seldom wrong."

Mom shook her head and started up the hill. "Let's just get this over with. And Frankie, you can have your phony negroni, but..."

"I know, I know," I interrupted. "One NA beverage and get out before I go on a bender."

"That's not what I was going to say. Have your drink, flirt with the bartender if you want, but remember Dusana is waiting for you at home."

"What's that supposed to mean? We're just friends." Even to my own ears, that sounded weak.

"For now," Mom said. "But that's going to change, and you're lying to yourself if you think it won't."

Images of Dusana flooded my mind, and I flushed. "Let's go in and get this over with, so we can go home with one more safe Valkyrie."

"Whatever you say, First," Mom said sweetly. "We can talk more about your love life later."

"Or not," I muttered.

Mom elbowed me. "Mark my words. The story of Frankie and Dusana will be sung about until the end of the world."

TWENTY-NINE

Walking into a wine bar, on purpose, between two people who knew about my addiction, curdled my stomach. Doing it after my mom talked about my not-yet-but-apparently-inevitable-in-her-eyes relationship with Dusana nearly triggered my gag reflex.

Stacy waved the second I crossed the threshold, and even though my mom had warned me about flirting with her, I couldn't keep the smile from my face.

"I heard you make a good mocktail," I said, leaning up against the bar.

"The best," she confirmed. She pushed a drink across the bar. "I was sure you'd be here, so it's made."

I took a sip. I hated negronis, and a phony wasn't an exception. Still, I needed to draw this out long enough for my mom and Lena to find our missing Valkyrie, convince her to come home with us, and get us out of here.

"Come here often?" I asked Stacy. Gah. I sucked at flirting.

She laughed. Maybe I didn't suck at this as much as I thought I did.

"I've been known to stop in from time to time. Like every Wednesday through Saturday from noon to eight." Stacy pushed a business card across the bar and wedged it under my drink. "Just in case…"

I picked it up. Stacy's name and phone number were scrawled on the back of the bar's card. I glanced behind me. Mom and Lena sat on either side of a young Black woman who looked seven or eight sheets to the wind.

"Didn't you just open?" I asked.

Stacy nodded. "About an hour ago. The owner, Betsy, opened for me today." She leaned over and looked around me. "There's no way we've been open long enough for your friend to be that wasted. Obviously, she's cut off now. Do you need to check on her?"

"My mom and aunt have it covered."

Stacy's hand clapped over her mouth. "I hit on you in front of your mom? Oh my god." Red stained her cheeks, and she cringed.

"It's not a big deal," I said. "My mom loves meddling in my affairs, and you made her day."

"Frankie!" Mom called from across the bar.

"See what I mean?" I asked before turning around.

Lena and Mom both had the kind of frozen grins on their face that I recognized as halfway between fear and frustration.

"Sorry, Stacy," I said, genuinely regretful. "I need to help out with my sister over there."

Stacy closed her eyes. "This is the worst flirtation I've ever done. I started off telling you I'd struck out with your sister, then hit on you in front of your mom and aunt. I am not humiliated often, but I am today."

"Don't worry about it. I spread chaos everywhere I go." I pushed my half-empty glass back to her. "Thanks for the drink and the conversation. It was really nice to meet you."

"Back at you. And if you find your way back to White Salmon, look me up. But only if you're here without your family. I can't go through this again."

I cracked up. "It's a deal."

I walked over to the other end of the bar, where the Valkyrie huddled in the corner. I slid in next to Mom.

"What's up?"

The Valkyrie—and she definitely was, if the connection that zinged between us when our eyes met—burst into tears.

"Okay. Let's get you out of here," I said. "Do you have a bar tab we need to close?"

She shook her head, flinging tears and snot across the table.

"No. Paid cash."

That made things easier. "What's your name?"

She picked up a bar napkin and noisily blew her nose. "Deb, daughter of Zara."

If I'd had any doubts before, that introduction erased them. I'd never met anyone besides a Valkyrie who identified their mothers without prompting.

"It's great to meet you Deb," I said. "I'm Frankie, daughter of Katrin."

Lena leaned in close. "I'm Lena, and this is Katrin, daughter of Hilda and mother of Frankie."

I flashed a grin at my aunt, thankful she hadn't busted out any "First" nonsense. I looked at Deb, whose tears seemed to be slowing, at least a little. "This is gonna sound weird, but you're in danger, and you need to come with us."

It sounded even creepier out loud.

"Do you know where my mom is?" Deb asked. "She told me she'd meet me in Portland, but I haven't heard from her since."

I didn't know everyone bunking at our house, but my mom's headshake told me what I needed to know.

"We don't. She hasn't made her way here yet. Where is she coming from?" I crossed my fingers that Zara hadn't met the same fate as too many of our other sisters.

"I drove from Chicago, but my mom lives in Dallas."

"Why have you been in White Salmon for the last week?" Mom asked. "Zara must have given you my number."

Deb's shoulders shook. She was three seconds away from bursting into tears again. I had to get the rest of my questions in quick.

"Will you come with us? We can keep you safe until your mom gets here." Fear rippled goosebumps over my arms. Something bad was about to happen. I rushed through my next words. "We really need to get out of here quickly. Where's your car?"

"Wrecked. I lost everything. Phone. Car. Luggage. All I have is my sword and my wallet." Tears streamed down her face again.

"Let's get you out of here," Lena said, wrapping an arm around Deb's shoulders.

Ye gods, this was creepy. I felt like an accomplice to a kidnapping.

Deb froze, then stared at me. "I recognize your name. You're the First."

"I am."

She reached across the table and clasped my hand. "You have to protect me. There are things after me."

I squeezed her hand. "I will protect you, I promise. But we need to go now."

The hairs on the back of my neck stood up. Lena nodded emphatically. "Now. Back to the car."

Deb swallowed visibly. "Yeah. That's a good idea."

"Where's your sword?" I asked, looking around.

"I stashed it in a bush outside," Deb said as she unsteadily got to her feet. "Can't bring weapons into bars."

The horror that'd been creeping over me intensified. "Cool, cool, cool. We'll snag it on our way by." I looked around. The only other patron who'd been in when we arrived was gone. Stacy stood by the front door.

"Are y'all heading out so soon?" Her tongue flicked over her lips, and my stomach curdled.

"We are. Gotta get my sister home. Thank you so much for the drink and for taking care of her. What do we owe you?"

Stacy smiled, showing all her teeth. Her grin got wider and wider, and her teeth lengthened into pointed fangs dripping with venom. "Not a lot," she hissed. "Just a kiss." She stuck her tongue out and wiggled it around. It was long and forked, like a serpent's.

Dammit. I'd flirted with a reptile. My taste in women was suspect.

Lena drew her sword and stepped in front of us. Mom followed suit. I reached behind me and pulled mine from the sheath I'd strapped over my back. This might be a serious situation, but for a moment, I felt like a comic book superhero.

"It's three against one, wyvern," Lena said. "You might as well run away now."

Stacy laughed. Her body shimmered, and her clothing split and fell away from her. Scales took the place of skin, and her body lengthened and twisted. "We knew you bitches would come for one of your own. Catching the First is a bonus I couldn't have imagined. Shame I had to leave the first one alive so you could find her. I would've preferred to take her out before you got here. But it's okay. I'm more than a match for a few Valkyries."

She slithered out from behind the bar. Ten feet of reptile with two short legs, stubby wings that couldn't possibly aid her in flying, and a beautiful head stood before us.

Her tongue flicked out. "I taste fear from the young ones."

"No shit," I said. "The cute bartender just turned into a weird-ass ugly lizard monster. I've wet my pants for less."

She hissed a laugh. "Thanks for stopping by. Don't forget to tip your bartenders and life-enders."

I rolled my eyes. Save me from monsters who thought they were funny.

Deb screamed and ran for the door, directly toward the monster.

"Oh, for fuck's sake," I muttered.

Stacy lunged for Deb, but the Valkyrie ducked and pulled the door open so hard, she almost yanked it off the hinges. Deb slid through the door, avoiding Stacy's fangs, and slipped down the stairs, barely keeping her balance.

"We've got this bitch," Lena said. "You grab your little sister."

I dashed forward, struck at Stacy, who slithered out of the way, and followed Deb out the door.

My newfound sister was halfway into a hedge, only her denim-clad legs visible.

"I don't think you'll be able to hide in there," I commented.

She wriggled out, sword in hand. "I wasn't hiding. I was retriev-ing." She climbed to her feet, swaying only a little, and brandished her weapon. Rather than the European style most of the Valkyries I'd met favored, hers was a saber. It had a thirty-two-inch curved blade and an arched, polished guard.

"That's a great sword," I said.

"It's actually a saber," Deb replied.

It took me a second, but then I burst into laughter. "Nice. Sword pun. Love it. Should we see if my mom and Lena need help with the stubby-legged monster in there?"

Deb rotated her wrist and grinned, all trace of drunkenness gone from her face. "Might as well. I've got nothing else to do today."

Mom and Lena did not need help. Broken glass littered the front room of the bar, but the damage didn't extend to the back room where most of the inventory was stacked.

It was difficult to focus on the bright side for the business, though, because the long bar in the middle of the room was covered in green ooze, bloody scales, and the body of a ten-foot-long mutant dragon, still sporting the head of Stacy the bartender.

"Oh my god, that's the mermaid nightmares are made of," Deb whispered. "What is it?"

"A French wyvern," Mom answered absently, walking around the monster. "Although I've never seen one keep its human face on before. I'm more interested in who she's working with."

"If you wanted to know, maybe you shouldn't have killed her so quickly," Lena said.

"She tried to eat you!" Mom shouted.

"I'm more than a match for a single reptile," Lena shot back.

"Should we clean up?" I asked before they could devolve into a full-blown argument. Disposing of bodies and cleaning up monster guts were not my areas of expertise.

"Already called in," Lena said, her voice returning to her usual placid tone. "And I've texted you the number of the company we use."

"Of course we have people." I rolled my eyes.

Mom smiled wryly. "We don't need them often. Usually, we're escorting the dead to the next life. But every once in a while, something like this comes up. It's good to have contacts."

"Can we get out of here?" Deb asked. "I need a hot meal, a shower, and a bed. I want to sleep for a week at least. And maybe then, my mom will show up, too."

My mom, ignoring the blood and guts staining her clothes, pulled Deb in for a hug. "I have Zara's number. We'll find her."

The unspoken phrase "dead or alive" echoed in the room and reverberated in my head. There were no guarantees. No more immortality. Only uncertainty, pain, and fear.

CHAPTER

THIRTY

By the time I'd gone to bed last night, six of the other search and recovery operations had returned victorious. The only group that hadn't reported in was Kara's, and the only Valkyrie who hadn't been found was Riley.

My stomach knotted, and I contemplated hiding out in my room, ducking any mention of responsibility.

My avoidance goals hadn't communicated themselves outward, though. Ten minutes after dragging myself out of bed and to the bathroom, someone knocked on my door. I crawled back under the covers and put my pillow over my head.

The door creaked open.

"I know you're awake," Becky said.

I flung the covers off my head and glared at my sister. "Who else knows?"

She held up her hand and ticked off the names on her fingers. "Mom, Dad, Dusana, Adele, Aunt Lena, Devin, the new girl, everyone else in the house, and Archibald."

I huffed a sigh. "Who *doesn't* know I'm awake?"

187

Her expression sobered. "Kara, Hope, Zofia, and the rest of the team looking for Riley."

"They aren't back?"

Becky shook her head. "Not yet, but Kara called Lena this morning, so they're okay."

"That's something, at least."

"Something good. Now get dressed and come get breakfast before the hashbrowns are gone." Becky backed out of my room and closed the door behind her.

I climbed out of bed, dressed, and went in search of potatoes.

I STARED at the drawing on the table in front of me. Two delicately feathered wings that trailed into long points formed a negative-space outline of a sword.

"I know it's not authentic," Grace Kim said, "But there's not a lot out there on Valkyrie symbols. I'll fit your scars into the feathers."

"It's fucking amazing."

When I'd finally pushed myself away from the hashbrowns and checked my phone, I found a text from Grace letting me know she had my initial tattoo designs ready for review, but she was in her Portland studio today.

My parents practically pushed me out of the house, and Dusana offered to drive me. I told myself it made sense to head to Portland since that's where Kara and her team had tracked Riley to, but in reality, I just wanted to get away with Dusana. I wasn't ready to take things further with her, but my mom's certainty eroded some of my objections.

"What changes would you like?" Grace asked.

I pulled my attention back to the drawing. "Honestly, nothing. Well..." My voice trailed off. I had an idea, but I wasn't an artist. Gah. I shook my head. My hesitance to offer feedback was why I had the most insipid rose in the history of tattoos inked on my left hip. "Do you do color work, or is that difficult over scars?"

"Color is great," Grace said. "What are you thinking?"

Thirty minutes and a lot of tweaks later, I walked out of Optic Nerve Tattoo with my ink date scheduled and a drawing in hand.

Dusana was waiting for me across the street, and she wasn't alone.

THIRTY-ONE

I slid into the passenger seat of the car and twisted around to regard Devin, the tall, Black man who was Becky's husband. I hadn't had much of a chance to get to know him yet. I knew he was some sort of supernatural creature who could converse with animals, but whenever I'd tried to talk to him about it, he'd been rather close-mouthed about what that entailed.

"Is everything okay?" I asked, glancing between Dusana and Devin. "Is Becky okay?"

"Maybe now he'll tell us why he's here," Dusana muttered. "He just showed up about twenty minutes ago, hopped into the backseat, and asked where you were. I just about had a heart attack. He's lucky I recognized him before I whacked him with Kella."

Devin grinned, and his white teeth gleamed against his dark skin. "My message isn't for you, reaper."

The hairs on the back of my neck rose. No one called Dusana reaper except Adele when she was in a jolly mood.

"And my car isn't your way station, kitty cat," Dusana shot back.

I grabbed my phone, made a note on my ever-growing list of questions to ask about the kitty cat comment, then turned my attention back to the other people in the car who were glaring at each other and completely ignoring me. "Um, as much fun as it is to watch you two trade insults, I'm tired and hungry, so if we could speed this up, that'd be great."

Devin twisted in his seat just enough to signal he was turning his back on Dusana. He reached into his jacket pocket, pulled out an envelope, and handed it over. Next, he hoisted a duffle bag from the shadows of the floor and waved it at me before dropping it. "From Becky." He flashed a grin again, hopped out of the car, and disappeared.

I opened the envelope and pulled out a piece of stationery covered in Becky's copperplate cursive handwriting.

Hey Frankie - I know you probably need a break from Mom and Dad's, especially with all the activity lately. Jackie and I have a house in North Portland you can stay in whenever you want. Mom knows where it is, but Dev and John don't know about it—not that we don't trust them, but boys, you know?

(Hopefully Dev doesn't know about it. Babe, if you're reading this, you will be celibate forever, I swear to god. Just because I trust you to deliver a message when you're already headed into PDX doesn't mean you get to read my private letters to my sister, you big jerk.)

AHEM. Now that he's taken care of...

House is on the corner of Leonard and Buchanan. Key entry code is 97113 & wifi passcode is noboysallowed!!

I've already cleared it with Mom & Dad tonight, but you're probably gonna want to let them know if you decide to crash there in the future.

*Happy birthday for all the ones we missed and have fun. *Winking emoji* *peach emoji x2* (Yes, I am writing out the names of the emojis. I'm hip like that.)*

xoxo-Bex & Jax

A slow smile spread across my face, and I looked over at Dusana. "Wanna crash at my sisters' secret hideout? Apparently, there are no boys allowed."

Dusana's expression mirrored my own for a second, then it became decidedly more wicked, and she winked.

Heat flared low in my belly, and I fought against the flush threatening to wash over my face. "Is that a yes?" I asked, altogether too breathlessly for my taste.

"It's a hell yes," Dusana replied. "Now, where are we headed?"

My sisters' bright-blue Craftsman bungalow stood out among the more muted colors of the other houses on the street. I grabbed my sword and the bag Devin had left in the car and led Dusana to the door. After punching in the code, we walked in.

The house was perfectly, if sparsely, furnished. The worn oak floors gleamed in the entryway and continued into the cozy living room, complete with fireplace. An arched wall opening led to a small dining room, and beyond that was a well-stocked kitchen. A bedroom was tucked away in the back, and a staircase led up to a second floor.

The large open space had clearly once been an attic. But now, built-in bookshelves lined the walls, and half of the floor was set up as a music room.

The other half featured a low, king-sized bed that couldn't have fit up the stairs, a rocking chair next to the huge, uncurtained window, and a small vanity table.

"This is amazing," Dusana said, looking over my shoulder. "We're going to have to buy your sisters a fruit basket or something."

I went back downstairs to find the bathroom. When I returned to the living room, Dusana sat on the overstuffed suede couch going through the duffle bag Devin had left behind, Archibald curled up next to her.

"Clothes for both of us and toiletries," she announced. "Becky knew what she was doing here."

I sorted through the items Dusana tossed my way. Another pair of jeans, a couple T-shirts, a clean flannel, and underclothes. "No pajamas," I said.

Dusana laughed, a low, throaty sound that curled my toes. "None for me either."

"Maybe she forgot." She hadn't forgotten; she was playing matchmaker. It was tempting. Dusana was hotter than sin and, unless I was reading everything wrong, attracted to me. But it'd only been a couple months since my engagement had ended—much too soon to jump into something else, even if it had the potential to be amazing.

I jumped off the couch before my imagination galloped away any faster than it already was. "I'll order pizza! Unless you want to go out. There are probably a ton of places around here we can walk to."

"Pizza sounds perfect," Dusana said. "And I have a metric ton of sparkling mineral water in the trunk. Becky asked me to pick some up at New Seasons while we were here, since they don't have the brand she likes in Estacada."

"Becky hates mineral water," I said absently as I scrolled through Google Maps, looking for a pizza place that would deliver. "She always made fun of me for drinking so much of it."

Dusana shook her head. "She planned everything down to the last detail, it seems."

"I'd forgotten how devious my sisters are. What do you like on your pizza?"

Dusana stood and walked up behind me, her breast softly brushing against my arm. She peered at the menu over my shoulder. "I'll eat just about anything, but I don't like fish on my pizza, and pineapple on pizza is an abomination."

I ordered a large prosciutto and pear pizza with gorgonzola and candied walnuts and crossed my fingers that it tasted as amazing as it sounded. By the time I'd hit the "confirm order" button, Dusana had run out to the car and back and shoved a half-dozen bottles of water in the fridge.

"What do you want to do while we wait for the pizza?" Dusana asked. The casual flirtation she'd had in her voice earlier had disappeared, and I couldn't decide if I was relieved or disappointed.

I opened the small closet in the living room. It was stuffed with games and DVDs. "We could play a board game or watch a movie. Or grab a book from upstairs. There aren't a lot of other things we can do unless you want me to play the harp for you."

"I vote movie," Archibald said. "Without thumbs, it's hard to play games or read, although if you'd let me sit on your lap, I could read with you."

"Do you play the harp?" Dusana asked, ignoring Archibald. She looked intrigued. "Because that would be wicked cool."

I laughed. "Not even a tiny bit. I can play a few chords on the piano, but Jackie got the musical talent, brains, and beauty. Becky is a gifted athlete and a champion swimmer. And I got the mental illness and addiction."

"Hey!" Dusana glared at me, and I took a step backward under the force of her ire.

"What?"

"You do not get to talk about my friend that way. You went to vet school—that's pretty fucking brainy if you ask me. And you've been sober and taking your meds for two months now, so don't pretend your mental illness and addiction define you. And my god, are you beautiful." She took a step forward and reached up to cup my face and run a thumb down my jawline.

I closed the distance between us and looked down at her, my earlier resolution to maintain things at a friendship level momentarily shoved to the back burner.

She licked her lips, and I groaned. I tangled my fingers into her hair and pulled back, angling her face toward mine.

And then I leaned in and brushed my lips across hers. They were so soft and sweet, and my breath hitched in my throat. But before I could take it any further, a heavy knock on the front door jolted me back to reality.

I stepped back and grabbed my sword. I rolled my eyes at myself. Kara would be so proud of my instinctive violent tendencies.

"Great fucking timing, pizza man," Dusana muttered. She stalked to the door and yanked it open.

Kara pushed her way past Dusana and looked at me. "Sorry to interrupt, but something's happened, and you have to come with me now." She spared a glance for Dusana. "I'll bring her back here later if I can. Otherwise, we'll see you at Katrin's tomorrow."

And with no additional warning, she grabbed my arm, yanked me close to her, and stepped. At the last minute, before the floor disappeared from under my feet, something sharp pierced my leg through my jeans.

"You are not leaving me behind, not now," Archibald said, his voice strangely flat.

I HIT the ground hard and stumbled forward. Once I caught my balance, I looked around. We were in an enormous, empty room. Four great cinder block walls surrounded us, capped by a high ceiling with metal beams and a visible HVAC system. "Where are we? What's going on?"

I shifted my sword in my hand until the grip felt right.

"Your Aunt Sasha, Jackie, Lenore, and John are missing," Kara said grimly. "I need you to take over my spot in the search for the missing Valkyries, so I can join your mother in looking for them."

"Wait!" I said when Kara turned around to leave. "If I'm taking your spot, where's the rest of your group? Where have you looked? Where the fuck are we?"

"Not far from where you were. Swan Island, where you had your last showdown with Loki. The others are through those doors." She pointed to the far end of the warehouse. "They are waiting for you. We've tracked Riley to this vicinity, but we can't tell if she's hiding from us after running scared for so long, or if something even more sinister is happening. I have to go. There's not a moment to lose if we're going to find your sister and your niece."

She took a step and disappeared.

I growled at where she'd stood a moment ago and looked down at Archibald. "You're sticking around this time?"

"Yes." His voice was nearly as grim as Kara's. "I won't leave you unprotected. I might not be much, but I hope I'm better than nothing."

I crouched beside him, scratching behind his right ear in the spot he liked best. "You're way better than nothing, and I'd be honored to walk into battle with you by my side."

He purred for a second, then head butted my chin. "Let's get going. The sooner we find Riley, the sooner we can get everyone to safety and concentrate on finding your sister."

I hefted my sword and walked toward the door Kara had indicated.

I opened it and peered into another huge warehouse space that looked just as empty as the one Kara'd dropped me in. I wrinkled my nose. I hoped the rest of the group hadn't wandered too far. I did not want to do this alone.

I stepped through the doorway, and all hell broke loose.

THIRTY-TWO

Sweat dripped down my face, and I gasped for air. I didn't know what kind of magic barrier had been on the door, but it'd kept me from seeing, hearing, or smelling the battle raging on the other side until I was in the thick of it.

I stepped back and risked a look around. The other Valkyries were still standing and more than holding their own, even Hope, but the tide of the draugr, Hel's undead soldiers, didn't seem to diminish, no matter how many of their heads flew across the room. The draugr not only looked like extras in a zombie movie, they smelled like the rotting corpses they were, making gagging a real danger while fighting.

I watch in nauseated horror as a headless monster rolled over, reached out toward a bodiless head, and attached it to the stump of its neck, screwing it in like a lightbulb into a socket. It stumbled to its feet, picked up an abandoned sword, and reentered the battle.

Our tactics weren't working, and I cursed my shortsightedness. After encountering draugr when we rescued Hope, I should've expected to stumble across them during other rescues as well.

"How do we kill them?" I hissed at Archibald, who, true to his word, had stayed by my side. He scrambled up the nearest zombie soldier's body and scratched out its eyes. I swung my sword, sending the head sailing away, and glanced down at my cat.

"I have no idea. Beheading should work. Beheading works on almost everything." He sounded as bewildered as I felt. "The only thing I can imagine is that Hel is here, and her presence is keeping them alive, for lack of a better word."

"So I need to find Hel and get rid of her if I want to stem the tide of her rotting army?" I raised my sword, swung wide, and beheaded the draugr coming straight at me. At least they weren't great warriors, and it seemed like the more times they were beheaded, the clumsier they got. That had to be at least partly due to the fact that they weren't always careful about whose head went on which body, and running around and fighting with a body you weren't used to must be confusing as fuck.

Archibald shook his head violently. "No. You do not confront Hel. What you need to do is get everyone out of here and retreat."

He wasn't wrong, but some hitherto unknown part of me balked at the idea of running away. "Won't that make us seem like cowards?"

"Do you care what a bunch of zombies think of you? And wouldn't you prefer that these people get out of here alive?" Archibald sounded absolutely disgusted with me, which was fair.

I waded back into the fray, conscious that for the most part, I'd let my sisters take the brunt of the attack while I stood in a corner and talked to my cat.

I elbowed past the draugr, removing as many limbs as I could in addition to heads, hoping that would slow them down more, as they had to search for compatible legs and arms to fight with.

Once I got to the knot of Valkyries in the center, I screamed, "We need to get out of here. Retreat toward the door behind us. Can any of you step?"

A tall, Black woman whose name I couldn't remember nodded. "I can." She swung her sword and lopped off the heads of two draugr with a single swipe.

"How many can you take?" There were a half-dozen women in the room besides her and me, plus Archibald.

"Three besides me."

She didn't waste breath on explanations or apologies, and I appreciated that.

"We are retreating. You lead the way back. Take their legs over their heads if you have to choose one. Once you get through the doorway, take the three closest people to the Aerie, and come back as soon as you can."

"It might be a while," she said. "I'll need a moment to catch my breath."

"Fine. We'll keep fighting until you get back." I arced my sword to the right, and a head dropped to the floor and rolled away.

Without another word, she pushed out of the tight circle we were in and carved her way through the room. I herded the rest of the Valkyries after her and brought up the rear.

Our new strategy of removing limbs instead of heads was working. They weren't dying, but they were slower to recover, and their mismatched limbs increased their shambling gaits, making them even easier to hobble.

When we got to the wall, I turned to face the oncoming horde again to give the others a chance to escape. Four Valkyries walked through the doorway and completely disappeared from view. I was about to order the rest to do the same, operating under the theory that the draugr couldn't pass the barrier that kept the fight contained and unnoticeable to the outside world, when a hair-raising laugh rang through the room.

The nausea I'd kept at bay overwhelmed me, and I leaned forward and vomited everything I'd eaten for what felt like the past three years.

A striking white woman with blond hair that flowed over her shoulders in braids and brushed against her hips appeared in the room. Her eyes were a brilliant blue, like the sky on a perfect, cloudless summer day, and looking into them was like gazing into heaven. She was the most beautiful woman I'd ever seen, and I took a half step forward. I wanted to bow to her, to offer to worship her, even though I felt unworthy.

Then she laughed again, and my gorge rose. The sound of the other Valkyries still with me throwing up brought me to my senses. As soon as I pulled my attention away from her eyes, her body writhed and morphed into a walking corpse, even more disgusting than the soldiers she commanded. Maggots the size of garden snakes wiggled in her left eye socket, and her right eyeball hung out too far.

"We have got to get out of here," someone said behind me. "There's no way we can win against her. Not with just four of us."

"Go," I ordered. "Get through the doorway. If anything breaches the room that isn't another Valkyrie, get out of there. Run, scatter, and do whatever you can to keep from being caught. I'm right behind you."

I inched toward the door, never taking my eyes off Hel as she glided toward me. Every draugr she walked by straightened up until they were once more whole—or at least as whole as an undead soldier could be.

I glanced behind me. Everyone else was clear of the room. Only Archibald and I were left.

"Get out of here," I yelled at the cat.

He hesitated.

"Go! You have to watch the rest of them, make sure they leave!"

Archibald dashed through the doorway and disappeared, leaving me with Hel and at least three dozen of her undead minions.

I scanned the room again. There were way more than three dozen. In the last few seconds, the number of draugr had at least tripled.

"What the fuck?" I whispered. I took another step back. My shoulder bumped the doorframe. Almost through. I hoped like hell that the rest of the Valkyries had gotten back to Mom's house, and that I was the only one left. I took a deep breath, crossed the fingers of my left hand, and raised my foot.

"Stop!" Hel shouted.

The draugr fell to their knees, swords and armor clanging.

I froze.

Hel smiled, and I shuddered at the sight of black teeth hanging loosely in her mouth.

"Don't you want who you came for?" Her voice sounded like a fork scraping over a plate.

"What do you mean?" I asked.

Her rotting maw gaped wider, and she took a single step to the right. There, standing behind her, was a young woman, no more than twenty, holding a sword and staring straight ahead.

"She's one of yours, isn't she, Frances? I couldn't find this one for ages, but when her sword woke, my father felt it." Hel slipped an arm around the Valkyrie's waist and pulled her close. The girl didn't resist, didn't show any sign at all that she was present in her body. "Didn't he, little sister?"

Oh shit. This was going to be a problem, but it needed to be a problem for future Frankie. Present Frankie needed to grab the Valkyrie, escape without getting either of us dead by Hel or draugr, and worry about who was related to whom later.

"Send her over," I said, my voice harsher than I'd ever heard it. "She's a Valkyrie, and that makes her mine."

"No," Hel said with mocking petulance. "She's my sister, and I love her."

"Give her to me, or I will take her."

Hel laughed. Maggots fell out of her mouth, bouncing off the Valkyrie's head and wiggled on the ground. "You and what army?"

"I don't need an army. I have my sword." I held it up and imagined the lightning hitting it the way it had when I'd battled Ash not far from where we stood now. A bolt of light blew through the ceiling and hit the tip of my sword. Blue electricity sizzled on the blade. I walked forward, swinging my sword to parry the blows leveled at me by the draugr. This time, when I beheaded them, they shriveled into dust and disintegrated.

By the time I reached Hel, the floor was grey with ash. Every step sent an eddy of gritty, dead warrior ash swirling up and around me.

I stopped about ten feet away from her and held out my sword. My muscles ached, and it was all I could do to keep my arm from trembling from the weight of it. "Give her to me."

"No," Hel repeated. She pushed the Valkyrie away. The girl stumbled but remained upright yet oblivious to the events around her.

Hel reached into her ribcage, rummaged around the sludge that was her internal organs, and pulled out a sword.

It was at least a foot-and-a-half longer than mine and looked heavier by far. I guess a giant, immortal goddess can heft a lot more weight than a short, mortal(ish) Valkyrie.

She raised the sword over her head.

I didn't wait for her to swing. Instead, I stepped forward, stabbed her through the stomach, wrenched my sword free, and grabbed the hand of the silently waiting Valkyrie.

"We have to run!" I screamed at her.

She blinked at me, but my words—or at least the volume of them—seemed to have gotten through to her.

She let me pull her along, and together we ran through the doorway and straight into the arms of Zofia, who'd been transporting the others.

"Zofia?" the girl at my side said, finally sounding a little less dazed.

"Riley! You're alive!"

Before Zofia could do more than pull Riley in close for a fierce hug, the wall behind us shuddered.

"We have to get out of here! Reunions later!" I reached out and grabbed Zofia's wrist. She took a step, and the surrounding walls disappeared.

It seemed to take forever between one step and the next, and for a few seconds, I was afraid we'd be drifting in nothingness forever.

Then my feet hit solid ground. I looked up and stared at my parents' house. It'd only been a few hours since I'd left home, but if fear aged a person, I was several lifetimes older than I had been this morning.

Dad rushed forward and pulled me into a hug, then dropped his arms and took several big steps back. "I'm glad you're safe, but you stink."

Archibald wound his way around my ankles and said, "He's right, you do, and not in a good way like tinned shrimp dinner."

"Jackie?" I asked, trying to dismiss the knowledge that I smelled worse than wet cat food.

He shook his head. "Still missing. Get showered and get back out here as soon as you can. Becky and Devin are on their way in now, and we'll need everyone who can fight ready to go." Anger flashed in my father's eyes, something I'd never seen on his easy-going face in all the years I'd known him. "I will get her back, no matter the cost."

THIRTY-THREE

I showered and raided the kitchen while we waited for Becky and Devin.

I texted Dusana in between giant bites of a roast beef sandwich to tell her I wouldn't be back to Portland that night. I got a thumbs up in response and spent the rest of my sandwich agonizing over what that might mean. Love-life—or lack thereof—angst was way better to dwell on than my missing family members.

A few minutes after brushing away the crumbs of my third sandwich, a car coming up the driveway pulled me from my navel gazing.

I ran out to the front porch and squinted against the headlights in the quickly darkening evening.

The car screeched to a halt, kicking up a cloud of dust, and Becky jumped out of the driver's seat. Devin emerged from the passenger side with nearly as much haste, and the mischief that'd been present when I'd seen him earlier was gone.

"Where the fuck is she?" Becky demanded, looking at the scattering of people in the front yard as if one of us was hiding our sister from her.

Dad opened his arms, and Becky stepped into them. I walked

forward and wrapped my arms around them both. Tentatively at first—I wasn't sure my comfort would be welcome after a decade of absence—but then more firmly.

"Mom, Kara, and Aunt Lena are looking for them," Dad said, finally breaking free of our arms and stepping back.

"Grab your sword, Frankie," Becky said. "We're going after them."

"Where?" I asked, fingering the hilt. I hated having to ask, and seeing Becky deflate made me hate myself even more. "Tell me where to start, and I'll be there. You know I will."

Becky's lip trembled, and Devin pulled her to him. "We stopped at her place," she whispered. "I thought we might find a clue, something everyone else missed."

"And?"

Becky dashed away tears with her right hand and stared at the ground.

"There was blood. A lot of blood," Devin said softly. "I thought Jackie was going to your Aunt Sasha's with the baby. Do you know if they were planning to stop at home?"

I shook my head. "She didn't say."

"Yes," Dad said. "She wanted to grab another few changes of clothes for the baby, since she'd used up everything she'd initially packed. It was a last-minute change of plans, but maybe they interrupted a home invasion or something?"

"But what about John? Isn't he missing too?" I asked.

"We assume so, since he's not answering my calls either, and their location apps have them in the same place," Dad said.

"How did you know they were missing? Did you stop by her house, too?" I hated playing TV-cop twenty questions, but I had to do something to get the pieces to fit together somehow.

"They didn't arrive at Sasha's when they were expected, and Michelle—that's the cat sitter—couldn't get ahold of Sasha and called me. Your mom tracked their phones, and they weren't anywhere near where they were supposed to be. Instead of Eugene, they were halfway to Seattle. Kara and Lena flew to the location they stopped at but found nothing but their abandoned phones and Lenore's diaper bag." Dad's voice was nearly as clinical as mine at this point. I recognized his powers of dissociating as being nearly the equal to mine.

A small crowd of Valkyries gathered around us. They'd obviously taken turns in the shower, because no one was covered with zombie guts anymore. Our newest rescue, Riley, was tucked under the arm of her mother, who didn't look like she'd ever let her daughter go again.

The memory of what Hel had said about Riley's parentage came back to me. "Your dad is Loki?"

Anja dropped her arm from around her daughter and ran at me so quickly I didn't have time to react. She slapped me across the face, raking her nails down my cheek and drawing blood. In another flash, she'd drawn her sword and pointed it at me. "How dare you?"

My jaw dropped, and I froze. My hand was on my sword, but I didn't unsheathe it in kind. "What the actual fuck is happening?"

Zofia walked up to us and inserted herself between Anja and me. "Put it away, Anja. Now is not the time to turn on each other. There's been enough loss lately."

Anja took a couple steps back but didn't drop her weapon. "Did you hear what she said?" she demanded.

"I did. And we can talk about it. She likely doesn't know how big an insult that is, and I'm sure she'll apologize once we get to the bottom of her accusation. But in the meantime, sheathe your weapon."

Anja finally lowered her sword, although she didn't sheathe it.

I looked back and forth between my family on one side and the Valkyries on the other, my head spinning. There was too much going on, and I didn't know which way to turn.

"Breathe," Archibald said softly from my feet. "Look around. It's dark. Everyone is tired and stressed, not just you. There is no immediate danger right here, and nothing anyone can do. Get inside, make some tea, and talk."

I hesitated before passing on Archibald's suggestion, but then plowed ahead. He was right. There was no use spinning our wheels outside when we could be warm.

"Everyone, inside. Devin, can you start the kettle? I'll make tea, and we can deal with both of the current issues at hand."

Devin nodded at me and gave me a tiny salute before leading the way inside.

I took my time with the tea, giving everyone a chance to get comfortable and chill out as much as possible. I wanted to ride in, guns a-blazin', to find my missing family, but there was nothing I personally could do at the moment. This was where my "cool head in a crisis" mode finally had a chance to shine. I would break down later where no one could see me, but for now... Well, now, I had to put on my big-girl pants and pull this room together.

Once everyone was seated and had tea or water, depending on preference—with only one mutter of disapproval and a wish for something stronger from Hope—I sat in the recliner Archibald had reserved for me.

I took a sip of my peppermint tea and looked at the assembled people—my dad, Becky and Devin, Hope, Zofia, Riley, Anja, and four others I didn't know well enough to put a name to, which was something I was going to have to rectify ASAP if not sooner. I huffed out a breath.

"Let's start with Loki," I said, wrapping my hands around the mug.

Anja jumped to her feet, but before she could yell at me again, Zofia pulled her back down.

"I did not know how insulting my comment was. I repeated what Hel told me without thinking it through. I don't regard her as a reliable source, and it would have been better if I'd phrased what I'd heard differently and in a more private setting." I bowed my head a bit without taking my eyes off Anja. "I hope you can forgive me for my misstep."

Anja's mouth was a thin, hard line, and she practically vibrated with anger. "Just because I do not know the name of Riley's father doesn't mean I would stoop so low as to fuck Loki."

Her daughter gasped, but whether she was surprised by the venom of her mother's words or the harsh, bitten-out f-bomb, I wasn't sure.

When Anja turned to her daughter, her gaze softened. "I'm sorry, Riley. I didn't want you to find out this way."

"I thought Dad was killed in a car accident when I was a baby. But if you didn't know who he was, then…"

Oh. So the gasp was a reaction to a public reveal of a twenty-year-old family secret. This night was getting better and better.

Zofia leaned forward and put a hand on Anja's knee. "I have to ask, and I am sorry, but are you sure your lover wasn't Loki? He can take any form, and seducing a Valkyrie would delight him."

Riley bit her lip. "It might also explain why everyone got my gender wrong at birth, right? Loki isn't exactly cis. It makes sense."

Her mother looked at her with a fierce protectiveness. "You are perfect, you know that? And unless every parent of every trans person throughout history had a one-night stand with the trickster, there's nothing to support your idea."

Becky tapped her fingernail on the wooden arm of her chair, drawing everyone's attention. "I think there's some merit to Riley's idea." She held up a hand to forestall arguments, but everyone was too shocked to offer any. "Obviously, I would never suggest there's something weird about the birth of anyone, cis or trans. But if a Valkyrie, who can only have daughters, gives birth to someone incorrectly identified at birth, that could be the result of the combination of gender-fluid trickster and Valkyrie genes."

"None of this matters," Anja said. "Loki is not the father of my child. I would recognize him in any form, and I would not lower myself so far. Hel was lying."

"Okay," I said.

She glared at me for a moment, then confusion knit her brow. "Okay? That's it?"

I shrugged. "You're right. It doesn't matter. She's your daughter and a Valkyrie; that's what's important. Now that that's out of the way, I want to talk about Jackie. Has anyone heard from Mom, Kara, or Lena recently?"

Dad shook his head. "Not since before you showed up. They should be back by now." Worry strained his voice.

Almost as if he'd conjured him, John stumbled through the front door, baby Lenore in his arms. Blood stained the tatters of his once-white dress shirt, and bruises bloomed on his face.

Becky ran forward and caught the baby before John could drop her.

He looked at the assembly, then focused on me. "You have to save them. You have to." His eyes rolled back into his head, and he hit the ground.

THIRTY-FOUR

John sprawled on the couch, where Dad and I had moved him after he'd passed out and covered him with the garish Afghan Aunt Sasha crocheted for Mom and Dad when they got married. After cleaning up the head wound that looked worse than it was, I stared at him, willing him to wake up.

Dad paced the room, alternately glaring at John and calling Mom. Neither action yielded any results.

Becky and Devin curled into each other on the couch, Lenore sleeping in Becky's arms.

The rest of the Valkyries had dispersed to give us privacy with the promise of help the second we called for them.

"What's taking him so long to wake up?" Dad growled.

"I'm a vet and not an MD, but I'd guess the head wound, possible dehydration, and shock now that the initial adrenaline rush has worn off," I said.

"Should we take him to the hospital?" Dad asked.

I shook my head but answered in the affirmative. "Probably. He might have a concussion, and although there's not much anyone can do for that, a CT scan would be a great idea to make sure there isn't any brain damage. But let's wait until he wakes up." My decision was purely selfish. I wanted to question him before the hospital claimed him and the cops were called. Besides, I reasoned, his injuries appeared entirely superficial, and the bump on his forehead was so slight as to be almost nonexistent. If there hadn't been blood crusted around it, I wouldn't have even noticed it.

"You said you're a vet," Becky said, the first words she'd uttered since John burst into the house.

I tilted my head and looked at her.

She read my confusion and didn't keep me hanging. "I haven't heard you call yourself a vet since you got back. Usually you just make lots of references to your perceived failure. But you haven't claimed your actual degree. This is good."

She might be right, but I didn't have time to examine that right now. I pulled out my phone, added it to my "discuss with therapist" note, and squatted next to the sofa.

Ten minutes later, John's eyelashes fluttered.

"Get me a glass of water and an ice pack," I commanded, not taking my eyes off my sister's partner.

It took a few more minutes for John's gaze to focus, and even longer for his memory to kick in.

He struggled to sit, and I slipped an arm around his shoulders and helped him to an upright position. He took the proffered glass of water and gulped it down.

"How are you feeling?" I asked. "Any lightheadedness, nausea, dizziness?"

He shook his head, then winced. "Headache."

Devin passed him the ice pack, and John pressed it to the back of his head and not to the bump on his forehead I'd assumed was the primary injury site.

"What do you remember?" I asked in my gentlest voice.

He pushed himself up the rest of the way, eyes darting around wildly. "Lenore? Where's Lenore?"

"Right here," Becky said. She carried Lenore over to the couch and sank into a cross-legged position on the floor next to him, offering the baby up to him.

He didn't take his daughter, but relief washed over his face with such intensity that tears rose in my eyes. "Oh, thank god she's okay."

He finished the water, handed me the empty glass, then whooshed out a long, noisy exhale. "Sorry. What did you ask me?"

"What's the last thing you remember?" I prompted.

He closed his eyes and slid the ice pack around to the side of his head opposite the goose egg. Whoever had kidnapped them must've really rung his bell. I looked at Dad. He nodded and went to grab his keys to pull the car around. John really needed medical attention, and I'd been an ass to delay it.

Devin gently pushed me out of the way and sat by John. "Let's start with something easier. Did you drive here?"

John nodded, then winced again. "Yes. I did."

"Good. What did you drive? Your own car?"

A line appeared on John's forehead, then he shook his head slightly. "I must have, right?"

Devin jutted his chin toward the front of the house, and I stood and headed outside. Jackie and John's car wasn't out there, and there weren't any cars that I didn't recognize.

I walked back into the living room and shook my head minutely at Devin, hoping he'd catch my drift.

"Did someone drop you off?" Devin asked. "You're not in any shape to drive."

"Maybe?" John asked. "I don't really remember. Everything is so fuzzy."

I took a deep breath to curb my impatience. Devin's line of questioning was more effective than mine, even if the answers weren't coming as fast as I wanted them to.

Dad walked back into the room. "Let's get him to the ER."

Devin scrubbed his hand through his short, black hair and let out a noisy breath. "That's a good idea. I don't think we'll get anything else out of him until he's a little less disoriented, anyway."

"No!" Becky stomped over and thrust her index finger into John's face. "He will tell us everything he knows right now. He will tell me where my sister is. I thought I lost Frankie once. I will not go through that again."

John shrank back from her finger. "I don't... Wait. I know. I know where they are!" Triumph rode his voice.

Dad straightened after bending to help John to his feet. "Where? Is Katrin there?"

"We were in the dark. It was cold and damp. And..." He screwed his eyes closed and appeared to be thinking. "Loud. Trains and cars and boats. There was a foghorn. The horn scared Lenore and made her cry."

"Was Katrin there?" Dad asked again.

John shook his head. "No. Just Jackie and me and the baby. And the old lady."

"What old lady?" I asked.

John waved his hands. "The psychic one. Although if she was a real psychic, she should've seen this coming, right?" He laughed, and I watched Dad's expression harden at the description of his sister.

"Aunt Sasha?" I prompted, a lot more gently than I wanted to.

"That's the one." He slumped against the couch. "She was pissed off."

"Last couple questions, now that you're feeling a bit more lucid," Devin said. He slipped an arm around John's shoulders and helped him sit up straight. "Who grabbed you and how?"

"I don't know," John snapped, going from tiredly pathetic to angry in a second. "I was at home. I heard the door open, then something hit me in the head. When I woke up, I was tied up in the dark with Jackie and her aunt."

"Okay, that's fine," Devin said soothingly. "Last question, I promise. How did you and Lenore escape when Jackie and Aunt Sasha didn't?"

"How am I supposed to know? Maybe they let me go. Maybe they needed someone to get the baby out of there. I don't know. Shouldn't you be the ones figuring things out? Where are all your powerful Valkyrie friends now that my wife has been kidnapped?"

"We'll find them," Devin said. "Now, let's get you some medical attention."

Devin and Dad helped John out to the car. I watched them situate him in the back seat. Dad drove off and Devin came back to the house.

I made another pot of tea and curled up in the recliner again. Becky deposited the sleeping Lenore in the bassinet that had a permanent place next to the couch and sat.

"Did something seem off about that?" Devin asked.

Becky ticked things off on her fingers. "He 'escaped' when Jackie and Aunt Sasha didn't, he showed up here with the baby but no car, he doesn't remember how he got here, but remembers a lot of specific but not helpful details about where he was being kept, and he didn't seem worried about Jackie until the very end."

"Also, he didn't seem to remember where his head injury was," I added. "He kept moving the ice pack around."

"A lot of it could be attributed to shock," Devin said. "But I don't want to miss anything, no matter how small. Frankie, do you have a laptop?"

I fetched my laptop from my bedroom and squeezed myself onto the couch on the other side of Devin.

He pulled up a map of the area. "Okay, based on the timelines we know, it's been six hours since Jackie was kidnapped. If they were held somewhere long enough for John to get those details and then get back here, I can't imagine they're more than a couple hours away."

"And on the water," Becky said. "Foghorns..." She stared at the map Devin had narrowed down to everything within a couple hours of Estacada. "Well, shit."

Within the area Dev had narrowed it down to were the Columbia and Willamette Rivers, both large enough to have significant ship traffic, and the Pacific Ocean.

"There has to be something we can do to narrow it down even more," Becky said.

I stared at the computer screen, willing it to give up the secret of my sister's location. "I don't understand the motivation. So far, everything's been about the Valkyries, not their families. Is this related? Is it random?"

"Frankie, most of the Valkyries don't have families," Becky pointed out. "Mom is different. She ended up with three delightful daughters, two sons-in-law, a grandbaby, and she's still with her husband, who is close to his family. Of everyone else we've met, have you seen any other men, much less extended family?"

My sister had a point. "But still... If her abduction is about the Valkyries, why take John, and why let him go?"

"There," Devin said, jabbing his finger on Portland. "We need to start looking there."

I squinted at the map. His finger was hiding a good chunk of North Portland. "Why there?"

"We have to start somewhere. Portland is close enough to Estacada that John could've gotten here quickly, especially if he had a ride. The St. Johns Bridge would have car traffic, and there'd be fog horns from the bridges. And it feels right to me." Devin said the last bit with more confidence than I would've managed if I was making a major decision based on a hunch.

"Six months ago, I would've scoffed at that reasoning, but the location fits our criteria. I just wish I could walk there the way Kara and the other full Valkyries can. There's got to be a trick to it, but the last time I tried, I stepped myself into a wall." I winced at the memory.

"Is anyone else here?" Becky asked. "I wasn't paying attention to who stayed and who took off to resume the search."

"Zofia is still here, but I'm sure she's tired from the fight and getting everyone out of that warehouse and away from the draugr." I glanced at the back hallway where the rescued Valkyries had claimed rooms. "I'll ask her, though."

I marched down the hall and tried very hard not to think about the outside dimensions of the house that didn't allow for this wing to exist in my parents' sprawling ranch. There were several doors on either side. I hesitated for only a second before knocking on the first. Shuffling feet approached the door, then Zofia opened it and peered out. I'd gotten the right room on the first try.

"Frankie?" she asked. Her hair was tucked into a sleep bonnet, and dark circles under her eyes marked her exhaustion. "Is everything okay?"

I chewed on my lip for a second. My desire to save my biological sister consumed me, but not at the expense of draining the resources of a woman who was a sister-in-arms. "We think we know where Jackie is. But I can't step the way you can, and I was wondering—"

"Of course. Let me get dressed. Come in." She left the door open and moved back into her room, flipping on the overhead light as she did so.

I walked in and looked around. A large rug covered most of the oak floor, and a king-sized bed piled high with soft, grey blankets dominated most of the room. On the far wall by the only window was a papasan chair and an end table. Another door opened into a large closet. There were no personal belongings in view, but it felt homey, nonetheless.

Zofia disappeared into the closet and emerged a couple minutes later in black leggings, a long-sleeved black shirt, and black leather boots. She held a sheath in her left hand and her sword in the other.

I watched her adjust the sheath over her shoulder and slide the sword in, wiggling it a bit until it settled comfortably.

"Ready," she said. "Let's go find your sister."

THIRTY-FIVE

Zofia and I stood in the shadow of a huge conifer, one of dozens that dotted Cathedral Park. We were mere blocks away from the house where I'd almost gotten to spend an evening alone with Dusana, and much too close to where the mass of eels attacked us.

I should've texted her, let her know where I was and what I was doing. She might not be a Valkyrie, but she could wield that scythe with deadly accuracy, and would be great to have by my side. Purely for battle reasons, obviously.

As if my thoughts conjured her, she glided over to me, joining us under the tree. I put a hand on Zofia's arm and nodded once, hoping to convey that Dusana was not the enemy.

"How did you know where to find us?" I breathed as quietly as possible.

In answer, she pointed at my feet. A large orange cat appeared, looking almost unforgivably smug. "Thought you might want some more help," he said.

"Where the hell have you been?" I winced. That'd come out much louder than I'd intended.

His body language gave the impression of a shrug. "Around. There are things going on that have nothing to do with you, and I'm trying to stay on top of them."

Something in his tone had me squinting at him in suspicion. He was hiding something. I pulled my phone out and made a note in my increasingly long "things to find out when we're not in mortal danger" list, once again, cursing my terrible depression memory.

"Fine." I jutted my chin at the large concrete base of the bridge. "There's a door there with a brand-new shiny padlock on it. The concrete step in front of it is muddy, and there are a lot of footprints in the area. Devin may have gotten the location right in one try."

The four of us stared at the door, then everyone looked at me.

"What's our play?" Zofia asked.

I bit my lip while I thought. I wanted to defer the planning to someone else, someone with way more experience than I had, but if I was going to be the one to lead, I needed to get comfortable making suggestions, if not decisions.

"The lock is on, which leads me to believe any abductors are absent. There may still be guards in there with them, but they're probably relying more on the secrecy of the location and the strength of that lock to keep Jackie and Aunt Sasha inside." I looked around the park—there wasn't another soul in sight or hearing distance. Even the cars overhead on the bridge were few and far between. "Watch my back. I'm going to give it a closer look."

I tucked my hair into my black hoodie and made a mental note to get it cut again. Then I pulled my sword from its sheath and paused to see if the sound had garnered any attention.

When the area stayed quiet, I sprinted from my cover in the trees to the doorway, cursing the bright light illuminating that part of the park. In my black cat-burglar-inspired outfit, a near duplicate of Zofia's, I'd stand out like a sore thumb.

I balanced my sword under my arm, glad Kara couldn't see me hold it improperly, and pulled on a pair of thin leather gloves. Then, sword once again held in a proper grip, I pulled at the simple padlock with my other hand. I berated myself for never having learned any useful skills, like lock picking, and yanked hard on it just in case it hadn't latched completely.

It had.

I walked around the concrete foundation. There were no windows or anything else that might serve as a secondary point of entry. If we were going in, we had to go through the door. And if we were going to get through the thick, reinforced door, we needed to pick the lock.

I sheathed my sword and sprinted back to Zofia, Dusana, and Archibald, glad the recent rains had soaked the leaves enough that they didn't crunch underfoot. "I don't suppose anyone here knows how to pick a lock?"

Zofia smiled grimly. "I don't know how to pick one, but I can get us in there as long as you don't mind telegraphing our presence."

I mulled that over for fewer than three seconds. "Let's do it. I need to get Jackie and my aunt out of there before whoever is holding them returns."

Zofia nodded once. "Follow me." She strode forward, drawing her sword as she walked. Dusana, Archibald, and I trailed after her.

She took a few moments to study the lock and the door, much as I had, but her examination looked more practiced than my quick scan.

"Stand back," she commanded.

We gave her some room. She held her sword to her face and whispered something too quiet to make out. Then she raised her sword and sliced at the door.

Sparks flew, and metal striking metal rang out like a clear bell sound and not like the screeching clang I'd expected. I walked forward. The lock lay on the ground, the shackle still in the hasp.

"Wow! That is more skill and precision than I've ever seen! Why aren't you the one training us newbies with the blade?" I reached out and pulled what remained of the lock from the door and pocketed it, along with the part that was on the ground. It'd be obvious it was gone, but there was a chance that whoever returned might assume one of their own had forgotten to return it.

"Once you have the basics mastered, I'll be stepping in more." Zofia pulled the door open slowly.

A long creak worthy of a haunted house accompanied the motion.

"Who's there?" a voice barked from inside.

We couldn't have been so lucky as to find my family unguarded.

I exchanged a look with Dusana. "Are you sure you want to be here?" I whispered, crossing my fingers that she wouldn't bail on me. "I've no idea what we'll find."

She reached into the air, and a long, wicked-looking scythe materialized in her hand. A black cloak swirled around her. Her visage flickered, a skull warring with her face for dominance as the power of death coursed through her. In a voice that echoed hollowly, she replied, "Wouldn't miss it."

I drew my sword, and we stepped up behind Zofia.

"Archibald, you should get out of here, or at least stay back. I don't want you to get hurt." I glanced down at the cat by my feet.

"Of course. I wouldn't want to be in the way." He sounded affronted and stalked away, vanishing after a few steps.

Cats.

"Barry? If that's you, you better give me the password, or I'll blow your head off in three seconds."

I pointed at the ground, then yanked the arms of my companions downward.

"It's not Barry!" I shouted, hoping Jackie and Aunt Sasha could hear me.

Muzzle flare shattered the darkness from the shadow-shrouded doorway.

Dusana rose to a crouch, then barreled forward. A loud grunt followed by a short, high-pitched scream echoed in the concrete chamber. A light switched on, and a warm glow invited us farther in.

Dusana stood in the middle of the room. "There's no one else here."

"Where's the guard?" Zofia asked.

"Gone," was all Dusana said.

Reapers didn't leave anything behind when they killed. Body and soul disappeared into the After, and what happened after that was something Dusana wouldn't talk about.

"What do you mean, no one else?" I demanded. "Do you mean no other guards or no one?"

"I can't sense another living soul, and there aren't any other rooms," she replied. "The only door is the one we just walked through. There are no closets or trunks or anywhere to stash a couple full-grown adults."

The room vibrated with the roar of a semi-truck passing four hundred feet overhead, and seconds later, a foghorn blasted.

"This has to be the right place," I muttered.

"Maybe they knew we were coming and had enough time to move them?" Zofia suggested.

"But how?" I asked. "We've been here less than ten minutes and had decided where to go only a little bit before that. No one else knew."

"Your other sister and her husband knew," Zofia said.

I shook my head, negating the unspoken accusation. "No. Neither of them would betray us or Jackie. Archibald is in the clear, too."

Zofia appeared taken aback. "I wouldn't presume to accuse a Guide of betrayal. Their training and mission render them blameless."

"A Guide?" I asked absently. My mind was turning over dozens of possibilities, from Jackie and Sasha being pulled out of here as soon as John disappeared, to them being relocated immediately before we showed up, to them never having been here at all.

"Frankie, come look at this," Dusana said, forestalling anything Zofia might've said about Guides and Archibald.

I walked over to where she crouched opposite the door. A small, rubber giraffe covered in mud and tiny smeared fingerprints was propped against the wall.

"That's Sophie," I said. "It's a teething toy. Lots of kids have them, and for some reason, they all love them. It's Lenore's. They were here."

"Listen," Zofia said.

Instant quiet fell in the room, and after the roar of another truck disappeared into the distance, it was completely, oppressively silent.

Except for a long, slow scraping sound coming from underneath us.

My eyes widened, and I dropped to my knees on the filthy floor. I shined my cellphone flashlight at the floor with one hand and used the other to feel the ground until I found what I was looking for. Seams in the concrete.

I traced the outline of the trap door, then looked for a way to open it. There was nothing, not even a groove where a pull-ring could be inserted.

"I don't suppose you can bash through this the way you did the lock?" I asked.

Zofia followed my lead and ran her fingers over the floor, then shook her head. "No. It's too thick, and my sword would never forgive me if I tried to blunt her edge like that."

We were so close.

I wanted to scream in frustration. The second I got down there, I was going to kill anyone who got in my way, especially if they'd hurt my sister.

Death tugged at me from below, and I gasped, thoughts of revenge pushed from my mind. I had to find Jackie and Sasha before whoever was down there decided they were expendable.

The tug disappeared immediately. I looked at my fellow psychopomps. "Did you guys feel that?"

Zofia nodded emphatically, while Dusana's agreement was more tentative.

"I thought I was going to get pulled down there, which would've solved our no-entry problem." I glared at the floor, anger tightening my chest and heating my body until sweat broke out on my brow. The fuckers who had Jackie and Sasha better be ready to die. I'd lost too many people lately, and I would not let anyone else go.

Death pulled harder this time, and I started to dematerialize. That hadn't happened before. All my previous encounters with death had been face to face, so to speak.

"Is this normal?" I asked Zofia, unsuccessfully masking my panic. I solidified again, and the sensation disappeared.

"Sometimes." Her voice was strained. "But it doesn't blink off and on like this. It feels like death in potential, rather than anything imminent."

"Potential like someone's life is being threatened, but the outcome keeps changing?" I asked.

She nodded and looked at Dusana. "Can you go down there and see what's happening based on the potential of death?"

"Not unless I can latch on the minute it starts again." She sounded as frustrated as I felt.

"Oh!" I concentrated on my rage and directed it toward the guards I knew were holding my sister. They would pay.

Instantly, death jumped to the forefront.

I let go of my concentration and thought about my niece instead, safe and sound with Becky.

The desire to choose someone for the afterlife vanished so suddenly it almost gave me whiplash.

"It's me," I said. "Whenever I concentrate on how much I want to kill Jackie's captors, the need to choose gets stronger, but when I get distracted from the weird feeling of needing to claim a soul and usher it into death, I lose sight of my goal and the surety of death goes away."

"That makes sense, in as much as anything about our lives makes sense," Dusana said. "I wonder what would happen if you held your homicidal rage long enough to appear at the side of the one you've marked but *don't* kill them? Would it create some kind of paradox?"

I didn't answer, as that was not something I needed to worry about. Unless the captor was my mother or someone else dear to me, they were going down. I concentrated all my rage—about the funerals I'd been to, the senseless murders, and the fear and anger swirling in me that'd taken hold when Jackie had been kidnapped—and focused it on whoever was below us, keeping my sister from me.

This time, when I felt my body fading into nothing and being sucked downward, I didn't break my concentration.

I reformed next to a tall, pockmarked, grey-skinned creature who looked like a reject from a Lord of the Rings orc casting call. It held a spear, the butt planted firmly on the ground, and wore a chainmail hauberk and a helmet that did nothing to hide the holes where its nose and ears should have been. Its mouth dropped open in surprise, revealing a half-dozen fangs dripping with what was likely venom.

I didn't give it a chance to react. I swung my sword and beheaded it. Zofia appeared beside me and yanked free its soul before it had a chance to register that it was dead.

I felt more than saw her shred his soul before sending it to Hel. "Now he cannot rise as a draugr," she said.

"Neat trick. You'll have to show me how you did that," I said. "I have an awful feeling I'm going to need to know that, and soon."

"You find your sister," Zofia instructed. "I'll figure out how to open the trapdoor so Dusana can come in, and we can eventually get out."

THIRTY-SIX

I assessed my surroundings. Bare lightbulbs hung along the ceiling at even intervals, their thick cords sporting too many exposed wires for my taste. We were in a tunnel that didn't look nearly as reinforced as I'd have preferred, especially since we were so close to a river and sitting right on the Cascadia Subduction Zone, which earthquake-ologists, or whatever they were called, had been warning for years was going to kill us all any minute.

I shuddered and thrust the fear of dying in a collapsed tunnel away. The corridor ran parallel to the river and ended a few feet west of where we stood. Only one way forward, then.

I didn't hear anything ahead of me, but I didn't know how much of a head start they'd had. However, in addition to the dank, musty smells of the damp earth and stale air, I could smell my sister's rich, spicy perfume, a fragrance like burnt amber and incense.

I walked as quickly as I dared, sweeping my eyes across the ground in front of me. An exposed root had nearly tripped me up a few yards back, and it'd be stupidly inexcusable if I missed saving my sister because I twisted my ankle.

Finally, I heard voices ahead. I slowed, not wanting to give away my presence with footsteps.

"What's wrong with her?" someone barked. "Pick her up and get her moving."

Jackie answered, and although I heard fear, anger dominated her tone. "She's old and tired. It's damp as fuck, we haven't eaten in hours, and I don't know what you did with my baby, you ugly fucker."

"I am not old, nor am I deaf," Aunt Sasha said. "I tripped over a root. I will be on my feet in a moment, and then you can continue marching us along to wherever you're not going to kill us next."

"Maybe we will kill you," a new voice said, sounding more like a petulant child than a kidnapper.

Shit. There were at least two.

"If you were going to kill us, you'd have done so by now," Jackie said. "We're more valuable alive than dead. No one wastes this much time and monster power on kidnap victims they're going to eventually kill."

"We want you," monster guard number one said. "But we don't need the old one any more than we needed the baby. If she can't keep up, we will leave her behind. There are rats in these tunnels, you know. I wonder what it feels like to be eaten alive?"

"No!" Jackie screamed.

There was a muffled grunt, then Aunt Sasha screamed.

I rushed forward, hoping there were only two of them I needed to fight and praying I hadn't waited too long to save Aunt Sasha.

It took longer than I expected to find them. The sound traveled funnily in the curved tunnels. I rounded a corner, and the tunnel headed away from the river and started climbing. Sasha was on the ground, pale and dripping in sweat. She cradled her left arm with her right.

I slowed, but she waved me on. "Just a broken arm. Get Jackie before something worse happens to her, then come back for me. I'll be fine."

I spared one more glance for her, then raced on. Either Dusana or Zofia would be along soon, and they'd take care of her.

Wherever they were taking my sister, it couldn't be good, and I wanted to stop them before that happened.

I skidded in a muddy patch as I took a corner too quickly and glimpsed Jackie tossed over the shoulder of a creature wearing the same kind of armor as the one I'd dispatched earlier.

The creatures were fast, but I had adrenaline on my side, and I pulled closer to them with every stride.

Neither looked around, even though I'd stopped trying to be quiet. My footfalls slapped against the wet earth, and my breath came in short gasps. I slowed to catch my breath, matching their pace and staying a few feet behind them.

I drew my sword in case they noticed me before I was ready, but they were remarkably oblivious.

Jackie looked up and stared me in the face. Her eyes widened, but before I could a hold a finger in front of my face to signal quiet, she screamed, "Run, Frankie! It's a trap!"

The two creatures spun around, and the one carrying Jackie dropped her unceremoniously. They pulled their swords and rushed me.

Two on one wasn't great odds, especially when they each outweighed me by a good hundred pounds of solid muscle, but the narrow tunnel kept them from flanking me. It also kept my motions shorter and less expansive than I was used to, which was a definite mark against me.

I ducked under one blow meant for my head and raised my sword to parry. The force of the creature's broad sword, wielded one-handed, sent reverberations of pain up my arm and through my body.

Note to self—avoid getting into duels with monsters. I rolled my eyes at myself like there was any way to avoid that.

I was fast, but not fast enough to dodge the blow that came from the second guard. I braced myself as his weapon arced toward my body on a collision course for my torso.

It made contact, rattling my teeth. I stumbled backward, resisting the urge to cradle my ribs, but I spared a moment to run my fingers down my side to assess the damage. Since it hadn't sliced into me, the blade must have twisted at the last minute, hitting me with the flat rather than the edge, but I wanted to make sure I wasn't dripping blood I might slip on later.

Instead of a torn cotton T-shirt, my fingers encountered metal. I glanced down. I was clad head to toe in Valkyrie armor. A tentative touch of my head proved I was helmeted as well.

A smile curved my lips. I wasn't immortal—the recent deaths of the other Valkyries had proven that—but I was difficult to kill, and these creatures wouldn't be the ones to do it. Now that I was clad in the fabled Valkyrie armor, I was next to invulnerable in the face of all but the most magical of weapons.

I took two steps backward to give myself some room and dropped my sword to lure in the one who'd tried to crush my ribs. It worked. He raised his sword and grinned at me. His fangs dripped, and where the liquid hit the dirt, it sizzled.

I raised my arm, took a step in to duck his blade, and slid my sword under the hem of his mail shirt and up through his abdomen. Then I twisted the grip and yanked my sword back out, carving a large hole and pulling a handful of stinking guts out with it.

His eyes widened, and he dropped his sword to wrap his arms around himself. He fell to the floor and tried to stuff his intestines back in, but they slipped out of his hands, squelching against the floor.

I didn't let him suffer long. There was still another opponent to deal with, and I didn't want to find out this monster had supernatural healing powers by getting stabbed in the back. I sliced his head off and kicked it away from the body. It rolled back down the long hall.

I advanced on the remaining guard. He looked between me, my

sister, and his dead companion, all the while backing away. I couldn't read his expression, but I wanted to imagine that fear was overwhelming him.

I smiled at him, aiming for sweet. If Jackie's gasp was any indication, I missed the mark.

The creature turned, tossed Jackie over his shoulder, and ran.

"Wrong move, asshole," I growled. I took off after him. I couldn't attack from behind, because Jackie's head was bouncing against his back, and I didn't want to risk hurting her.

Her eyes were closed tightly and sweat dripped off her face. She was more prone to motion-sickness than anyone I knew, and between fear, the smell of blood and guts, and the jarring rhythm of the monster carrying her, she must have been nauseated beyond belief.

"I'm going to barf," she moaned, confirming my guess.

Then she screamed. It was a sound so agonizing that I nearly dropped my sword to cover my ears.

The monster dropped her and took off, even faster than before.

I stopped and crouched next to her, rolling her onto her side as she vomited. That was when I saw the blood staining her side.

"He bit me," she said weakly once she'd stopped heaving.

I yanked down the waistband of her jeans and pulled her shirt up and hissed in horror. A large chunk of her hip had been torn out, and the edges of the wound were black and sizzling.

She screamed again.

"I will get you out of here," I promised. "We'll get this taken care of. Lenore is with Becky, and Sasha is gonna be fine, too."

I was babbling, but I didn't know how to stop myself.

"Lenore's okay?" she whispered.

I nodded and gulped as I watched black streaks crawl across her skin, radiating outward from her wound. I didn't know what kind of venom this monster had, and I certainly didn't know how to treat it, but someone must.

"John's okay, too. He's in the hospital, but nothing serious."

"John?" she wrinkled her nose, then cried out in pain again.

I held her against my body until the spasms stopped. "He brought Lenore home after he escaped with her."

"He didn't... He isn't..." Spasms shook her again, and tears streamed down her face.

"Shhh," I murmured, rocking her gently. "You're going to be okay."

"You have to go," she whispered. "Stop him before he talks to Hel. I told him things, things about our home he shouldn't know. He did things to my mind..." She shuddered again. "I'm sorry, but you have to stop him."

I looked at her, uncertainty warring in me. She was my baby sister, and I could feel her soul being tugged away from her body. It wasn't like what I'd felt with Gwen, not yet, but death was near.

"You said it yourself. I'll be okay. Go. Please. I'll be here when you get back."

Dusana burst around the corner and took in the scene with one look. "I will stay with her, and no one else will take her until you return."

I heard the meaning hidden in her words. She was a reaper, and she could hold death at bay.

I stood and picked up my sword from where I'd dropped it.

"I love you, Jax. See you soon."

"Love you, too. Tell Lenore every day how much I love her." Her voice faded, and I had to strain to hear her.

I choked on a sob, then blinked away my tears. "You are going to tell her yourself, Jacqueline Sasha Ström." I looked at Dusana. "Take care of her for me," I mouthed.

Dusana nodded once, then knelt by Jackie's side.

I turned and ran, chasing the monster who was the reason my sister was dying.

THIRTY-SEVEN

I'd been running for more than ten minutes by the time I caught sight of my quarry. I pushed harder and gained on it. Now I had to get it to stop long enough for me to kill it before it could share whatever my sister had told it.

Before my adrenaline-fueled brain came up with a plan to do that, I saw the end of the tunnel and the door that blocked it.

I was out of time.

I put on a last burst of speed, crashing into the monster's back when it skidded to a stop in front of the door and grabbed the handle. I wrapped an arm around its neck and hauled it back. I needed a dagger for situations like this, but for now, I'd have to make do with what I had.

I shifted my balance to my left leg, pulled back and down on its neck, then kicked the back of its knee as hard as I could.

It groaned and sagged but didn't hit the ground like I'd hoped. I stomped on its insole, and it fell to one knee.

That was the opening I needed. I stepped back and kicked again, this time aiming for the area where the left kidney would be on a human.

It screamed and fell forward. I drew my sword and sliced off its head.

The adrenaline drained from my system in a *whoosh*, and I wobbled with exhaustion. It was over.

I took a deep breath and exhaled slowly, then turned to jog back to where I'd left my sister. Whatever lay beyond the door could wait until I had backup.

Before I'd gone more than a few steps, the door behind me creaked. That was not a good sign.

I hesitated. If I turned around, I'd have to walk through the doorway and find out what the creature had been running toward. But if I kept going, I could pretend everything was okay and get back to Jackie's side.

A faint breeze blew by. Seconds after I registered that, I was hit with a stench so foul it made my eyes water and engaged my gag reflex.

I knew that smell.

Draugr.

I couldn't walk away from the undead soldiers now that I knew they were there. They couldn't be afforded the opportunity to escape and wreak havoc among mortals, and I had zero doubts that Hel wouldn't care if her army killed humans in their march to find and take out the Valkyries and usher in Ragnarök.

I turned reluctantly. A thin crack just big enough for one person to slip through broke the expanse of the heavy metal door. I couldn't go through that doorway alone, not without knowing how many there were. I needed backup, and the only other people who knew I was here were too busy taking care of Jackie to help me.

I mulled over the possibilities. Right now, the draugr didn't know they'd been discovered, so although I didn't want to leave them indefinitely, I had time.

I crept toward the door to peek in and get an idea of their numbers. If there were fewer than a dozen, I'd be able to clean them up myself with only a little trouble. More than that would necessitate me calling for help.

I stayed in the shadows and paused before I reached the doorway. I heard movement on the other side, but no conversation.

I slipped through the opening and stopped, dumbfounded and confused. I was in a tiny circular room, barely six feet tall and less than that in diameter. What the fuck?

I looked up. A rope ladder had been tied off to one side, and the trapdoor at the top was open. We were underground—of course there had to be a way out.

I snagged the end of the ladder and pulled it down, then climbed it, wincing each time the rope creaked.

Finally, my head was even with the floor above, and I peered cautiously over the edge.

My chest tightened and nausea surged and threatened to overwhelm me. I was at the far end of a massive warehouse—much bigger than an American football field—and the space was teeming with activity.

Draugr were packed in like sardines, and more appeared through a hole in the ground every second.

"Holy shit," I whispered, confident they wouldn't be able to hear me above the sound of milling bodies. This was definitely more than I could deal with on my own. Probably more than all the remaining Valkyries could deal with together. An airstrike might be the only thing that could get rid of this horror.

I ducked back out of view. My best option now was to rally the rest of the Valkyries to make a plan. Unfortunately, I didn't know where I was, and bringing an army of Valkyrie through the narrow tunnels wasn't a practical battle strategy.

I peeked into the room again, looking for another way out. Maybe if there was a window or door near me, I could sneak out without drawing any attention to myself. Most of the undead were focused on the center of the room, where the floor was belching forth new draugr, and it wasn't like they were independent thinkers at the best of times.

The only door I spotted would require me to skirt the draugr for at least a couple dozen feet. They might be focused on something else, but trying to get through scot-free was a risk I didn't want to take.

There were no good plans. Heading back to Jackie and recruiting help was the only plan that made even a modicum of sense.

I took a hesitant step down the wobbling ladder, freezing when it rocked beneath me. Before I could take a second step, something grabbed me by the collar and yanked me up into the room.

I squawked in surprise and flailed as my feet dangled a couple feet off the ground.

"So, you found my hideout," Hel purred, swinging me around so I'd have to look at her hideous visage. "Took you long enough. I was beginning to think I should've lured you here with cocaine and whiskey rather than your kidnapped sister."

I stiffened, both at the reference to my addictions and at the admission that she'd been the one behind Jackie's abduction.

Hel dropped me to the ground without letting go of my collar. Then she dragged me across the room and up onto a dais I hadn't seen through the ocean of draugr.

"Do you know what's going on in here?" she asked me in a casual, conversational tone.

I looked around but didn't answer. It seemed obvious—she was raising a zombie army in the middle of North Portland. But if I knew anything about the bad guys, and I really, really didn't, it was to never tell them their plans. Let them monologue themselves into a confession.

Hel shook me hard enough to chatter my teeth, but I clamped my mouth shut and tried to will the armor that'd disappeared while I'd been chasing the monster back into place. I wasn't sure if it would protect me against Hel, but it'd be better than nothing.

"My father told me everything about you," she said sweetly,

changing the subject and mood so abruptly it gave me whiplash. "I can't believe he put up with you for as long as he did. I've never heard of anyone so needy and whiney in my life. Nice job on ruining every job you ever had *and* your love life. It takes a truly incompetent moron to make that many catastrophic mistakes in just a few years."

This hurt more than the bone-rattling shakes she was still giving me, but I was not going to let her see it. Fuck Ash and everything he'd done to me. It hadn't been all him, of course. I'd been more than willing to be led down the garden path of drugs and alcohol, but he'd been right by my side, paving the way.

I smiled tightly at Hel but continued to hold my tongue. I didn't know what came after mild physical discomfort and verbal taunting, but I doubted it was mani-pedis at the day spa down the street.

At least she hadn't taken my sword yet. I didn't know if I could kill a god; so far, I hadn't had any luck with Loki aka Ash, but perhaps I'd try for decapitation and find out.

Hel dropped me, this time letting go of me altogether. I hit the concrete floor hard.

The death goddess reached down and picked up my sword. I hadn't had any wood to knock on a moment ago, and now I was paying the price.

Hel ran her thumb down the edge of my sword, slicing her skin. Black, tarry liquid oozed out and stained the blade. She held it above her head and examined it from that angle.

"I haven't seen a Valkyrie without her armor before, but then again, I never thought I'd meet a Valkyrie dumb enough to lose her sword to me. And to have it be a First? That's too precious." Hel snorted and stabbed my sword into her stomach.

My mouth dropped open as I watched. No wounds appeared this time. Instead, my sword disappeared.

"What the fuck?" I whispered.

Hel smiled at me but said nothing.

I looked around, desperate to do something, *anything*, that wasn't standing in front of the goddess who'd stolen my sword and was probably deciding on the best way to get rid of me.

She grabbed my arm, yanked me forward, and pushed my head down until a swirling pit, an inky whirlpool that stretched down to Hel's kingdom, filled my vision.

I watched in horror as a blueish, undead warrior swirled to the top and was yanked out of the hole by another draugr.

"I have countless soldiers, but raising them in such great numbers leaves them vulnerable."

She wouldn't be telling me this if she had any intention of letting me live, but I wouldn't give up hope until I was dead, so I paid attention to everything spoken and unspoken.

Her glance raked my body, and an avaricious light appeared in her eyes. "You are the solution to my little problem. Your blood, harvested at the moment of your death, will make them all but invincible. And without you to lead your precious little army, as diminished as it is, there will be no one to stand against me. Ragnarök will begin, and the world will burn."

My body betrayed the indifference I tried to maintain, and I dropped out of her hold to my knees, vomiting until my stomach was empty and my ribs ached.

Hel reached back into her abdomen and retrieved my sword. "What do you say we get started?"

She grabbed my hair, held me upright, and dropped me into a contraption that looked like a stainless-steel bathtub. Then she raised the sword, grinned madly, and plunged it downward.

THIRTY-EIGHT

I closed my eyes and waited for the blow, hoping it would at least be quick. Dying by my own sword would be embarrassing, but dead is dead in the end.

Funny, now that death was imminent, I didn't want it anymore.

I felt the movement of air that signaled the blade was in motion and tensed.

The clang of metal on metal caused my eyes to fly open. The sight in front of me pushed them wider.

My sword, wielded by Hel, was mere inches from my face, held in place by another. The blades slowly moved upward and away from my body. When it was far enough away, I rolled over the side of the tub, tumbled to the floor to get out of the way, and pushed up to standing.

I didn't have a weapon, but at least I could make my rescue easier for my savior.

Kara stood in front of me, grim-faced but barely seeming to strain against Hel. "Get out of here, Frankie," Kara grunted.

I shook my head. "I can't leave you on your own."

"You're exhausted, under-trained, and unarmed. How will any of that be useful in this situation?"

She was right, but it didn't change my mind. I didn't have a weapon and the hordes of draugr were starting to take an interest in what we were doing. But if I stayed, Kara might have a chance. If I left without her, she wouldn't make it out, nor would my sword. Neither should end up in Hel's hands.

I backed up and scanned the draugr nearest me to see if any had a weapon worth stealing.

A young-looking white man with bulging muscles that strained his *Beavis and Butthead* T-shirt stood nearest me. Although he looked like he'd be comfortable taking any comers in a fist fight, his seeming modernity meant he probably didn't have a lot of battle training. He wasn't carrying a sword, but he had a pitchfork for some reason, and the tines were shiny and sharpened.

I smiled at him, trying to dazzle him with my beauty. When that didn't work, I reached out and took the pitchfork, flipped it around, and shoved it into his body. He hit the ground without a groan. He didn't disintegrate like I'd hoped; he didn't even bleed. The draugr might not have the invincibility a properly armed and armored Valkyrie received with her blood, but their regeneration powers were still off the charts.

In a couple seconds, he was back on his feet. The mindless expression he'd sported before had morphed into a berserker rage, and he ran at me.

I flipped the pitchfork around and swung at his head like I was playing horror T-ball. His head didn't sail off like a wiffle ball as I'd hoped, but his skull collapsed inward. He staggered forward and reached out to grab me. Without my armor, he'd be able to crush me. I swung the pitchfork around again, took a step backward, and stabbed the tines up into his eyes, heaving like I was mucking out a stall. Goddess bless the hated large-animal rotation I did when getting my DVM. It hadn't all been sticking my arm in places arms shouldn't go.

The draugr's head didn't detach, but the body went flying into the crowd, laying a few others flat when it landed.

As one, the draugr in that area turned, looked at me, and took a single step forward.

Shit. Maybe tossing an undead soldier wasn't a great idea after all.

The draugr took another step.

I looked around desperately. The pitchfork might've done in a pinch, but it wasn't my weapon of choice and had already proved to be ineffective at beheading, which was one of the easiest ways to keep the draugr from chasing me, at least for a while.

Kara and Hel were dueling, Kara with the sword she'd named Kaldheim, and Hel with my blade. Seeing my weapon in the hands of the death goddess woke a rage in me I hadn't known I was capable of, and I roared my anger at her.

Hel looked at me, dropping her guard for a second. Kara took the opportunity to run her sword across Hel's abdomen, which had no effect except to increase the goddess's stench and dribble out a few more intestines. Kara followed it up with another, higher swipe that would've removed Hel's head if she hadn't dodged.

I dashed forward to grab my sword while she was distracted, but the goddess whipped around and nearly impaled me with it. I ducked under the blade and reached forward to grab her wrist and twist until she dropped it.

Instead, my hand penetrated her abdomen, squishing through her rotting internal organs and scraping along her rib cage. From the inside.

My gorge rose, and it was all I could do not to vomit on her, not that it would've made anything grosser. I withdrew my hand, but as I did so, I felt something harder than guts and longer than rib bones. I gripped it before I had time to think about what it might be and pulled.

My hand grasped a long dagger as it squelched out of Hel's abdomen.

"Nooooo!" Hel screamed. "You cannot have that!"

She spun around and screamed in a voice like the bass turned up high enough to vibrate my liver. "Kill her!"

She tried to make good on her own order by swinging my sword at me.

I stared at her, then raised her blade to deflect the larger weapon. "I am a fucking Valkyrie, and you cannot take me down."

I felt a crawling sensation, and again supernatural armor designed by Freyja herself protected me.

I extended the dagger and nicked Hel's arm with it. Instantly, the draugr who'd started toward me at Hel's order pivoted to stare at her.

"You fucking bitch," she said to me coldly. "I will kill you for this."

"I thought you were gonna kill me anyway. If you're going to threaten me, you might want to up your game," I said in a cocky tone I barely managed to sustain.

"I will kill your family, your stupid Guide, and every last Valkyrie. And then I will butcher your sister's baby right in front of you. Finally, I will take you."

Okay. She'd done a pretty good job of upping the stakes. But still. "Good luck with that, Hel. First you have to survive them." I spun the blade, pointing it at the draugr that were closing in on her now.

She screamed, swung my sword around, and beheaded the first row of undead.

Hel dropped her sword arm and stared out at her army of draugr. Kara took a step toward me, and I slid sideways and reached out my hand so she could step us out of here. But before our hands met, Hel raised my sword again and swung it through the air.

I ducked under it and lunged forward to grab Kara.

She sagged to the ground, nearly pulling me with her.

I stared at her headless body, Hel's dagger hung limp in my suddenly nerveless hand.

Kara lay at my feet, and I watched her armor dissolve away from her lifeless body. I looked up and met Hel's eyes, then pointed her dagger at her.

"For that, you will pay."

"You were going to kill me anyway," she mocked. "You're going to have to up the threat level for this to mean anything."

I picked up Kara's sword and shifted Hel's dagger to my left hand. I advanced on the death goddess. A helm formed on my head, and my armor thickened. A mail collar formed around my neck.

My sword sparked. Unfortunately, Hel still held it.

She startled, staring at my blade with suspicious anger.

"Every torture you've undergone since your birth will pale in comparison to what I'm going to do to you. You had a chance to side with the light, to fight against the gods who seek to bring Ragnarök out of boredom, but you chose this path. And now, not only will you have to live with your choice, you get to die with it."

She stumbled backward into the arms of the advancing draugr.

She screamed again. "Garmr!"

A giant dog, way bigger than I could've ever imagined, crashed through the wall, picked her up in his mouth, and leapt through the ceiling, my sword still in her grasp.

Metal, insulation, and debris crashed to the floor, pinning several draugr. The uncrushed undead slowly and mindlessly marched through the hole Garmr had made and into the night. The Daimler building visible through the ranks of the draugr told me where we were. Once again, we were on fucking Swan Island.

I sank to the floor, cradling Kara's body. I couldn't stop them, and I couldn't help Kara.

I couldn't save my sister.

I bent my head and cried for Kara, for Jackie, and for myself.

THIRTY-NINE

It might have been minutes, or it could've been hours before Archibald head-butted my knee, and I came to my senses again.

It was raining, and I was soaked through.

Archibald crawled into my lap and curled up. "Your father and Dusana will be here in a couple minutes to take you and Kara home."

"I failed her," I whispered to my cat. "I've failed everyone."

He stretched up and bumped his nose against mine. "You didn't. You saved your aunt and your sister. You prevented Hel's minions from gaining knowledge of the Aerie, and you have Hel's knife, Famine. Kara is just as much to blame as you—maybe more so. She shouldn't have fought. She should've grabbed you and stepped out of there. She was too confident in her ability to face Hel and a horde of undead. She should've known better, and she died because of her hubris."

I heard what he was saying, but I couldn't agree with him. I shook my head. "She tried to save me, to give me a chance to get away. Instead, I lost my sword, distracted Kara at a crucial moment, and was too slow to save her when it counted."

Tears trickled down my face, but they didn't bring insensibility with them this time. I wrapped my arms around Archibald and held him close. He didn't protest, even though I knew he didn't like being squeezed like this. Then some of the words he'd uttered, almost as a throwaway, penetrated my grief fog.

"Did you say I saved my sister?"

Sunlight pierced my brain when I opened my eyes. I blinked several times to clear my vision and figure out where I was. I hadn't woken up so uncertain as to my location in months, and a moment of panic curdled my stomach. Too much whiskey and a boatload of cocaine had caused my last blackout and morning-after confusion.

I breathed deeply. No pounding headache or uncontrollable nausea. Not a hangover then.

I pushed myself to a sitting position and looked around. I was in my room at my parents' house, and from the light streaming through my window, I guessed it was late morning at the earliest.

A glass of orange juice, condensation dripping down the sides, sat on my night table, a Smurf glass full of sparkling water next to it. Thirst burned my throat. I grabbed the Smurf glass and gulped the contents down, then did the same with the OJ. As soon as both beverages were gone, two sensations penetrated my brain fog, both pushing me toward the bathroom.

After peeing, I turned on the shower. I stunk. A quick glance in the mirror showed that someone had at least cleaned me off before dumping me in bed, but the stench of the tunnels, of the draugr, of death, clung to me.

It took four cycles of rinse and repeat and fifteen minutes of scrubbing until my skin tingled to feel clean again.

I dressed in a pair of soft yoga pants, a cotton bralette, and a dark-green hoodie that looked like a skinned muppet. After pushing my feet into a pair of faux-fur-lined slippers, I ventured forth.

The house, lately awash with the chatter and energy of a dozen and more Valkyries, was quiet. The soft murmur of conversation, the only human noise I could discern, drifted out from the kitchen.

I padded forward, the thought of food had hunger gnawing at my stomach. I entered the kitchen in time for my stomach to yowl in protest of missing the pizza I'd ordered with Dusana the evening before and not being able to do anything about it for nearly twenty-four hours.

Three people turned toward me as my hunger announced my arrival.

Dad, Dusana, and Devin looked at me. Lenore was asleep in Dad's arms, so I forgave her the inattention.

Dusana was on her feet and at my side in an instant. "How are you? Are you okay? Do you need anything?"

"Jackie?" I rasped.

"She's at Legacy in Portland. Critical but stable. Lena knew the antidote." Dad's words were robotic, and the grey pallor to his skin and the bags under eyes did more to indicate the lack of sleep than anything else could have. "Becky's with her, as is your mom."

I sagged into a chair in relief.

The microwave dinged, and he pulled out a plate of lasagna and set it and a fork in front of me.

"Kara?" I whispered.

Dusana shook her head. "You already know. Her funeral is tomorrow."

Tears pricked the corners of my eyes. Another Valkyrie gone. Another life lost.

"This has to stop." Of course it did. What a stupid thing to say. No one with any compassion or sense would argue otherwise.

"Can you stop it?" Dad asked. "Stop it before you're lost? Before your mother dies?"

I wanted to jump in to say, "Yes! Of course!" But I paused. My dad needed a real answer, not an empty promise. I picked up my fork and took a bite of lasagna, chewing while I considered.

"I think so," I finally said. "But Hel has my sword, and we've lost too many in the last few weeks. I don't know what to do, and I need to figure it out. I don't want to lead, but apparently, I have no choice. And if I'm going to be forced into this position, I need to do it right." I sighed. "The problem is, I don't know how. I've never managed so much as a single employee, much less an army of supernatural shield maidens. What do I do, Daddy?"

Dad handed Lenore to Dusana, who looked utterly terrified to be holding a baby. He slid his chair over to me and wrapped me in his arms. "You will do what you have always done. Your best."

A bitter laugh escaped me before I could stop it. "I've always done my best? You have to be kidding. I spent ten years hiding from you after a failed suicide attempt, and the last three years spiraling my life down the toilet with drugs and alcohol. I ended up in a bar a week ago, and seeing John there was the only thing that stopped me from ordering a drink. I am the last person anyone could accuse of always doing their best."

Dad squeezed me tighter. "Doing your best isn't always fairytale perfect. Sometimes, it's surviving for another day. Everyone struggles with things almost too big to handle, but what matters is perseverance, not perfection."

I wanted to believe him as much as he seemed to believe in me, but he didn't know the truth. No one did. I closed my eyes and whispered, "I am not okay."

"You don't have to be okay all the time. There's been a lot of stress and grief lately. But if your baseline is depression, you need to find a psychiatrist and switch your meds," Devin said. "Sadness in the face of what you've gone through is normal, but it's okay to expect to be happy most of the time."

"Are you?" I challenged him, looking up from where I'd buried my face in my dad's shoulder.

He shrugged. "Yeah, usually. I have a great life, a fantastic partner, and her family is amazing. I like my job. I have good friends, and I can watch the sun rise over Mt. Hood almost every day. Sometimes

I'm really happy, and sometimes I'm really, really sad. But I am usually content, and I smile more than I don't. That should not be an unrealistic state of being."

"Okay. When all this"—I waved my hands, trying to encompass the events of the last few weeks—"is over, I will find a shrink."

"No," Dad said. "If you wait for a break in events, it'll be too long, and you'll not be at your best, something you need to be if you're going to save the world."

I blanched. My shoulders crept up around my ears, and heat flared on my face. "What if I just concentrate on saving myself and the Valkyries first?" I whispered.

Dad dropped a kiss on the top of my head, then unwound his arms from around my body. "That sounds like an excellent place to start. I'll make some phone calls and find a psychiatrist who has an opening."

"Good luck," Devin muttered.

Dad shot him a quelling look. "I don't need luck. I will have a short list by the end of the day tomorrow."

Dad took Lenore back from Dusana and left the kitchen. Devin made some polite noises that didn't really register and walked away, leaving me alone with Dusana.

I finished my lasagna, trying to appreciate the taste of it instead of dwelling on the panic threatening me every time I thought of my sister, Kara, and leading a bunch of Valkyries into battle to save the world.

I mechanically rinsed my empty plate and put it in the dishwasher. When I turned around, Dusana stood behind me. I didn't want to meet her eyes, didn't want to see the judgment that I knew would be there.

Dusana grabbed my hand. "Let's go for a walk. Fresh air and sunshine will be good for you, and maybe a change of pace will get your brain moving so you can come up with a plan to stem the tide of Valkyrie deaths."

I let her pull me to my feet and followed her out the door.

We walked in silence for a few moments. The air was cool but not yet crisp. The deciduous trees that were interspersed within the conifers had begun to change color, and the air smelled of pine and autumn. The sky was a brilliant blue, with nary a cloud in sight.

We rounded a bend, and Mt. Hood towered in front of us, perfectly framed by the trees on either side of the road.

I stopped in awe. "That is so beautiful."

"It really is. I miss the desert sometimes, since Percy and I spent most of our time in New Mexico and Arizona when we were tied to Route 66. But this lush greenness and the mountains are awe-inspiring. Thank you for letting me stay with you." Dusana glanced at me, a soft smile on her face.

"Thank you for coming," I replied. "And thanks for getting me out of the house. I needed this break."

She slipped an arm around me and side-hugged me gently. "You're not alone in this. In addition to me, you have your family, a host of Valkyries, your Aunt Lena..."

"And me," Archibald said from my feet.

I crouched beside him, sliding out of Dusana's embrace that'd felt way too right for this stage in my life. "Thank you, Archibald."

"For what?" He head-butted my hand until I scratched between his ears.

"For staying with me after Kara..." I choked on the words. "Until Dad and Dusana showed up."

He pushed his head harder into my hand. "That's my job. I'm your Guide *and* your companion."

"And my friend." I scooped him into my arms. "And I think I have an idea. Let's go back and gather the troops."

CHAPTER

FORTY

The only room large enough for the full contingent of remaining Valkyries, both past and present, as well as our other allies, was the basement.

I stood in the center of the room while I waited for everyone to find seats and get settled and tried not to think about all the training sessions I'd gone through with Kara in this room. That was over. She was gone, and I had to hold back my grief.

Once the noise of scraping chairs and broken murmurs of conversation stopped, I looked up and spun slowly around and made eye contact with every person in the room. I thought about my armor, about the way it felt on my body, about how much it made me feel like a true Valkyrie. I willed it to appear.

It didn't.

Shit.

I closed my eyes and took a deep breath. I didn't need the armor. I was a Valkyrie with or without it, just like I didn't need a flying horse, or my sword or...

Nope. Not going down that path. I was a Valkyrie.

"Kara. Göndul. Regan. Prima. Arya. Mathilda. Agnes. Seta."

253

Small gasps and quiet sniffles accompanied the names of the dead.

"Of the twenty-four of us who make a full contingent, only fourteen are left." I took a deep breath. "And it's not going to be enough, especially since not all of us are trained."

"Some inspirational speech," Hope muttered from the corner.

I turned to her and stared directly into her eyes. "I'm not trying to be inspirational. What would that even look like, Hope? People have died. Our *sisters* died. And it won't stop if we don't do something different. We cannot hide out here and stay safe. It would do the world, Portland specifically right now, a disservice. None of you saw what I did in that warehouse. There were countless draugr, and more being pulled from the earth every second. Hel may have cleared out of there, but you have to know that she has already found somewhere else to keep pulling legions of the dead to form an army."

Zofia raised her hand, and I nodded at her. "I didn't see the draugr Frankie's talking about, but Hel has new minions as well. You all know the First's younger sister is in the hospital in Portland, where she's still unconscious after what she underwent during her abduction. But you might not know that the injury that nearly took her life was the bite of one of the venomous children of Ymir. It is lucky for her, for all of us, that Lena knew of an antidote that would work. We killed a half dozen of them, but there will be more."

One of the younger Valkyries, a new one whose name I hadn't stored yet, said, "What are we supposed to do? Someone's trying to kill us all and Portland is being overrun by monsters. We can't stop it, and we're all going to die." A note of hysteria pushed her voice up several registers while she spoke.

"No." My voice echoed in the room. "We are not going to die. I will not lose another one of you to assassins or overwhelming odds. And I won't leave the ordinary humans in Portland to be butchered by armies of the undead." I picked up the sheath at my feet and pulled out the long dagger I'd stolen from Hel's chest cavity. The accompanying noise, like a fork scraping across a ceramic plate, made me shudder, and from the "ughs" and other noises around the room, I wasn't the only one who hated the sound.

"Hel stole my sword." Soft gasps of horror greeted my statement. No one had known except for my parents.

"How can you even pretend you're the First?" Hope challenged. "You don't have armor, your mount has not chosen you, and now you don't even have your Valkyrie sword."

My mouth pressed into a thin line. I was getting really tired of Hope, even though she hadn't said anything incorrect or unexpected. "I have Hel's weapon, and I have a plan."

FORTY-ONE

The wind whipping my hair around my face was colder on the coast than it'd been near my parents' house, and it carried with it the smell of rain and ocean spray. Waves broke and crashed on the craggy rocks below me.

The lighthouse where we'd said goodbye to too many Valkyries in the last week was barely visible in the distance, and soon the grey of dusk and storm would hide it from my view.

I was alone, sitting on the rocky cliff, and staring out to sea. The others were already at the lighthouse, preparing for Kara's funeral. Dad and Becky had stayed in Portland so they could be with Jackie and take care of Lenore—John was still in the hospital for his head injury—but everyone else who'd become part of our extended family was here to celebrate and mourn.

Two birds dived and swooped in the distance, the last rays of visible sunlight occasionally glinting off their beaks. They didn't move like raptors, and they weren't seagulls. A year ago, I would've said they were crows. But now I knew better.

I pretended I hadn't noticed them and drew Hel's weapon, Famine, from the makeshift sheath I kept it in. The screeching noise was weaker this time, or else I was getting used to it, but the malevolent aura it exuded when air hit the blade hadn't lessened one bit. This dagger hated me. Hated all living things. It didn't want to kill though. It wanted suffering; it starved for it.

The birds flew closer. I glanced at them, as a person would if two big-ass black birds came within a stone's throw, then forced myself to dismiss them.

I set the dagger on the ground in front of me and crossed my arms in front of my chest, shivering against the wind and wishing I'd worn more than just my hoodie.

Archibald appeared next to me and crawled into my lap. "What's wrong, First?" he asked, his voice pitched louder than usual.

I shook my head. "Everything. There are too few Valkyries to fight against the draugr Hel's released in Portland, especially now that she has my sword. She said it'd make her undead army invincible, and I don't know what effect it'll have on her."

"Do you think she'll try to take the throne, or is she still focused on Ragnarök?"

"I only wish I knew. Either way, I'm going to have to fight her. But if she's changing course from bringing about the end of the world to making a power grab, that might make things easier." I scratched Archibald behind his ears. "If I knew how to use her stupid knife, that might make things simpler as well. I know there's more to it than stabbing, but I don't know how to activate it. Having a magic dagger in battle would be great, but not if it I can't access its true power."

"What are you going to do?" Archibald asked, curling into an even tighter ball in my lap.

I sighed. "I don't know. I'm supposed to lead, but no one will follow. Without my sword, my armor, or my steed, I'm a Valkyrie in name only. I'm not even at Kara's funeral."

It didn't take any acting skills to infuse dejection and hopelessness into my voice. The plan I'd laid out to the Valkyries was simple, put no one but me at risk, and still there'd been arguments. It wasn't even the objection my mother had brought forth, the potential danger to me, that caused the dissent. No, they just worried about whether I was fit to make plans, whether or not it was my fault Kara died—that was Hope—and if I shouldn't let the actual planning be taken over by some of the more experienced Valkyries until I got the hang of it.

In the end, I'd overruled them all, and here I was.

Someone had to be watching us. Between Jackie's abduction and the way the new Valkyries had been scattered in the Pacific Northwest to draw us out on rescue missions, that much was obvious. No one could see past the wards around my mother's house, but I hadn't been careful to stay within them when I was running, and based on the squirming and uncomfortable looks I'd gotten last night when I'd asked, the others hadn't always been circumspect, either.

No one would notice a pair of ravens hiding in the shadows on high tree branches, but that didn't go far enough to explain how someone had killed seven Valkyrie—six in almost a single moment. But it did maybe shed a little light on how our movements were being tracked.

The ravens wheeled out of sight. I stood, holding Famine in a casual grip, and waited.

Thirty minutes later, my shoulders slumped. I'd been so sure that a sad, pathetic loser Valkyrie would've made an excellent target, and that I could prove how our actions were being monitored. I'd been wrong. Again.

Sighing, I pulled my flashlight from my belt and started back up the path to where I'd left my dad's car. I had twenty minutes to get to the dreaded helipad for the white-knuckle trip to the lighthouse.

The leaves crunched satisfyingly under my feet, and I scuffed my shoes through them, throwing them into the air. The cracking of a branch yanked me to a stop. Footsteps continued for a second longer.

I drew Famine from its sheath and continued down the path. The steps started again, drawing closer with each stride.

When I judged the distance between me and my stalker to be less than the length of the blade, I whipped around and slashed it across my follower's chest.

A nondescript white man dressed in tan hiking pants, a beige flannel shirt under a khaki-colored jacket, and brown hiking boots stood, mouth open in a silent scream and hands clasped to his chest. Blood leaked from under his fingers.

Fuck. A human. I'd just stabbed a hiker.

I dropped the blade and started forward to render first aid before calling 911. But the minute the dagger hit the ground, the person in front of me blurred and shifted into a familiar figure.

"Ash." I squatted and picked up the dagger before he could. "Or should I call you Loki? Have you come to kill me? That didn't work out for you so well last time."

He twisted his lips into the smug, sneering smile I hated. "You lost your sword. You were an easy target this time."

"I have your daughter's blade though." I pointed it at him.

He yawned. "You really think it has the power to hurt me? It is forged from my blood and bone, and I gifted it to her on the occasion of her quinceñera."

I rolled my eyes. I couldn't help it. "Either attack me or get out of here. I don't have time for your bullshit."

"I merely wanted to see if the rumors I'd heard were true, and it looks like they are. You're failing—again. You can't manifest your armor. You have no steed to fly you into battle. And you don't have your Valkyrie sword. From the looks of it, you don't have the trust of the people you're supposed to be bossing around, either. You are weak. You've always been weak."

I smiled at him and reminded myself that he no longer had the power to hurt me.

Loki took a step back and glared at me. "Why do you have to be so very boring? I want a challenge, and you've never presented one. I thought it would be fun to destroy your mind and body before you came into your power, but it was too easy. And then I thought driving you mad after you became a Valkyrie would be more satisfying, but you escaped me. This is not the satisfaction I deserve." He produced a blade, although I didn't see where it'd come from. Perhaps he carried his inside his body the way Hel did. "I cannot kill you now, and your sisters are out of reach for the time being."

Loki showing up had been the pivotal part of my strategy. His refusal to fight with me because I was boring had not entered my plans. "You'd better come for me now. I nearly beat you last time. If you wait, I'll be even more skilled. It won't even be a contest." I darted forward, blade outstretched.

He stepped out of reach and laughed. "Pull yourself together, babe. Get stronger. And once you do, keep an eye out for me, because I am watching you, and I will come for you."

Loki melted back into the forest, his threat lingering in the air.

I turned and headed back to the car. My plan had failed, and I had to return to the Valkyries without proof I could lead them.

Once again, I had nothing.

EPILOGUE

Lena and I knelt in front of the wooden boat that held Kara's body, which was draped with a white sheet. We hadn't found her head in the warehouse, and I shuddered to think what might've become of it.

I laid the sword on the front of her body, then closed my eyes.

"She died for me," I said to Lena. "Why would she do that?"

Lena laughed harshly. "Kara was my best friend for over three thousand years. She was brave, loyal, a brilliant swordswoman, and an excellent strategist."

The lump that'd been in my throat for the last two days increased as more guilt surged to marry with the grief. "I'm sorry."

Lena continued as if I hadn't spoken. "She was also stubborn, hubristic, and too ready to throw herself into situations that she shouldn't have. This was not the first time she took on an army with no backup to save a young Valkyrie. It was just the last." Tears streaked down her face. "Do not feel guilty because you were present at her death. She would've done the same for any of us."

Lena rose to her feet and picked up the bundle of kindling behind her. She arranged it around Kara's body and turned to face the rest of the mourners who stood in a half circle behind us. Every Valkyrie was clad in her full armor, and they all—both past and present—held their swords.

"Today we say goodbye to a legend among Valkyries," Lena said. "We mourn her now, but we will always remember her quick wit, her sharp blade, and her willingness to walk through fire for any of us."

The wind gusted off the ocean, misting us with salt water that matched our tears.

The Valkyries walked to the shore. Six horses alit behind them and another landed next to Kara's boat. He bent his neck gracefully and whickered softly. Then he leapt into the air and circled the lighthouse twice.

Lena took a torch from one of the retired Valkyries and lit the kindling. A burst of wind threatened to blow it out, but the flame quickly strengthened.

Lena and I bent and pushed the boat out to sea. Kara's mount followed it as it disappeared into the night.

When I turned around to face the Valkyries again, each of them stood with their horse, and one came forward to nuzzle Lena. Joy and wonder lit the faces of the new Valkyries, and their armor gleamed in the torchlight.

"We've been chosen," Sydjea said.

Hope's face glowed with awe. "I could never have imagined this."

Mom nodded, a wide smile on her face. "Our Valkyries have their battle steeds. Even from an event this sad, we can find joy." She smiled at the newly chosen, all of whom had their arms draped around their pegasi's necks.

Mom looked at me. She didn't have to say anything. No one did. Out of all the Valkyries there, I was the only one who hadn't been chosen, and the only one not clad in gleaming armor.

"It will happen," Lena whispered to me, low enough that no one else could hear. "Have patience and faith."

"What if it doesn't?"

"Then something has gone very, very wrong, and the prophecies can no longer be trusted," she replied, her voice less confident than it'd been a moment before.

A shiver unrelated to the cold ocean wind raced over my body. "What would that mean for us?"

Lena turned to look at me, fear present in her gaze, and said, "There may be no way to stop Ragnarök, and we'll have to stand by and watch the world burn around us."

Keep reading for an excerpt from Chapter One of Waking the Fire, or preorder now!

WANT MORE AMY CISSELL?

And why wouldn't you?

Love it, hate it, somewhere in between? Please leave a review for **Calling the Blood** at Goodreads, Bookbub, or your favorite online retailer.

Links to all retails sites are at:
https://books2read.com/callingtheblood

Reviews are always appreciated & allow me to keep writing what you love!

Sign up for Cissell's Epistles at https://amycissell.com for new release updates, exclusive content, and a bevy of book recommendations! (You'll also get to choose a free book as a thank you for hanging out!)

Come hang out in my Facebook Reader Group - the Amyzonians can always use another shenaniganator. (It's a word. Promise.)

https://www.facebook.com/groups/amycissellauthor/

Join my patreon for early access to books, free copies of my digital books, free paperbacks, and access to my entire back catalog!
https://www.patreon.com/ACissellWrites

WAKING THE FIRE

GHOSTS OF VALHALLA BOOK THREE, CHAPTER ONE

The stench of rotting flesh buffeted my senses. I gagged but kept what little stomach contents I had left where they belonged.

I swiped my forearm over my face to push back my hair and wipe the dripping sweat. Salt stung my eyes and burned in a dozen small cuts. I adjusted my borrowed sword in my hand and twisted around, narrowly avoiding a rusty machete aimed at my head.

I struck, neatly disarming the draugr. The arm in question dropped to floor, joining piles of limbs, bodies, and heads. Another took his place. I decapitated her, and her head sailed across the enormous, windowless room. I ran my sword through her heart, but she didn't drop until I sliced off her left leg below the knee.

More came, an unending undead stream of stinking zombies appearing in an abandoned warehouse on Swan Island in Portland, Oregon. There were dozens more than we'd expected, and even with the legitimate kills by my sister Valkyries, they draugr still outnumbered us by at least ten to one, maybe more.

"Riley! Report!" I screamed over the melee. I'd led nine Valkyries into this mess, and regardless of what we left behind, I would get them all out.

For a second, I heard nothing, and fear tightened my chest.

"Ready to get the fuck out of here," Riley yelled. "We're making zero headway."

"Hope? Deborah?"

Deborah replied with a string of expletives that made her agreement with Riley perfectly clear.

Hope's reply reinforced everything she'd said to me or about me during the last two months since we'd watched our sword teacher's funeral boat drift out to sea. "In over your head? How many Valkyries will you get killed on this stupid adventure?"

I saw red, and it wasn't blood from the blow on my head I'd taken earlier. Then I forced my breath to slow. Deborah, Riley, and Hope were the strongest fighters of our generation of Valkyries. They coordinated their squads of three each, and I oversaw the whole group.

Behind me, Lena and Zofia, senior Valkyries, watched and waited. They'd wade in if they thought the danger to us overwhelmed the lesson of fighting draugr with little credible intelligence, but their role was to observe and critique. As if that didn't make a deadly battle even more fraught.

"Begin retreat formation A!" My mother, a retired Valkyrie, Aunt Lena, the oldest living Valkyrie, and Zofia, who was about my mom's age but still on active duty, had stepped in when Kara died to save my life. Lena imparted me battle tactics and strategy, Zofia took over weapons training—what she could do with a sword was nothing short of artistry—and Mom taught me leadership. Or at least she tried. I was a pretty hopeless case.

However, I had learned one thing. Never, ever count on Plan A. Best not count on Plan B, either. Plan A had been to destroy the draugr and get home in time for mashed potatoes and side dishes. That had been discarded as soon as we arrived at the place our scout had told us about. The warehouse was on the western edge of the industrial Swan Island jutting into the Willamette River. Large holes gaped in the ceiling, the walls inside and out were tagged, and bird shit covered just about every surface.

There was no clear entry point into the warehouse. No roiling hole spitting up Hel's soldiers from the underworld she ruled. No secret trapdoors. They just kept appearing. So now I needed to get my people out and execute Plan D.

I stepped into the fray, concentrating more on removing limbs than heads. Killing the undead is a tricky deal in the best of times, but with Hel, the goddess of the underworld and creator of the draugr, close, the zombies regenerated quickly. If one lost a head, it would search the ground until it found one, shove it back on, and keep fighting. Same with any other limb. The one thing that worked in our favor was that they weren't terribly discerning about which body part they put on, and after a while, they were a jumble of limbs, torsos, and heads that didn't fit together. It put the "shamble" in "shambling horde," and it slowed them down enough to deliver the killing blow.

The only way to kill a draugr was to remove its head and penetrate its heart with a Valkyrie blade. And since I didn't have one of those anymore, my role was to slow them down and let the teams of three coordinate the actual takedowns.

Riley and Deborah and their squads reached me. Their Valkyrie armor, which shone like a beacon when clean, was covered with gore.

I looked to my left. Hope and her team were still on the other side of the room.

"Hope! Retreat!" I yelled.

She paused long enough to give me the finger.

I drew a breath and clenched my teeth. She challenged me at every turn, not only ignoring my orders but actively defying me.

I almost looked back at Lena and Zofia but stopped myself. If I asked them to reinforce my authority, that meant I had none.

"Why don't you put on your armor, grab your sword, and join the real fighters over here where the action is instead of hanging back and hamstringing zombies?" Hope called.

A couple of the Valkyries near me snickered. I glared at them, which shut them up, but did nothing to dampen their amusement. A quick look at Riley and Deborah proved they weren't laughing at me, but neither were they about to jump to my defense.

"Retreat to Lena and Zofia and hold there. Protect them and yourselves, but do not be lured into attacking again. Defense only." I paused to meet Riley's and Deborah's eyes and garner their acquiescence. Assured that they, at least, would follow orders, I headed back into the fight. By the time I reached Hope and her group, I had a dozen new slices on my unprotected arms and torso and had beheaded five more draugr.

"Nice of you to join us, First," Hope said. Her gleaming helmet disappeared, revealing her [description].

"I called retreat," I ground out. A draugr with mismatched legs, one arm, and a head that hadn't fully reattached stumbled toward us. I beheaded it, and before it fell, Hope thrust her blade into its chest. The faint spark of life that animated it flared and disappeared.

"I heard," Hope replied coolly. Her helmet covered her once again. She spun gracefully, crouched low, and kicked the legs out from under another draugr. It crashed to the ground. I disemboweled it. While it scrambled to shove its guts back into its body, Hope decapitated it and finished the job.

"So retreat," I barked. I hid the wince my harsh command caused me. I did not want to lead. My idea of leadership was imparting a team goal and deadline and letting everyone get there in their own way. Mom had impressed on me that was not a winning battle strategy.

"Make me," Hope snarled. She took off the head of a draugr with a swing that looked more like a casual tennis lob than a sword strike.

I ground my teeth. "There are too many to keep fighting like this. Maybe you're not tired yet, but you will tire before they disappear.

We discussed the plans. You know what to do. Why aren't you doing it?"

"Because you're wrong." She flicked a piece of rotting skin off her arm. It hit my unarmored chest.

It might be my imagination, but I thought one of the other Valkyries—Aster, I thought from the pale grey eyes visible beneath her helm—gasped at that.

I turned my head, slashed out to behead another, and tried to count how many remained. I gave up at forty.

"Maybe I'm wrong, but it doesn't fucking matter right now. Aster and Sydjea, retreat back to the others. Hope and I are right behind you." I gave them my hardest stare. It wasn't that hard, but it looked like it would be enough.

"Stop!" Hope said.

Sydjea and Aster halted. This was so stupid. Hope was going to get us all killed.

"Valkyries, I am the First, and you will obey me," I said. Anger rolled over me, and with it the feeling of completeness.

My Valkyrie armor appeared, although without a helmet.

"Yes, First," Aster squeaked. She and Sydjea took off, hacking their way back to the others.

I jabbed my borrowed sword at Hope, enough to pull her attention to me for a second, but not long enough to completely distract her and put us both in danger. "You will retreat with me now. Everything is set for Plan D. If you've forgotten what that is, let me know."

Hope scoffed. "Whatever. I'm coming."

I walked back to the others, slicing limbs and cutting off heads as I made my way there. Every couple steps, a draugr's life spark would flare and die as Hope took out the headless undead I left for her.

We finally got to the doorway. The eight Valkyries I commanded there were more than holding their own, and although Lena and Zofia had their swords out and ready, they weren't using them.

"Out!" I commanded.

I don't know if it was the authority in my voice or the armor that still hadn't disappeared, but everyone walked through the door as if I'd lit their asses on fire.

Which is more or less what I was about to do.

"Now!" I screamed.

A half dozen former Valkyries lifted their bows and shot flaming arrows into the warehouse. Another volley. And a third. A few draugr headed toward the still open door but were cut down by my warriors before they took more than a couple steps.

After the fourth volley, the interior of the warehouse caught, and the building roared into an inferno.

Seconds later, the flames reached the explosives set around the interior perimeter, and the warehouse exploded.

PREORDER TODAY! Waking the Fire will be released on June 27, 2024.

THE CARDINAL GATE

AN ELEANOR MORGAN FANTASY
ADVENTURE #1

I am faced with an impossible choice: destroy the world of my birth or the world I call home?

I was minding my own business, giving Hedge Antilles—my laurel hedge big enough to warrant its own name—a much-needed trim when bam! Vampire! At least that's what he called himself, and he did have pointy fang, try to bite my neck, and died with a stake to the heart. He also called me a fairy before he bit it—literally and figuratively.

Now I'm in a race I don't quite understand to open gates I'm not entirely sure should be opened to save the Fae Realm, the home I don't remember. Finn—up until now, my best friend—is guiding me on this quest, but we both need some personal growth if we're gonna make things work. He needs to get over the hope that I'll ever be in love with him, and I need to get over the fact that he deliberately infiltrated my life by order of my absent Fae father.

Not everything on this whirlwind quest is bad, though—Isaac, Mr. Tall, Dark, and Handsome werewolf, is along for the ride (that's what she said...). There are too many secrets to sort out, and I feel like I'm the only one playing this thing straight.

275

Everyone seems to think I'm going to shatter this world, but only some believe I'll save it. Am I trusting the right people, or will my faith in my friends be the straw that destroys it all?

Meet Eleanor Morgan as she begins her quest to open the gates between Earth & the Fae Plane. Come for the magic, stay for the puns.

The Eleanor Morgan Fantasy Adventure series is a contemporary/urban fantasy series with adult themes (read: explicit naked times and a fair amount of violence). It is a complete series at seven full-length novels.

https://books2read.com/cardinalgate

ACKNOWLEDGMENTS

I'm grateful to my editor Andrea at Two Birds Author Services and my proofreader Christopher Barnes for their feedback, plot hole discoveries, and comma rehabilitation.

My favorite local coffeeshop and wine bar kept me going in the mornings and evenings respectively, and I'm not sure I would've gotten through this book without frequent libations.

Chris - thank you for encouraging me, even when I quit writing about 30 times each book. I'm glad I married you and can't wait to visit you in Portugal!

Of course, no acknowledgment section would be complete without mentioning my amazing daughter Liana. She's my regular coffeeshop writing companion, brainstorming partner, and graphic design consultant. Love you to the ends of the universe, then through a wormhole to a parallel universe. And back.

MAGIC & MAYHEM AT THE END OF THE WORLD

Amy Cissell is a USA Today Bestselling Author of urban fantasy and paranormal romance novels. She lives in Portland, OR with her husband, her haunted house-obsessed daughter, their two cats, and the murder of crows she's conspiring to turn into her vengeful army.

When she's not working or writing, she's sleeping because that's all she has time to do! There are few things Amy loves more than a well-timed pun, a good book, a glass of wine, and making calf eyes at Portugal when she thinks no one's looking.

Although she reads anything and everything, her first love has always been fantasy. Eleven-year-old Amy discovered fantasy when she 'borrowed' her father's copy of The Hobbit and an enduring love affair (mostly with dragons) was born.

facebook.com/acissellwrites

instagram.com/acissellwrites

bookbub.com/authors/amy-cissell

goodreads.com/acissellwrites

tiktok.com/@acissellwrites

patreon.com/ACissellWrites

Also by Amy Cissell

Contemporary/Urban Fantasy

Ghosts of Valhalla

Haunting the Route

Choosing the Slain (December 2023)

Calling the Blood (2024)

Waking the Fire (2024)

Raising the Dead (2025)

Seeking the Frost

Breaking the World

Drawing the Blade

Burning the Gods

Riding the Storm

An Eleanor Morgan Fantasy Adventure

(complete series)

The Cardinal Gate (February 2017)

The Waning Moon (June 2017)

The Ruby Blade (October 2017)

The Broken World (March 2018)

The Lost Child (June 2019)

The Iron River (May 2020)

The Dark Throne (February 2021)

Box Sets (ebook only)

Eleanor Morgan Books 1-4

Eleanor Morgan Books 5-7

Paranormal Women's Fiction

Vamps in the Vineyard

Stakes and Stems: A Prequel Novella (September 2022)

Here to Slay (September 2022)

Slay Bells Ring: A Holiday Novella (January 2023)

Midlife Magic in Eden Valley

(complete series)

Raising a Demon (June 2021)

Devil and the Deep, Blue Lake (September 2021)

Valley of Angels (November 2021)

Guardian of Eden (February 2022)

Eden Valley World Novellas (ebook only)

Match Made in Hell (June 2021)

Hell's Bells (December 2021)

Fall From Grace (January 2022)

Devil May Care (February 2022)

Box Sets (ebook only)

Midlife Magic in Eden Valley (Collection One)

Midlife Magic in Eden Valley (Collection Two)

Paranormal Romance

Psychics of Oracle Bay

Not in the Cards (October 2018)

First Hand Knowledge (November 2018)

Wing and a Prayer (January 2019)

Belle of the Ball (December 2019)

Hell and High Water (June 2022)

Tempest in a Teapot (April 2023)

Elements of Surprise (April 2023)

Dead Giveaway (2024)

Bad to the Bones

Shoot for the Stars

Fun and Prophet

Box Sets (ebook only)

Seeing is Believing in Oracle Bay (Books 1-4)